KT-523-084

Cal hadn't counted on the intimacy that came with sharing a house with someone.

Even in the two short weeks that Amber had been there, as nanny to the kids, he'd grown accustomed to finding her in his kitchen when he got home from work, to seeing her there in the mornings when he awoke, to coming upon her bath gel in his shower, with its floral scent that lingered on her skin.

Worse, somehow Amber had got *under* his skin. He couldn't recall wanting a woman more.

But she was Amber Campion, spoiled, indulged daughter of one of the state's wealthiest men. Cal was the sheriff. Raised poor, he'd had to work his rear end off for everything he had.

He and Amber had nothing in common. Nothing.

Except the wanting…

Dear Reader,

Welcome to the spot where you get a brief glimpse at the titles now available in Silhouette Special Edition®.

Our **That's My Baby!** book this month comes from the talented pen of veteran author Sherryl Woods and is an absolute delight; it features an older child and a father who isn't ready to be a father, yet! It's another in the author's novels about the Adams family, where **And Baby Makes Three**.

We also have a new novel from the small town in **Montana** full of big secrets—*Cinderella's Big Sky Groom* by Christine Rimmer. There are, of course, more of these to come at Christmas and in January's books.

Lindsay McKenna has the third of her Hunter family stories *Hunter's Pride*, part of her **Morgan's Mercenaries** mini-series, the next one of which is coming next month in Desire™.

There are also terrific books from *New York Times* best-selling author Patricia Hagan, Penny Richards and Jodi O'Donnell.

Happy reading!

The Editors

The No-Nonsense Nanny

PENNY RICHARDS

™ SILHOUETTE
SPECIAL EDITION®

*Silhouette, Silhouette Special Edition and Colophon are
registered trademarks of Harlequin Books S.A., used under licence.*

*First published in Great Britain 2000
Silhouette Books, Eton House, 18-24 Paradise Road,
Richmond, Surrey TW9 1SR*

© Penny Richards 1999

ISBN 0 373 24279 4

23-1000

*Printed and bound in Spain
by Litografía Rosés S.A., Barcelona*

This book is for my unique Ambur with a 'u', even
though they wouldn't let me spell it that way.
First grandchild, first granddaughter, a true
joy and blessing in my life. Love 'U'!

PENNY RICHARDS,

describes herself as a dreamer and an incurable romantic. Married at an early age to her school sweetheart,
she claims she grew up with her three children. Now
that only the youngest is at home, writing romances
adds an exciting new dimension to her life.

Dear Reader,

Sometimes a character demands his or her own story, and that's what happened with Kim McShane's sister, Amber, from my previous Special Edition™ book, *Their Child*.

Amber started out as the 'bad sister,' but I soon realised she wasn't truly bad, that she'd been spoiled and indulged as a child (not her fault), that she never felt she measured up to the 'the perfect Kim,' and that the cocky snooty demeanour she presented to the world was to hide her insecurities.

In *The No-Nonsense Nanny*, Amber has come home to Louisiana after being in L.A. for ten years, ready to make some lifestyle changes and eager to build a closeness with her family. But the town's preconceived notions of her make finding and keeping a job an impossibility.

Sheriff Cal Simons, also from *Their Child*, is having a hard time finding anyone to look after the niece and nephew he's been raising since his brother was killed and his sister-in-law took off with the insurance money. When Amber's name keeps cropping up as a candidate for a live-in baby-sitter, Cal is more than hesitant. He can't forget the crush he'd had on Amber in school, when he'd wooed her with poetry and flowers and she disdained his romantic attempts. But Cal is a desperate man. Summer is coming and he can't let the kids run amok. Reluctantly he offers the job to Amber.

Just as desperate for employment, needing (for her own reasons) to be needed, she agrees. When Amber finds herself falling in love with the entire family, she knows she's in trouble…

While there are plenty of serious issues in *The No-Nonsense Nanny*, it is a much lighter book than I normally write. I had a great time with it, and I hope you enjoy it as much as I did. I wonder what kind of hero Beau will make in ten or twelve years… Enjoy!

Penny Richards

Chapter One

Wanted: Reliable lady to sit with ailing octogenarian with heart problems. Light housekeeping. Eleven o'clock till 7:00 a.m. Minimum wage.

Amber Campion picked up the felt-tipped pen, made a bold X through the ad and laid the pen aside with a shudder. "Not if I starve."

Her rose-hued fingernail trailed down the list of job opportunities, and her delicately arched eyebrows drew together over troubled brown eyes as she perused the meager offerings of the *Vanity Voice*'s classified section.

Be your own boss. Make your own hours. Full-time. Part-time. Commissions paid to individuals willing to work long hours selling Dynamic Dynamo Dietary Supplements. Must have transportation. Good telephone skills a plus.

"Like someone's going to go pound the pavement door-to-door to sell *that* stuff."

There wasn't much pavement to pound in the small town of Vanity, Louisiana, population 3,694. And door-to-door was a problem, too, since anywhere from several yards to several miles separated the houses once you got out of the town proper.

Besides, any phone skills she might possess didn't enter into the equation since the phone company had cut off her phone the day before. Not even her most seductive smile or the flirtatious fluttering of her eyelashes had budged the coldhearted young man who'd come out to do the dirty deed. The sigh that filled the tiny living room was the embodiment of weeks of frustration. Amber picked up the pen.

Mabel has the gout. Short-order cook needed desperately. Apply in person at the Snack Shack. Ask for Bubba.

The felt tip screeched another bold X. Cook? Ha! She could barely boil water.

"'Looking for hardworking, temporary stock person at the Vanity Value Mart,'" Amber read aloud. "'Minimum wage. May work into full-time position.'"

Amber swept the small weekly newspaper off the minuscule, Formica-topped table in the rented travel trailer she'd called home for the past three months. She ground the heels of her hands into her eye sockets to hold back the tears that threatened on a regular basis. Not even the cheerful sounds of the chirping birds outside the open windows and the unfolding of new life around her could banish the defeat that seemed to take a tighter grip on her each day.

When she'd made the decision to come back to Louisiana after nearly ten years in California, she'd felt she was ready for the change, was in control of her life and was finally making a good decision. She'd been in L.A. since graduating from the Art Institute in Dallas with an interior decorating diploma a few months before her twenty-third birthday. She'd lived a fairly hedonistic life, getting involved with the wrong kind of man and going through life without any specific goals or plans.

Almost exactly a year earlier, she'd come back to hit up her father, Gerald Campion, for a hundred thousand dollars because she was being blackmailed by David Perkins, her biological father. David had been squeezing her for more than three years—ever since he'd seen her picture on the front page of the tabloids for being drunk and disorderly in a swanky L.A. club. He'd recognized her because she was the spitting image of her dead mother at the same age. He'd gone out to California, looked her up and threatened to tell Gerald the truth about her paternity if she didn't, as he put it, "come up with the scratch."

Gerald had suffered a heart attack after reading about her in the tabloid, and Amber had always felt responsible. There was little doubt in her mind that he'd be as upset as she was to learn that he'd been duped by his first wife. Rather than risk his having another spell with his heart, Amber had kept asking him for the money David demanded of her, even though it meant painting herself as shiftless, money-hungry and selfish to both her father and her estranged sister, Kim.

But the last time she'd asked for a "loan," Gerald had been strapped for money himself and couldn't help her. In desperation, David, who was being pressured by loan sharks for gambling debts, had kidnapped Amber's niece, Hannah. Amber had figured out that David must be behind the kidnapping and was left no choice but to tell her father and her brother-in-law what was going on.

The good news was that everything had turned out okay, and she and Kim were closer than they'd ever been. The bad news was that Amber had taken a bullet during the standoff. She'd run between David and Kim, flinging her arms up in a defensive gesture. The bullet had gone through the fleshy part of her upper arm, barely missing bone, and grazed her cheek.

Gerald had seen to it that she had the best plastic surgeon in the area, and to the doctor's credit, the scar was nothing more than a thin white line, easily masked with makeup. She could live with that. What she'd realized she couldn't live with was the emptiness and lack of direction in her life.

Amber considered the whole incident to be the third major turning point of her life. The second had been her arrest, which had prompted her to get professional help for whatever was behind her self-destructive life-style, something she'd be eternally grateful for. The first had been giving up the child she'd secretly borne five months after she'd announced to a stunned Gerald that she was leaving Louisiana State University in the middle of her junior year and enrolling at the Art Institute in Dallas.

But she didn't want to think about that. Couldn't. Not yet. Maybe never. It was a secret known only to herself and her psychologist.

Healing the rift with Kim and basking in the new closeness with her family had doubled the restlessness Amber had been feeling the past few years. A new, often painfully sharp awareness of life's uncertainties had kindled a longing to try to make a more meaningful life for herself by coming back to Louisiana and starting over. Still, there was something to be said for the familiar, no matter how unsatisfactory it might actually be. It had taken Amber eight months to get up the nerve to box up her possessions, load them in a rental moving van and head home.

She'd arrived just after New Year's, hoping to start a new life in a new year, but it was nearing the end of April, and so far, things weren't working out as she'd planned. Neither her interior decorating skills nor her knowledge of art was in much demand in a place the size of Vanity. The Vanity furniture store handled the basics at mid-price range, and the local artist, eighty-year-old Percy Stovall painted primitives, a form that had never been one of Amber's favorites.

She'd been forced to go into Thibodaux to find work, but even there, she'd been unable to find anything but a clerk's position at a clothing store. She was a pretty fair salesclerk, but there was a certain amount of resentment among the women she worked with. Part of them were intimidated by the Campion name; the others were secretly amused that a high and mighty Campion was working at such a commonplace job. Every suggestion Amber made was met by resistance from her co-workers or her boss.

Make that bosses. She'd had three bosses at three different stores since she'd arrived. She'd been "let go" the previous day after having told one of her co-workers—who just happened to be her boss's niece—that she didn't think it was very nice to spread gossip. The girl, who was in her early twenties and had no sense of style, had resented Amber from the first. It was a foregone conclusion that she'd use the criticism to find a way to oust Amber from the job and her life.

Amber could deal with jealousy, snide remarks and snickers. They had been a way of life where she came from. Her biggest problem was that for whatever reason, she couldn't seem to find and keep a decent job. It wasn't that she was too good to work as a clerk. Gwen, her stepmother, had taught both Amber and Kim to give their best, whatever it might be, and that all work was good, if it was honest.

Amber could buy that. It was just that her weekly checks—minimum wage plus commission—were a far cry from what she was accustomed to making in California. She'd brought some major bills along with the move, and even though the cost of living in Vanity was peanuts to that of L.A., she was badly in debt.

Amber reached for the pack of cigarettes lying on the table. Her hand hovered in midair. Her shaky finances meant she had to ration out the cigarettes. A wry smile curved her lips. She'd tried unsuccessfully to give up smoking before. Maybe this time she'd manage it. At least something good might come from being in a money bind.

She let the cigarettes lay and picked up the newspaper. It would be so easy to take up her dad's offer to live with him at Lafourche Farm—Gerald was lonely since Kim and Hannah had moved to Kentucky to be with Drew—but stubborn pride and a determination to make it on her own held Amber back. Indulged and spoiled all her life, she'd taken too much from her dad as it was, taken the easy way out too often. It was time to prove to herself and everyone else that she was a mature, capable adult. Sighing again, Amber focused on the newspaper.

Baby-sitting in my home. Three boys, ages nine months to four years. Minimum wage. Meals provided.

The marker screeched; a tear fell.

Clerk/stockperson needed. Minimum wage. Apply in person to Rose at the dollar store.

Instead of crossing through the ad, Amber drew a ring around it. Beggars couldn't be choosers—not too choosy, anyway.

"I hated to call you, Cal," Maggie Otwell said two afternoons later as she sat on the floral sofa wringing her hands. There was an apology in her eyes as she spoke.

Sheriff Cal Simmons forced a smile and let her finish.

"I know you have enough on your plate with your job, but I can't let Timmy come over to play with Beau after school anymore if there isn't an adult around to supervise them. Claudia just isn't able to keep them in line. You know how kids are—especially boys. One is fine on his own. Two or more manage to get into things they'd never dream of doing alone."

Cal set his glass of sweet tea down on the plastic coaster his hostess had provided. "Don't apologize, Maggie," he said. "Beau is my responsibility, and if he's doing things he shouldn't, I need to know about it."

"That's what Jake said." Her cheeks turned red. "Of course, he made *me* call. I know you're in a bind with Dudley being at the rehab and all, and if the boys were just fussin' or being generally ornery I wouldn't think a thing about it. But smokin' and lookin' at girlie magazines..." Her voice trailed away, and bright red stained her thin cheeks. Her right hand fluttered above her heart, as if the very thought might make her swoon.

A rowdy, mouthy handful, Beau didn't understand why his dad had died, and he resented his mother, Georgina, for leaving. He was a challenge for Cal, even with his background in law enforcement. Unfortunately, you couldn't treat kids the way you did the criminal element. There were times, like now, when he'd like nothing more than to lock Beau up until he turned eighteen and was ready to leave home. But that wasn't an option, and, as Cal had told Maggie Otwell, Beau was his responsibility, and he'd have to deal with this newest escapade.

Cal stood, and the petite birdlike woman sitting across from him sprang to her feet, a startled expression in her eyes. "Don't worry about it another minute, Maggie," he said. "I'll take care of it."

The assurance did little to erase the anxiety from her eyes. "Thanks, Cal." He started for the front door, Maggie hard on his heels. "How much longer is Dudley going to be out of commission?"

"I'm not sure," Cal said. "It depends on how well his arthritis responds to the new drugs and exercise."

"Not having any luck finding someone to take his place, huh?"

"Nope."

"I know it's hard," Maggie sympathized now as she trekked along behind him. "Most teenage sitters just want to sit in front of the TV or talk on the phone with their boyfriends. Worse yet, they want their boyfriends over. Now that's a problem I don't want!"

Cal stifled a shudder, remembering with frightening clarity the heavy necking sessions that had taken place during his visits to the homes where his high school girlfriend had baby-sat. He didn't want that problem, either.

"Most moms want to keep kids in their own homes, and older women don't seem to want the bother." Maggie gave another jittery laugh. "My mama told me she raised hers, and it was my place to raise mine." Then, remembering about Georgina, Maggie muttered, "Sorry, Cal."

"It's okay, Maggie." He pushed through the screen door and turned to face his reluctant hostess. Poor Maggie's face was a study in mortification. "Thanks for the tea."

"Sure," she said with a quick, nervous smile. "You know, school will be out in another six weeks."

Cal stifled the urge to snarl that he didn't need reminding that Beau and Claudia would have even more unsupervised time and that he didn't have the slightest idea how he was going to get through the next few weeks without Dudley, much less the upcoming summer. Instead, he just flashed his most charming smile and said, "Yeah, time flies, doesn't it? Tell Jake not to worry. I'll have a talk with Beau."

"Okay."

Cal was opening the cruiser's door when she called his name.

"You might try Ginger Elliott," Maggie said. "She seems responsible for a fifteen-year-old, and I hear she's looking for a summer job."

"Thanks. I'll think about it," Cal said, already dismissing the idea. Ginger Elliott was sweet, shy and tended to fall to pieces under the slightest pressure. Claudia suffered from asthma, and when the attacks occurred she needed someone calm around—not someone who'd go into a panic. He turned the key in the ignition and put the car into gear. As he started down the driveway, he happened to glance in the rearview mirror. Maggie was running along behind the car, waving her arms.

What now? He slammed on the brakes and backed up, counting to ten.

"Is something wrong?"

"Oh, no!" she said breathlessly. "But I just thought of someone else. Amber Campion."

Cal's heart took a sudden nosedive. Amber, whom he'd had a tremendous crush on in high school, who'd made it clear that the poems and flowers he'd left in her locker were nothing but a source of amusement. Amber, who had given her own parents their share of misery as a teenager. Cal knew firsthand that she'd grown into a gorgeous, sexy woman. And, if rumor was to be believed, she'd left a trail of broken hearts from here to California.

"Amber Campion?"

Maggie nodded. "Yeah. You know. To watch the kids. Becky over at the beauty salon told me Missy Cavenaugh over at The Fashion Shop in Thibodaux fired her the other day. I don't know what the problem is, but she can't seem to keep a job since she's come back."

There might be a lot of problems in the parish, but a short in the community grapevine wasn't one of them. Though he hadn't set out deliberately to keep tabs on Amber since she'd moved back, it seemed there was always someone somewhere who was more than happy to give him an update on how her life was going. The general drift was that it wasn't going too well.

"Becky said some of the folk around here think she's just too darn highfalutin, comin' from California and all," Maggie rambled. "But then Missy let slip that what happened at her place was that Amber got on to Missy's niece for talkin' bad about one of the customers. She might have been in the wrong, but blood's thicker 'n water. You know that as well as I do, Caleb."

"Yeah, Maggie, it sure is."

"Well, I'll let you go," she said, backing away from the car. "Good luck."

Cal thanked her and drove away, wondering what the heck he was going to do. Dudley Millsap, his seventy-something neighbor, had been Cal's after-school baby-sitter ever since Cal's brother had been killed in a crop dusting accident four years ago and Dean's widow had taken off to Europe with the quarter-million-dollar insurance settlement, looking for a good time and a new husband, leaving her kids behind. None of her relatives had offered to take them, which left Cal.

After four years in an unsuccessful marriage, Cal was newly divorced at the time. He was at a loss as to how to deal with the rest of his life, much less care for two small children, but he was unwilling to put them in foster care, so he had taken them into his home and his life. Working as a sheriff's deputy meant Beau and Claudia would be at home alone from the time school let out until his shift ended. Thankfully, Dudley had stepped in. The old man had been a godsend, offering after-school supervision, snacks and homework help.

When Cal had been elected sheriff two and a half years ago, he'd often needed someone on hand at a moment's notice. Dudley was always available. Then, a month ago, the old man's chronic arthritis had taken a turn for the worse and, hoping for some relief, he'd gone to a rehabilitation center for an indefinite period, which left Cal's charges without anyone to look after them until he got off work.

Claudia was no problem. At twelve, she was old enough to lock the doors and read or watch TV until Cal got home. Beau was another thing altogether. There weren't too many people willing to take on a kid like Beau.

Good luck. Maggie's words lingered in his mind. With people like Ginger and Amber the only ones available as baby-sitters, he'd need it.

Still, he couldn't get the image of the last time he'd seen Amber out of his mind. Lying in the hospital bed hurt, vulnerable, but with that gorgeous mouth still spouting sass. Amber, who'd redeemed herself with her family by getting between her sister and a madman's bullet.

* * *

"The kids here?" Cal asked his dispatcher as he walked through the doors to the sheriff's office.

"Yeah. They're in your office," Jimmy Rowell said.

At Cal's request, one of the teachers who lived in the area had recently started dropping off Beau and Claudia at the sheriff's office after school. It wasn't a good arrangement, but until Cal could find someone to stay at the house in the afternoons, it was the only way he could keep Beau out of trouble. He'd made an exception the afternoon Timmy and Beau had played together, wrongly assuming that Claudia could handle the situation for an hour or so.

"Anything happening?" he asked as he passed the desk and headed toward his office.

"Nothing but a little domestic problem out at the Masons. I sent Lawson out."

"Good."

"Did you hear the news?"

"What news?"

"They shut Amber Campion's phone off a few days ago."

Cal stopped and faced the deputy. "Who told you that?"

"Dave Fielder. He's the one who shut her off. That's a hoot, iddn't it?"

"Only for someone who likes to kick stray dogs," Cal said, hoping the dispatcher got his drift.

The embarrassment that stained Jimmy Rowell's chubby face told Cal he'd scored a direct hit. After the way Amber had treated him when they were kids, the news of her bad luck should have given him some pleasure, but having borne the brunt of many snickers himself, Cal wasn't one to kick anybody when they were down. And Amber Campion was obviously down. Instead of satisfaction, he felt something closely akin to anger, which he carried with him into his office.

The kids were waiting for him—Claudia, too thin, too pale, her strawberry-hued bangs too long, that haunted look in her eyes and the sweet smile on her lips. And ten-year-old Beau cocked back in Cal's chair, hands behind his head, his sneaker-shod feet resting on Cal's desk, and the stub of a yellow pencil stuck in the corner of his grinning mouth like a cigar.

He looked so much like Dean as a kid, Cal stopped in his tracks. A bittersweet pang of nostalgia washed over him. He missed his big brother. A lot. But missing Dean was no reason to let Beau run amuck.

"Get that pencil out of your mouth and your feet off my desk."

Leisurely, Beau took the pencil from his mouth and pretended to tap ash from the tip. His grin widened, his devilish green eyes sparkling with mischief. The freckles spattered on his face added to his look of roguery. "Please, Beau."

Cal's lips tightened. The little brat was throwing the rules back in his face. He fixed his nephew with a look that had caused many an insolent, in-your-face lawbreaker to back down. The impish smile vanished, and Beau lowered his feet to the floor.

"Thank you very much," Cal said with exaggerated politeness. He turned to Claudia with a smile. "Hi, honey. How was your day?"

"Fine," Claudia replied, but she turned red to the roots of her hair. "I need to talk to you, Uncle Cal."

"Sure thing, honey, but I need to talk to your brother first." He reached into his pocket and pulled out some dollar bills. "Why don't you go into the break room and get you and Beau a snack?"

"Okay."

As Cal watched her go, he was filled with an inexplicable sadness. Claudia was such a sweet kid, but she was so shy and insecure. She needed something Cal couldn't give her. She needed a woman in her life. Needed her mother. Both the kids did. He cursed Georgina to hell and back and turned to face his nephew.

"I had a call from Maggie Otwell today." The statement extinguished the glimmer of playfulness from Beau's eyes. "She said Timmy couldn't come over anymore unless there was someone around to keep an eye on the two of you. I'm sure you know why."

Beau's gaze slid from Cal's.

"Where'd you get the cigarettes?"

Beau crossed his arms over his chest and refused to answer, taking refuge in a stance that had become all too familiar. It wasn't so much defiance as Beau just seemed to go blank, to pull into himself.

"Tell me, or you'll be grounded until school's out."

Beau's startled gaze flew to Cal's. "But that's weeks."

"Life's tough, kid."

Beau dropped his head and mumbled something under his breath that Cal suspected was a curse. "What did you say?"

"Mike Miller."

Mike Miller was a big, buff, good-looking football player, who'd never been in any trouble. He was the kind all moms wanted their daughters to date and little boys looked up to. His mama had been right: you really couldn't judge a book by its cover. "He give you the *Babes* magazine, too?"

"Yeah."

Cal lifted a hand to his ear and cocked his head as if he hadn't heard correctly. "What did you say?"

Beau scowled, his dark eyebrows drawing into a single line. "Yes, sir."

"Why'd you try the smokes? And don't tell me everyone does."

Beau shrugged. "You used to."

"Yeah, and I quit. I couldn't even get through a thirty minute workout session without gasping for air. If you want to play sports, you'd better start thinking about that stuff."

Beau rolled his eyes, but Cal knew he'd scored a hit. Dean's greatest wish—and Beau's—was for Beau to have the college baseball career he'd had, and maybe make it to the majors.

"You know the rules. No smoking. If it happens again, I'll pull you from Little League."

Once again, Beau's startled gaze flashed to Cal's. "You wouldn't."

"Try me." Cal stared the boy down and went on to the next topic. "Why'd you look at those girlie magazines?"

"Why do you think?" The expression in Beau's eyes seemed to imply that if Cal didn't know why, he was the one with the problem.

"I know you're…curious…about all that," Cal said, "but you're just a little too young for that sort of thing. Besides which, that kind of trash is demeaning to women."

"What's that?"

"It means that by posing for those pictures, they've given up their dignity, the same way people do when they get drunk or do drugs and lose control."

Beau considered that a moment. Shrugged. "All I know is that when I look at them I get all, uh…h—"

"I know!" Cal interrupted. Thankfully, Claudia stepped through the door carrying a couple of soft drinks and candy bars. "There's your sister. No more smutty magazines, bud. Got it?"

"Or what? You gonna put me on bread and water?"

"Maybe I will," Cal shot back. "But it'll be worse on your buddy Mike. If I ever find out he's given you anything like that again, I'll haul him in for contributing to the delinquency of a minor. Tell him that next time you see him."

That erased the cocky gleam from Beau's eyes.

"Come on in, Claudia. Beau, you go harass Jimmy while I talk to your sister." Rowell had three boys of his own, so Cal figured he could handle anything Beau might dish out, at least for a few minutes.

"Sit down, Claudia," Cal said, motioning toward a chair and taking the place behind the desk Beau had vacated. "Is anything wrong?"

Claudia colored again. "N-not really." She took a deep breath and a gulp of her soda, then plunged. "We had a film today about...umm...starting our periods—" If possible, her face grew even redder. Cal felt his own face grow hot. "Mrs. Tidwell said we were all getting to the age when we should, uh, have some feminine, uh, products on hand, so we'd be prepared."

Searching his mind for some reasonable comment, Cal rubbed a hand over his face, covered with end-of-the-day stubble. "Good idea," he said at last.

"And I really need to get some bras, Uncle Cal. I'm the only girl in my P.E. class who doesn't wear one."

In a knee-jerk reaction, Cal's gaze flew to her chest, then as quickly moved away. Dear sweet heaven! Why hadn't he noticed that even though Claudia was skinny as a rail, there were breasts budding under those T-shirts she was so fond of wearing?

"I thought...I mean, I know you're real busy and don't

have time to go…like shopping or anything today, but maybe we could stop at the dollar store when you get off work.''

"Sure thing, honey,'' Cal replied. A look of relief swept over Claudia's finely featured face. If he could have gotten his hands on Georgina at that moment he'd have strangled her.

Amber hooked the brightly-hued swimsuit straps in the notches of the plastic hanger and loaded an armful onto the shopping cart. Thank God, there's only an hour to go until quitting time, she thought, wheeling the cart out into the store. She blew back a strand of hair. She was desperate for a haircut and a touch up on her roots, too. Unfortunately, both took money.

Instead of complaining, Amber knew she should be grateful the store manager had hired her on the spot. Of course, she didn't deceive herself into thinking it was because she possessed any special skills. Running the cash register and pricing and stocking inventory didn't require the mentality of a rocket scientist. The truth was that one of the clerks quit without notice and they needed another warm body to share the load.

Determined to do her job well, Amber wheeled the cart past boxes of toilet tissue and paper towels. She had turned down an aisle and just passed a bin filled with throw pillows when she stopped dead in her tracks. Cal Simmons stood in front of a display of bras, turning a hanger with one of the lacy undergarments this way and that and frowning fiercely. Her first reaction was to wonder why he was shopping for a bra.

Her second was that she hadn't seen Cal since she'd been back. In fact, she hadn't seen him since he'd come to visit her in the hospital a year ago, and that hardly counted since she'd been almost completely out of it from the pain medicine.

She'd heard plenty about him, though. Everyone in the parish thought he was the greatest thing since sliced bread. They praised his ability as sheriff, commended him for taking his brother's kids to raise when their mother abandoned them and bemoaned the fact that so far none of the local beauties had managed to lure him to the altar.

She tucked her hair behind her ear in a self-conscious gesture. Cal had grown into an attractive man, she thought, admiring the impressive breadth of his chest and the finely developed musculature of his arms and thighs. And he was good-looking without being conventionally handsome. His jaw was too square, his nose had obviously been broken once or twice, and the fine line of an old scar angled across his left cheek, cutting through the hint of a groove hiding behind the shadow of beard.

His hair was cut short and brushed to the side, a no-nonsense haircut that was probably easy to care for. Then there were those eyes—a warm, golden-brown surrounded by ridiculously long lashes for a man—and that mouth, a Sean Connery kind of mouth. The kind of mouth that was designed to drive a woman crazy.

Whoa! Just hold on a darn minute, Amber! This is Cal Simmons. Cal Simmons. The guy who'd had a major crush on her in high school. The skinny kid with holes in his jeans who'd stuck flowers and poems in her locker. She'd thought he was cute back then, though she'd never have admitted it to anyone. Even though she'd been touched by his acts of devotion, she'd blown him off because he was two years her junior. *Be honest.* Okay, the truth was that she'd been a spoiled snob back then, and Cal Simmons hadn't run in her crowd. Cute and sweet though he might have been, she hadn't thought he was good enough for her. The attitude she'd sported back then wasn't something she was proud of now.

She took a deep breath. She couldn't ignore him. As she saw it, there were only two courses of action available. She could either wait for him to look up and see her or she could walk over and thank him for coming to visit her in the hospital.

Gripping the cart of swimsuits, she started toward him, stopping within a couple of feet. He glanced over at her, and her heart seemed to stumble for the space of a single beat. He looked as surprised to see her as she felt to her reaction to him. Fortunately, her smart mouth came to the rescue.

"Is there something you're hiding from everyone, Cal?"

He actually blushed. She remembered that from their high school days but she'd have thought he'd outgrown the habit by now.

He shook his head, shrugged and slammed the bra back onto the display with such force the plastic hanger snapped. Reacting instinctively, Amber reached over to pick it up. So did Cal. Their foreheads collided with a muted thud as she grabbed at the scrap of lace. Amber gave a yelp of pain. Cal swore. She started to rise, and he grabbed her elbow in an involuntary gesture. Her breath tangled in her throat, and her gaze lifted to his. They stood, their gazes locked. All Amber could think was that his eyes were the most incredible color. And his hand was warm. Warm and gentle.

"Claudia," he said, as if that explained everything.

"Claudia. Right." Amber nodded, even though her thoughts were so scrambled she had no idea what he was talking about or what she'd just agreed to.

Cal released her arm and stepped back a pace. Amber's

head began to clear. Irritation replaced the chaos of her thoughts. She gripped the bra and stared at the tag, telling herself to get a grip. It was ridiculous to have such a reaction to Cal Simmons.

It's been nearly two years, Amber. Right. Two years. Too long. Her body was just crying out for a little tender loving care, that's all.

"My niece," he said, bringing her gaze back to him and her focus back to the conversation—if the inanities they were exchanging could be considered a conversation. "Claudia."

Niece. Of course. Claudia was his niece, and Beau was his nephew. Amber remembered the ornery little brat from Hannah's party the previous year.

"She said she needed a bra," he explained, his color deepening.

"Not a 36-C I hope," Amber said.

A look of astonishment flickered in his eyes. "No. I guess not."

"We don't have any training bras," she said, making an all-out effort to gather her scattered thoughts. "But we have some sports-bra-and-panties sets in cotton—sort of a one-size-fits-all thing that might work until you can get her to a store with a larger selection."

He opened his mouth to say something, but a girlish voice interrupted. "I found them, Uncle Cal." A young woman was coming down the aisle toward them, her arms filled with various boxes. "I wasn't sure what to get."

Cal's niece was preteen and would be stunning in another few years—if she could lose the frown and get a decent haircut. As she grew nearer, Amber saw that Claudia was carrying a selection of feminine products.

The bewilderment and embarrassment on Cal's face matched the expression on his niece's. Cal might be a take-charge kind of guy when it came to law enforcement but he didn't have a clue about how to handle this situation.

Amber was surprised by the sympathy that swept through her. Cal was raising Claudia and Beau alone, no small feat for anyone—man or woman. Claudia was about to embark on the often confusing journey into womanhood, if she hadn't already. A memory of her own first initiation into those hallowed halls surfaced. Unlike Claudia, who had no one but her uncle to guide her through the awkward and sometimes frightening passage, Amber had had her stepmother to calm her fears and help her make her choices. Amber certainly couldn't imagine Gerald Campion doing for her what Cal was doing for his niece.

"Need some help?" she heard herself ask in a bright, cheerful voice.

"That's okay," Cal said. "You don't have to bother. I'm sure you have better things to do."

Amber couldn't decide if he was being polite or if the comment was a deliberate dig. "Actually, it's no bother. I'm just doing my job." Seeing the blank look on his face, she added, "I work here. Why don't you go check out your other things and leave some money with Claudia. I'll help her find whatever she needs."

The relief on Cal's face was palpable. "You will? That'd be great. I really need to get back to the station. I left Beau there sweeping floors."

Amber smiled at the image that came to mind. "Then by all means go, before he decides to let all the prisoners loose. I'll see that Claudia gets back okay."

"I really appreciate it," he said, already turning his cart in the aisle. He brushed a kiss across Claudia's cheek. "See you in a little while."

Claudia grabbed his shirt. "But Uncle Cal."

"It's okay, Claudia. Amber is an old…schoolmate. She can help you better than I can."

Claudia nodded reluctantly and, with another kiss, let him go.

Amber watched him as he wove his way through the store's displays, his back straight, moving with an athlete's grace. Regret stung her heart. So many regrets.

She wondered what it would have been like to be Cal Simmons's girlfriend, to have had someone bring her flowers and write her love poems on a regular basis. She wondered if Paul—the man who'd sworn he loved her but wouldn't marry her when she got pregnant with his child—had ever married and had children. She wondered if their child had been a boy or a girl and if he or she had been lucky enough to be adopted by someone who loved them as much as Cal obviously loved his niece and nephew.

Amber drew in a trembling breath and forced herself to smile at Claudia Simmons. Though she should be used to it, Amber didn't think she'd ever get used to the way the old, nagging memories sabotaged her when she least expected it. Cal had said she didn't have to help Claudia, but he was wrong. She did have to. It was a small enough thing and, as penances went, a negligible one. She was glad to help Claudia, but it wasn't enough. Nothing she did for other kids would ever be enough to ease the pain of her remorse.

Chapter Two

"We weren't even properly introduced, were we?" Amber said to Claudia after Cal had disappeared through the dollar store's doors.

"No ma'am."

"I'm Amber Campion. My father owns the thoroughbred farm down along the bayou. You must be Beau's sister, Claudia."

Claudia nodded. "I know about Lafourche Farm. Our class went there for a field trip when I was in the fifth grade."

"Really?"

"I loved the horses," Claudia said with a wistful smile. "But I got asthma from being around them."

"Asthma's no fun," Amber said. "My friend had a few attacks when I was a kid, but she outgrew it."

"She was lucky."

The wistfulness on Claudia's petite features brought an

ache to Amber's heart. The child was on the cusp of womanhood, at the brink of her teenage years, a transition that would be hard because she was so shy and insecure. Amber had often been insecure herself, but no one had known, because she'd perfected the art of hiding her uncertainty behind a facade of snobbery and sarcasm.

Her sister, Kim, had always been the one who knew exactly where she was going and what she was doing. Kim had been the good sister, the dutiful daughter, the one everyone loved because she always did the right thing. If she'd ever suffered any of the usual teenage angst, it didn't show. And even though she'd been doted on and indulged by her father, Amber had been the one who stayed in trouble, the one with the attitude.

She thought about the mother who'd abandoned Claudia and Beau. Georgina had been the same age as Cal, both two grades behind Amber. More ambitious than smart, and pretty as a picture, Georgina had seemed like an okay person when they'd gone to school together, but as Amber knew all too well, time and circumstance often made people do things they shouldn't. Things they later regretted.

Amber wondered if Georgina Simmons ever thought about the kids she'd left behind. Did she ever think about how her actions had affected Cal's life—all their lives? Did she miss seeing Beau play Little League? Did she ever think that Claudia might need help with something as simple as choosing the right feminine-hygiene products?

"Dump those boxes in this empty cart." Amber told Claudia. "I don't think you'll need all of them."

"Stop using store time to chat with the customers, Amber," Rose Milford, the store's manager said. "The back room is full of merchandise that needs to be priced and put on the floor."

The censure in the woman's voice grated on Amber's

nerves, but she bit her tongue to keep from saying something she shouldn't. Amber knew that if the store weren't empty except for her and Claudia, and if Claudia had been an adult instead of a child, Rose wouldn't have said a word.

"I'm helping the young lady make a selection," Amber said, biting her tongue to keep from saying more. Rose frowned but turned back to her own task without further comment. Amber smiled at Claudia, encouragingly.

A few minutes later, after some questions that left the young girl with a red face, Amber suggested that Claudia buy two different products and see how she liked them when the time came. Then they moved on to the sports bras.

"These aren't what you really need," Amber told her, reciting what she'd told Cal, "but they'll serve the purpose until you can get to a store that has a bigger selection."

Claudia chose three different bra-and-panties sets, and Amber took them to the front to ring them up. There was no hiding the gleam of excitement in the girl's eyes. Amber remembered how thrilled she'd been when Gwen took her to buy her first bras, and how grown up she'd felt.

"Thank you," Claudia said, clutching her change in her fist. "You've been awfully nice, and it's sure a lot easier to talk to you than to Uncle Cal."

Amber was touched by the gratitude she saw in the child's eyes. "I know what you mean. Men just don't get it." She handed Claudia the plastic bag and turned to her boss. "Rose!" she called. "I promised the sheriff I'd get his niece back over to the station when she finished shopping. I won't be gone but a few minutes."

Amber waited for the supervisor's reply. Rose liked to flaunt her authority, and Amber knew that as a new employee she was pushing her luck. But she had promised Cal, and she wouldn't be gone long.

The look of censure in her eyes would have made a lesser woman shake in her shoes, but all Rose said was, "Make it quick."

When Amber and Claudia reached the station, Claudia shyly thanked Amber again and pushed through the door. With her heart filled with a curious ache, Amber turned and headed back to the waiting swimsuits. She was halfway down the block when a masculine voice called her name.

She turned and saw Cal, with his head stuck out the door. She wasn't even aware that she sucked in a nervous little gasp of air. All she knew was that she had a sudden longing for a cigarette to calm the covey of butterflies that seemed to have congregated in her stomach.

"All hell's broken loose in here," he said shoving his hand through his short hair, "but I wanted to thank you for helping Claudia."

"It was no big deal. She's a sweet girl."

"Yeah, she is. Well, I gotta go. Thanks again."

Amber nodded and watched him disappear through the door. Her day, which had perked up a bit when he and his niece had come into the store, suddenly went as flat as a bottle of day-old champagne.

The rehab where Dudley was taking his treatments was in Thibodaux, a thirty-five minute drive from Vanity. Cal tried to take the kids for a visit once a week, if his workload and Beau's ball games didn't interfere. They usually made a night of it, checking Dudley out long enough to get something to eat, and, if they were lucky enough to get away on a Friday or Saturday evening and the Hollywood offerings were something Cal didn't feel would warp the kids' minds too badly, they took in a movie afterward.

Though Dudley went along, grateful for a change of scenery, he complained that Cal should be squiring around some pretty girl, not an old man and a couple of kids.

Cal couldn't have agreed more. God knew he wished there were someone to talk to besides the kids...someone to stir him into a raging passion, but it had been more than a year since he'd met anyone who inspired the slightest interest. It had been so long, in fact, that he was beginning to worry that there might be something wrong with him.

Now, as they sat at a favorite restaurant, the bones of some delicious barbecue ribs in front of them, the buzz of a couple dozen conversations creating a lively background, Cal was gripped by an unexpected memory: His head cracking against Amber's as they both stooped to reach for the plastic hanger. The sexy, exotic scent of her perfume filling his nostrils and swamping his senses. The way his heart had revved up for a second or two as her startled gaze collided with his. The smooth warmth of her upper arm beneath his hand as he'd reached out to steady her.

"Uncle Cal's got a girlfriend."

The taunting observation snapped Cal's attention back to the present. Beau was regarding him with a smug expression on his freckled face. "Why do you think I have a girlfriend?"

"'Cause you got that goofy look on your face you used to get when you and Darlene used to sit out on the porch swing and kiss."

"You watched us?" Cal asked, wondering why the notion of Beau spying on Cal and an old girlfriend surprised him.

"Sometimes. When there wasn't anything good on TV."

Even though he tried to be circumspect and had never had a woman share·his bed at the house since getting guardianship of the kids, Cal racked his mind for memories of anything he and Darlene might have done to further Beau's sex education, which—if Maggie Otwell were to be believed—didn't need any furthering.

"That isn't very nice, Beau," Claudia said. "How would you like it if Uncle Cal watched you with your girlfriend?"

The boy's face turned beet-red. "I don't have a girl-friend."

"Liar," Claudia said with an angelic smile. "What about Tammie Thompson?"

"Shut up, snot face!"

"Make me."

Dudley's sharp blue gaze followed the volley like a fan at a tennis match.

"Both of you be quiet," Cal warned in a low voice. The look in his eyes told them he wasn't playing around. "We're in a public place, not out in the woods."

"Yes, sir," Claudia said promptly. "I'm sorry."

"Apology accepted." Cal glanced at his nephew whose face was a study in defiance. "Beau?"

"Sorry."

"A definite lack of sincerity, I think," Dudley said, wiping a speck of barbecue sauce from his Clark Gable moustache with a paper napkin. "But coming as it is from the young ruffian, I suppose it will have to suffice."

"If you two are finished eating, go feed the ducks until Dudley and I are ready to go."

"Are we going to the movies, Uncle Cal?"

"Not tonight, Claudia," Cal said. "There's nothing much good playing, and I'm beat."

"Oh, man!" Beau moaned.

Cal cast him a sharp look. "If you behave yourself until we're ready to go, we'll rent a couple of movies for the weekend."

Beau nodded grudgingly and started for the exit that led to the duck pond. "Beau!"

"Sir?" he said, turning.

"Try not to get into any trouble while you're out there, okay?"

"Yeah. Sure."

Cal watched them go, closed his eyes and pinched the bridge of his nose at the thought of the upcoming weekend. He dreaded the weekends, since there was no supervision for the kids.

"I'm sorry to leave you in the lurch this way," Dudley told Cal for the dozenth time since he'd been forced to go to the rehab. "But I should be out of here by the time school's out."

Cal regarded the old man fondly. As usual, Dudley was impeccably groomed, from his carefully combed shock of snow-white hair to the tips of his expensive shoes. Blessed with plenty of money, a legacy of a lucrative law practice, Dudley continued to stay on top of current styles and was always fashionably dressed. Age, he maintained, was no excuse to let oneself go. If he'd been born a couple centuries earlier, he'd have been a dandy.

"Stop worrying about it, Dud. It's my problem, not yours. Besides, you should spend your time fishing or something, not baby-sitting."

"Yeah. Sure," Dudley said, sounding so much like Beau, Cal had to smile.

"So what's Beau gotten himself into this week? I sensed more tension than usual between the two of you."

"Oh, nothing much. Just smoking cigarettes and looking at pictures of naked women."

"My idea of heaven," Dudley said. "So what will you do with the kiddos this weekend?"

"Maybe I'll call Peggy Jamerson and see if she'll watch Beau," Cal said. "She raised two boys and she can always use a few extra bucks. Claudia can stay by herself."

But she shouldn't have to. She should be helping her mom around the house, polishing her fingernails, talking with friends on the phone and having sleepovers or whatever girls her age did for fun. She should, by golly, have a life, not spend her Saturdays with her nose in a book or watching hours of television.

"What you need, my boy, is a wife."

Cal gave a dry laugh. "I tried marriage, Dudley, and it didn't work out, as I'm sure you remember well. My job is the kind that makes most women uneasy. I have no desire to try it again."

"I told you Carol wasn't right for you, and never say never."

One corner of Cal's mouth hiked up in a wry grin. "I'm smarter than that."

"So is Beau right? Is there someone? You did have a rather…goofy look on your face there for a moment."

Was he so easy to read? Cal wondered. If so, his law enforcement career would certainly be short-lived. "Just thinking about a girl I used to have a crush on," he said, opting for the truth. "Nothing to get excited about."

"You must have some feelings left for her."

The stunning observation robbed Cal of speech for a moment. Feelings for Amber Campion? No way. Not beyond thinking that she was still a gorgeous, sexy woman. "She's the glamorous type. Not the kind who'd be willing to settle down in a place like Vanity with a hayseed sheriff."

"You don't give yourself enough credit, my boy," Dudley said. "You have a lot to offer a woman. You're a fine-looking man. You're kind, honest, have a good, though sometimes dangerous job, and you're intelligent and sensitive. I'd think most women would be happy to hook up with the likes of you."

Cal grinned at Dudley's assessment of him. "Thanks, Dud. You're good for my ego. Intellectually, I know you're right, but to tell you the truth, I haven't met anyone in a long time who interests me."

"True."

"And even if I did find someone who interested me and who could handle my job, who'd be insane enough to marry into my crazy household?" Cal added.

A scene from the previous year flickered through his mind: Amber and Beau at Hannah McShane's birthday party. Beau being his usual obnoxious self. Amber threatening to have Cal throw him in the slammer.

"You have a point," Dudley commented thoughtfully, "but people marry people with kids all the time—just look at the number of blended families out there." He smiled. "Though I have to admit most of the kids aren't like Beau."

"Thank God."

"He's angry with his mother, you know."

Cal picked up his glass of tea. "Aren't we all?"

"That's why he behaves so badly. He's hurting, so he lashes out at everyone, tries to make everyone feel as bad as he does."

"Well, he's succeeding. When did you become an armchair shrink?"

"Since you bought that piece of land next to mine, as I recall. At least I've been listening to your woes since then."

"Yeah, you have," Cal said, grinning. "And I appreciate it."

"You may have to get Beau some counseling. Claudia, too. She holds her feelings in."

"I know." Cal raked a hand through his short, sunbleached brown hair. "I just keep hoping things will get better on their own. I love them both, and I'm doing the best I can for them. But I have to do my job if I'm going to keep a roof over our heads and food on the table."

"I'm sure they understand that. What they don't understand is why their mother left them."

"I don't understand that, either." Cal exhaled harshly. "I guess Maggie Otwell was right. I need to hire a babysitter for the summer. Someone to keep the kids corralled and the house straight. Give them some sort of stability and routine."

Dudley's face wore a thoughtful expression. "I heard Amber Campion got fired from The Fashion Shop."

"I heard that, too. I also heard they shut off her phone, but I know for a fact she's working at the dollar store. Claudia and I saw her there today. Besides, I don't think Amber Campion is the kind of person I'm looking for. She's all fluff and no substance."

"She's awfully easy on the eyes, though," Dudley said with a lewd smile. "Still gorgeous and sexy."

Having his thoughts about Amber thrown back at him by Dudley—however innocently—made Cal shift in his chair. "I'm not looking for a pinup."

Dudley shrugged in a manner that said, "Too bad."

"I'm looking for someone who'll take responsibility for the kids, not just a warm body who wants to collect a paycheck. The problem is, only some high school kid would be happy to make what I can afford to pay, and what I need is someone mature enough to handle the job. A person like that is going to want the big bucks.''

"Why don't you look for someone older? Maybe a widow woman who might be having a hard time financially. You could offer her a wage and room and board. You have that spare room.''

"I'm not sure I'd like having a stranger around.''

"You're hardly ever there. You can give her the same day off you have, and that way she won't be underfoot much when you are there.''

"It's a plan,'' Cal said. "I'll think about it.'' He glanced at his watch and stood. "Time to get the troops home.''

"And the old geezer back to his cell.''

"It isn't that bad, is it?''

"Actually, it's not bad at all,'' Dudley said. "There's always someone I can beat at dominoes, and there's a little seventy-year-old down the hall with the cutest dimples and a spunky attitude who helps pass the time. But I will be glad to get back home.''

Cal smiled at his friend. "That makes two of us.''

Cal was glad to get home. It had been one heck of a day with one thing and the other. He turned off the car's engine and glanced at the kids. They were both asleep. Claudia's head rested against the passenger side window, and Beau was curled into a fetal position in the back seat. Both the picture of innocence.

His anger and his frustration over the whole situation melted like a fudge bar left in the sun, and a surge of love rushed through him. He wasn't the victim here; they were. No one had forced him to take responsibility for them. Social services would have been happy to find foster homes until Georgina came back, but the thought of his own flesh and blood being farmed out to strangers had left a sick feeling in the pit of Cal's stomach.

"It was your decision to keep them," he muttered under his breath. "So stop complainin'."

He reached out and gave Claudia's shoulder a gentle shake. "Wake up, sunshine," he said softly. "We're home."

Claudia's eyes fluttered open. She smiled and stretched and opened the Explorer's door. Cal got out and opened the back door, reaching in and lifting Beau into his arms and grunting with the effort. The kid was deadweight.

Moments later, Cal laid Beau on his bed with the faded Ninja Turtles bedspread, pulled off his sneakers and pulled an afghan over him. Beau smiled in his sleep, an incredibly sweet smile that tugged at Cal's heart.

He tiptoed from the room with a new resolve. He would do his best to change his attitude, and he would find someone loving and responsible to take care of his charges while he was at work. Somehow....

The next morning found Amber sitting on the back *galerie* of the house at Lafourche Farm, having breakfast with her father, something she'd gotten into a habit of doing on Saturdays since she'd been back, whenever she wasn't working.

"I tried to call you yesterday," Gerald said, slathering red plum jam on a slice of toast.

Her face flamed with embarrassment, but Amber lifted her gaze to his. There was no getting around the truth, something she was learning more and more as she grew older. "And you found out my phone had been disconnected."

Gerald nodded. "I'll write you out a check before you go."

"No you won't," she told him in a firm voice.

Their gazes engaged in a silent battle for several seconds. Finally, Gerald said, "I suppose I can always leave a message on your cell phone, and you can call me back."

"Sorry. I've never gotten one since I moved here."

"What?" Gerald shook his head. "Look, I know you think you need to prove something to yourself, and after what we all went through last year, I appreciate your determination to make it without my help, but you can't live without a telephone."

"Of course I can. I never talked to anyone but you anyway." She blushed. "I know it's humiliating for you having a daughter in such a financial bind, but I really need to do this by myself, Daddy. No matter what the outcome."

"I understand," he said, but she could see that he really didn't.

"Thank you. You should also know that I got fired from the dress shop. I'm at the dollar store in Vanity, now."

"I see."

"The work isn't so bad, but that Rose is an ogre," she said. "She'd make a good drill sergeant."

"Rose is legend in Vanity," Gerald said. "She goes through help like most people go through a box of tissues."

Amber's mouth twisted into a wry smile. "Well thanks loads for that bit of news. It really made my day." She and Gerald laughed together.

"Cal Simmons and his niece came in yesterday." As soon as Amber broke the news to her father she wished she hadn't. Ever since she'd come home, Gerald had been after her to find a "suitable" young man and start dating. She didn't want him reading more into the encounter with Cal than there was.

"Really? He's a nice guy. And eligible."

"Daaad." Both her expression and her tone of voice warned him to stop right there. "Cal Simmons and I would be like oil and vinegar."

"Ah, but when a few spices are added and oil and vinegar are shaken up, they're a delicious combination."

Amber laughed again, surprised by his analogy. "Why Gerald Campion, I do believe you're a romantic."

"Yes, I am," he said. "Maybe more than you or your sister realize."

"And what's that supposed to mean?" There was no denying the gleam of pleasure in his dark eyes. "Don't tell me you're interested in another woman?"

"What if I told you I am?"

Surprise left Amber speechless momentarily. "Who? Not some gold digger half your age, I hope."

Gerald chuckled, and Amber reflected how good it was to see the happiness in his eyes, to hear him laugh.

"It's Maria Antonia."

"Maria Muldair?" Amber asked. If possible, she was even more shocked. Maria Antonia Muldair was the widow of an old friend of Gerald's. Soon after Larry died, Maria had married David Perkins, who, in one of life's strange twists, happened to be the man who'd blackmailed Amber for so long.

"Yes. And it is Maria *Muldair* again. She took back Larry's name after David's arrest. Her divorce was final about five months ago, and we've been sort of seeing each other when I go to Kentucky."

"I never knew you were interested in her—romantically."

"I wasn't. She married David too soon after Larry's death. They say some people do that trying to find the happiness they had with their dead partner. And I was still grieving over Gwen. But I've always liked and admired Maria.''

Still in a state of shock, Amber asked, ''So how did this all come about? I mean, did you just look at her one day and know you loved her?''

Gerald looked uncomfortable. ''I don't know. We were thrown together a lot trying to straighten out the breeding mess with Flight of Dreams.'' He reached for the silver coffeepot. ''We went out to eat a few times as friends, and it just—'' he shrugged ''—happened.''

''So it's serious?''

''I've asked her to marry me. She's said yes.''

Amber's mind reeled. In a million years she'd never have thought her dad would remarry. ''What will you do with the farms? Will you move there, or will she come here? Or will you do like Kim and Drew did and have one of those modern marriages where you live apart?''

''We certainly aren't going to do that!'' Gerald said emphatically. ''And thank God Drew and Kim aren't anymore, either. Maria wants to come here. She's ready for a change. She's already talked to Drew about buying the farm, and he's interested. So we'll see what happens.''

''Well I'm thrilled,'' Amber said, meaning every word. ''Shocked, but thrilled.''

''So you don't mind?''

''Why would I mind? You and Maria are both wonderful people.'' A sudden thought came to Amber. Her own mother had died when she was three, and she'd never known her. Gwen, Kim's mom, had died five years ago, and Kim might be unhappy about another woman taking her mother's place in her father's life. ''Is Kim okay with it?''

''She's fine,'' Gerald said. ''Hannah is already calling

Maria Granny Ree. I just wanted to make sure you weren't opposed to it.''

"Well, you can stop worrying. Personally, I think it will be nice having a woman around to talk to.''

Gerald turned serious. "You still haven't made any friends here?''

"Nary a one,'' Amber said. "You've heard of preconceived notions? Well, if you ask half the people in town, I'm that wicked Jezebel from California. Ask the other half, and I'm that flake from California.''

"It may take some time, but they'll change their minds,'' Gerald said.

Amber reached for the pack of cigarettes she'd been avoiding all morning. "I'm not worried about it.''

But she was, and they both knew it.

On Monday morning, Cal stood shirtless and barefoot on the porch of his Cajun-style house, a mug of coffee clutched in his fist. He watched the yellow school bus trundle down the road with a feeling of profound relief.

Thankfully, there hadn't been too many incidents over the weekend that called him away from the kids, and those had soon been set straight. On Saturday he'd even managed to watch one of Beau's Little League ball games without interruption. They'd made plans to go to church on Sunday, but Cal had been called to the site of an accident so he'd dropped them off, instead. When he'd returned just as services let out, Beau's Sunday school teacher had given Cal an earful about the boy's disrespectful behavior.

When Cal tried to talk with Beau, he was met with stony silence. Beau just crossed his arms over his chest, rolled his eyes and refused to be drawn into a conversation about his actions. Cal sentenced Beau to an afternoon cutting the grass, while he and Claudia cleaned house and did the laundry.

Deciding to follow Dudley's suggestion, Cal called a couple of widowed women whose husbands had passed away and asked if they'd be interested in a job. Neither was.

Now a new day had dawned—without any milk for the cereal or bread for toast—and a new week was at hand. Cal knew it would fly by and that everyone was counting down to the start of summer vacation. There was so much to do and so little time to do it, he thought, bringing the cup to his lips and taking a healthy swig of the chicory-laced brew.

He needed to go to the school and see about getting a teacher for Beau next year, a teacher who could handle him. He needed to sign up the kids for swimming lessons and the summer reading program at the library. He needed to take time to sit down and write a check for his light bill. He needed to buy groceries. And he needed to find someone willing to take on two kids for the summer, which was just three weeks away—all while trying to keep peace in the parish. Heck, as hairy as it sometimes got, his own job seemed like a piece of cake compared to his home life. What in sweet heaven was he going to do?

"You're late."

Amber didn't miss the ominous overtones in the words or the smoldering anger in Rose Milford's pelletlike dark eyes. "I know, Rose, and I'm really sorry. I had to stop and get some gas. The station was really busy."

Amber didn't tell her boss that she'd put the bulk of her scant paycheck from the dress shop in the kitty reserved for her car payment and the remainder on a few groceries.

She'd had to roll some change to scrounge up enough money to put five dollars' worth of gas into her car.

"Well don't make a habit of it, or you'll be history around here."

Amber forced a smile. "Don't worry. I won't."

At his desk that afternoon, surrounded by paperwork, Cal called the library and found out the time of the story hour. Beau would have a fit at being forced to go to something for "babies," but maybe Sally Potter could help him find some books on subjects that interested him—assuming he was interested in anything besides cigarettes, nude women and wreaking havoc on the world. Claudia, an avid reader, would love the time spent among the books. The bottom line was they'd be supervised for an entire morning every Tuesday.

Fighting the beginnings of a headache, Cal called and put the kids into swimming lessons at the pool in Thibodaux. How he'd get them there was another problem, but he'd deal with it later. In a moment of desperation, he called Ginger Elliott's mother to ask if Ginger might be interested in a baby-sitting job for the summer, but Mrs. Elliott said Ginger would be keeping the Marlow children. Cal couldn't help feeling relieved. Tommy and Evelyn Marlow's kids were angels. Beau would have made mincemeat out of Ginger in less than a week. *Back to square one.*

At midafternoon, his headache was a raging pain, but he'd managed to find time to go to the school and talk to the guidance counselor about finding a teacher who could handle Beau. His choice was either one who treated her kids like a Marine drill sergeant or a new pretty one just out of college. Over the counselor's protests, Cal chose the new teacher. More rules would just rub Beau the wrong way. On the other hand, if he developed a crush on the young, pretty teacher, maybe he'd toe the line.

As he left the school, his beeper went off. There was a domestic disturbance on Elm Street. Cal got into this cruiser with a feeling of relief. This kind of problem he could deal with.

On Tuesday, Amber woke up to a gorgeous spring morning. With the exception of being ogled by Joe Bob Milford, Rose's smarmy husband, she'd had a good day at work the previous day. She'd been unfailingly pleasant to the customers, spent every minute she wasn't at the cash register unpacking merchandise and stocking the shelves. She even worked through her lunch hour to make up for her tardiness. Rose hadn't been able to find a single thing to complain about. *Hope springs eternal.*

Smiling, she poured coffee into a delicate rose porcelain cup, added a spoonful of sugar and carried it out to the small tin-roofed porch attached to the front of the travel trailer. She plunked down in the molded plastic chair provided by her landlord and propped her bare feet on the matching table.

The morning sun poked through the canopy of leaves provided by the oak trees surrounding the trailer. A variety of birds sang a springtime medley while others hopped along the ground, searching out breakfast. Two squirrels played tag at the base of an aging willow oak and ran across the grass alongside her car, which, Amber noted idly, had a flat tire on the front driver's side.

It took a few seconds for the disaster to sink in. When it did, she scrambled to her feet, spilling coffee and turning over the small table, screeching with rage, frustration and disbelief.

Maybe it was a trick of the light, she thought, racing

down the steps and out into the yard. Maybe she was hallucinating. She stepped in a sticker patch and yelped in pain. *And maybe you're kidding yourself.* She came to a sudden stop and balanced on one foot while she pulled stickers out of the other one. They were the round, clingy kind that pricked her fingers as she pulled them out.

Sucking a drop of blood from her fingertip and favoring her sore foot, Amber limped over to the car. It wasn't a trick of the light or a vision. The tire was definitely flat. She could see the split from where she stood. This wasn't something a can of flat fixer could solve. The tire would have to be changed.

Wonderful. She was going to be late again.

"Don't make a habit of it, or you'll be history around here."

Amber's throat tightened and she felt the hot sting of tears prickle behind her eyelids. She fought the impulse to throw herself to the ground and bawl and kick and scream the way Hannah did when her day was going wrong, but as Kim always said, tears didn't solve anything. There was nothing to do but have her dad come over and change the darn thing and call Rose to tell her what had happened. Surely, Amber thought, Rose would understand that this wasn't her fault.

She was halfway to the trailer when she remembered she didn't have a working telephone. She'd have to change the tire herself, something she'd never attempted to do before. Once more she felt the urge to cry, but instead of giving in to her tears, Amber swore, a string of curses that would have done the most seasoned sailor proud. *You wanted to prove your independence? Well, honey, this is your chance.*

She went inside, changed into some old clothes and went to open the trunk. Twenty minutes later, she had the spare—one of those little tires that didn't look as if it could go a mile—out of the trunk and had the jack placed in what looked like the right spot.

Recalling that her dad had once told her stepmother that if she ever had a flat and couldn't reach him she should loosen the lug nuts before raising the tire completely off the ground, Amber tried to do just that. But no matter how much force she exerted, Amber couldn't get the nuts to budge. After another thirty minutes of trying, she threw the tire iron to the ground in defeat. As much as she wanted to make it on her own, she had no choice but to call her dad.

She swiped her sweat-damp hair away from her face with a blistered palm, then planted her hands—sans a couple of nails—on her hips. She looked down the road one direction and then the other. Her nearest neighbor and a telephone were at least a mile away. Biting down on her bottom lip to stop its trembling, Amber started down the driveway, her sandal-shod feet creating small puffs of dust as they hit the thirsty earth.

Finding no one home at the first house, Amber doggedly slogged on to the next. By the time she'd walked the nearly two miles back home, Gerald had arrived. He'd changed the tire while she got cleaned up. By the time she walked through the dollar store's doors, she was more than two hours late.

Rose was at the register checking out a customer when Amber limped to the back, but despite her pleasant way with the elderly man, she spared Amber a spiteful look. Amber was putting her purse away when Rose stepped through the doors of the stockroom.

"Don't bother putting that up," she said, a triumphant gleam in her eyes. "You're fired."

Chapter Three

"Anything important going on?" Cal asked his dispatcher as he strode through the outer office and headed for his own private domain on Wednesday morning. There was a spring in his step and hope in his heart. He and Dudley had put their heads together over the phone the night before and come up with a list of nine possibles for a summertime baby-sitter. Jimmy Rowell's voice followed Cal down the hallway.

"We've got two drunk-and-disorderlies locked up, and Bobby and Don responded to a domestic situation outside of town about 5:00 a.m. Carl over at the ambulance service said Judge Danvers's wife had a stroke or something about midnight, and Amber Campion got fired from the dollar store yesterday."

Cal absorbed the first two bits of news with no visible effect. A typical night. The news about the judge's wife and Amber affected him more profoundly, both items of interest leaving him with a feeling of sorrow. The first he understood. The second he didn't. He turned toward the front desk. "How's Nancy Danvers?"

"Stable."

Remembering Amber's helpfulness with Claudia, and recalling the unfair reasoning behind the loss of her previous job, he strove to keep his voice noncommittal. "What did the infamous Ms. Campion do this time? Wear real Georgio to work instead of one of those copycat scents?"

Rowell hooted with laughter. "That's a good one, Cal, but you're right. If what I hear is true—and it came from my wife, who knows Linda, who works for Rose part-time, so she must know what she's talking about—Linda says Rose only hired Amber because she was in a bind. Said she went to school with her and never liked her, 'cause she put on too many airs. Anyway, Linda told my wife that Amber was doing a real good job, but then Joe Bob came in the other day and couldn't take his eyes off her. Rose was fit to be tied."

Joe Bob Milford was legend in Vanity, a womanizer who might have thought the town was named for him and him alone. He'd been trampling Rose's self-esteem into the dirt with his fancy cowboy boots for years. It was no wonder she had such a bad attitude. "Joe Bob Milford is a jerk and who thinks he's God's gift to women." Cal said.

"Yeah, but he is Rose's husband. Anyway, after that, Rose wouldn't cut Amber any slack. She stayed on her like tick on a dog's back. Linda said she even got in trouble for bringing Claudia back here the other afternoon."

Cal frowned. Wasn't that a great payment for an act of human kindness?

"Amber was about five minutes late for work on Monday morning, and Rose told her it best not happen again. Then, yesterday, she was more than two hours late. Said she had a flat tire. Rose said she didn't give a flying fig what happened, she was fired.''

"Did she have a flat, or was she just skipping out on work?''

"It was a real flat, all right. Harry down at the garage said Mr. Campion brought the tire in. Had a split in it. Mr. Campion had the car towed in and put two new tires on the front.''

Jealousy, Cal thought, was a sad thing.

"They're all just jealous that's all,'' Rowell said, the words echoing Cal's thoughts. "I remember back in school, a lot of the girls resented Amber and her sister. They were both always nice enough to me, though. Amber even flirted with me a little.'' He laughed and patted his paunch. "Course, I was about twenty-five pounds lighter back then and had a little more hair.''

Cal smiled, and the phone rang. "I'll be in my office,'' he said as Jimmy answered the call.

Inside the silence of his home away from home, Cal made a cursory examination of the papers on his desk and decided that everything could wait until he'd made his phone calls. He picked up the receiver and took his list from his pocket. "Anne Mason,'' he read aloud. "Divorced. Needs a job to supplement her child support.''

He punched in her number, forming his inquiry as the phone rang. Three minutes later, he hung up and scratched a bold line through her name. It seemed that Anne's own children were old enough to be left at home alone for a few hours at a time, and she didn't want the responsibility of one who couldn't be—even if Claudia was an angel. She'd decided to sell cosmetics door-to-door.

Cal dialed the next number, fighting the small bud of

anxiety taking root in his mind. Anne was the first on the list, for crying out loud. There were eight names to go. No need to panic just yet.

Due to the demands of his job, it took until quitting time for Cal to catch everyone at home. When he slashed a dark line through the last name on the list, Cal gave himself permission to be alarmed. Evidently, Beau's reputation had preceded him. Hell, Cal thought, raking a hand through hair that already stood on end, there were rock stars and bestselling writers who had less name recognition than Beau Simmons!

He buried his face in his hands. What was he going to do?

Amber Campion is looking for a job.

The thought came from out of nowhere. Low, sarcastic laughter filled the small room. Amber looking after Claudia—maybe. Beau? Not in a million years. He'd have her in tears within thirty minutes.

Naw, she's tougher than that. Actually, she's just mouthy enough herself that she might last a few days. Maybe even a week.

And there was the fact that Beau and Claudia still had more than two weeks of school left, which meant Amber would only have to deal with the kids in the evenings. It would give her time before school let out to settle into the routine Cal expected of her.

He brought his thoughts up short. Was he actually considering Amber Campion as his baby-sitter? A live-in baby-sitter at that?

"Darn right," Cal muttered aloud. Desperate times called for desperate measures.

What makes you think Amber will want to baby-sit for you? After all, she's never seemed too fond of kids.

He didn't know. And he didn't know her any better than the people in town who'd had so many preconceived notions about her. She'd been away for years. People changed. He certainly had. Amber couldn't have been kinder to Claudia, and she seemed crazy about Hannah.

And she's desperate for a job. Don't forget that.

True. Maybe he could put his situation to her in a way that would elicit her sympathy. Yeah. If he chose his words just right, maybe she'd jump at the chance to stay at his nice, quiet home in the country—rent-free, meals included—with his dead brother's poor grieving children…whose mother had left them for greener pastures.

Cal smiled at the scenario he was painting in his mind. With a few more embellishments, it ought to work.

What about living under the same roof as Amber Campion?

What about it? The tiny bit of resentment he'd felt for the way she'd treated him in high school was nothing but a memory. Kid stuff. As Dudley had pointed out, he had the spare room at the back of the house and he'd be gone most of the time. And, as Dudley had suggested, she could be off the same days Cal was. It should be okay, because they weren't kids anymore, and whatever tender feelings he'd once felt for her had been long forgotten.

Unexpectedly, a memory surfaced from years ago: watching from behind a corner…Amber opening her locker and finding the rose he'd spent ten minutes in his mother's garden looking for…bringing the perfection of the scarlet petals to her nose and inhaling…smiling in what looked like genuine delight…a friend coming up and questioning her…hearing his name as the rose was thrust into her locker. Both of them laughing while Cal's heart bled.

He pushed the memory away. Old news. Water under

the bridge. He wasn't so easily taken in anymore. Or so easily hurt. This arrangement would be business only.

Cal headed for the door, anxious to leave before his common sense overrode his desperation. If Amber accepted the job, she'd keep house, watch the kids, cook the meals. He'd give her room and board and a small salary. It was a workable plan. One mutually beneficial. The house was big enough that they could keep out of each other's way except for mealtimes. Surely they could get through a few dinners together in a civilized manner.

At five o'clock, Amber was sitting out on the porch, slurping the dregs of a chocolate milk shake from a paper cup and putting off going inside the small trailer until she had to. During the hottest part of the day, she'd been inside, cleaning the already spotless interior just to have a way to pass the hours. She'd washed windows and cleaned upholstery and carpet with the fancy vacuum she'd brought from California and was still making payments on.

By four-thirty, she'd been positively claustrophobic and starving. As usual when she was into something, she'd forgotten to take time to eat. She'd showered and driven back into town, deciding that what she needed was a chocolate milk shake—a large one—from Dot's Dairy Bar. She rationalized the expenditure by telling herself it was dinner as well as a treat. Thick and rich, it tasted heavenly, she thought, as she attempted to suck up the last of it.

Feeling better than she had since Rose fired her, Amber set the empty cup on the step beside her and let her gaze roam the front yard. It was a pretty lot, but it needed some landscaping. Maybe some ferns, hostas and caladiums under the trees, and some crape myrtles out near the road. She was contemplating a plan—not that she had the money to buy any of the plants—when she saw the sheriff's car approaching.

Her mouth went dry, and a nebulous fear clutched her by the throat. What now? Surely she wasn't so far behind on her bills that someone would be suing her—was she? Her mind and heart were both racing so fast she couldn't force herself to her feet. She just sat there waiting, while a feeling of foreboding grew inside her. When Cal Simmons got out of the car, she didn't know whether to laugh in relief or cry in embarrassment.

He looked good, she thought. Solid, dependable, definitely handsome in a ruggedly, manly, jock sort of way. Sexy. And here she sat in old cutoff jeans shorts, a worse-for-the-wear Betty Boop T-shirt hanging almost to the bottom of the shorts, and no bra. That bothered her less than the fact that she hadn't put on a smidgen of makeup when she got out of the shower. In spite of herself, her hand moved upward and her fingertips drifted over the scar on her cheek.

"Hi," he said. "You okay?"

The sound of his voice broke the spell of misery binding her. The concern in his eyes caused the tears to threaten again. Years of practice at hiding her true feelings called up her trademark sarcasm. "I'm fine. What's wrong? Did Rose accuse me of stealing, along with general shiftlessness?"

Cal's finely shaped lips lifted in a half smile. "No. Nothing like that."

"Then what brings you to this neck of the woods? If this isn't official business, what is it?" She raked him from head to toe with a look designed to jump-start any man's stalled libido. She'd have been happy to know that despite Cal's denials to the contrary, it worked.

He cleared his throat. "I'd call it something like personal business."

"Sounds intriguing," she said, wondering what the heck

he was hinting at. "Would you like to go inside where it's cooler? The co-op hasn't shut off the electricity yet. Of course, I'm sure you know it's just a matter of time."

"No, this is fine," Cal said.

Taking her by surprise, he dropped onto a lower step, stretching out his long legs on the grass. He leaned both elbows on the riser where her bare feet rested and focused his gaze on the Brangus cattle grazing in the pasture across the road, while Amber worked at regulating her breathing. His nearness was intimidating, but she realized it had less to do with his size than the sexy scent and raw masculinity that radiated from him like the heat waves off the asphalt road at high noon.

Amber wasn't sure she'd ever been so aware of a man and so uncomfortable with that awareness. He wasn't even looking at her, but she felt the effect of his proximity, of his *presence*, as if he were pinning her with his sharp sheriff's gaze. She couldn't help noticing how flat his stomach was or how the sun had bleached the hair on his muscular arms or the tautness of the skin covering his biceps. Her toes curled involuntarily.

"Good-looking cattle."

The mundane comment derailed the turn of Amber's thoughts. "W-what?"

Cal crossed his legs at the ankle and glanced at her over his shoulder. "Bob Maxwell's cows. They're fine looking."

"If you say so."

"Not much interest in beef, huh?" he asked, slanting her a grin over his shoulder.

"Only as a rib eye or a pot roast."

His grin widened. "How's your dad?"

"Just dandy, thanks. He's getting married again."

Cal's surprise was evident. "Really?"

"Really. I can't believe the Vanity grapevine hasn't picked up on that one yet. I mean, he actually proposed a few weeks ago."

"The grapevine's pretty good," Cal admitted with a nod, "but it hasn't gotten into mind reading yet. Who's the lucky lady?"

"Maria Muldair from Kentucky. She'll be moving to Lafourche Farm."

"And how do you and Kim feel about a new step-mother?"

"Kim and I both think Maria will make Daddy happy, and that's the bottom line for both of us."

"Tell him congratulations for me," Cal said. "And you can be sure I won't mention this conversation to anyone until Gerald makes the official announcement."

"He'll appreciate that."

"How do Kim and Hannah like living in Kentucky?"

"They love it."

"And how's the new baby?"

"Fine, the last I heard."

"That's good. Tell Kim I said hello. And tell Drew the bass fishing has been great over at Blue's Pond."

"I will."

Cal turned his attention back to the cattle grazing across the road, and Amber tried to do the same. It was hard with him so near. He recrossed his legs a couple of times and cleared his throat.

You are such an idiot! Amber barely refrained from smacking herself on the forehead with her palm. The man was thirsty and too polite to ask for something to drink. If she were still alive, Gwen would be appalled by her older daughter's shocking lack of hostessing skills.

"Would you like something to drink? I have some iced tea in the fridge."

Cal glanced up at her again. "No, thanks."

"Okay."

Another silence stretched out between them. Amber was aware of every breath Cal took, of the way he laced and unlaced the fingers clasped across his stomach, of the way the fabric of his brown slacks stretched tautly across his thighs....

An alarm she didn't understand sent her surging to her feet, her heart pounding. Cal reacted by doing the same thing. "What's wrong?" he asked.

"That's what I want to know," she said, confusion clouding her eyes. "What do you want, Cal? You didn't drive all the way out here to chitchat about cows and my family's welfare."

A grimace of discomfort flickered across his face.

"You're right. I didn't."

"Then why *did* you come?"

Cal planted his hands low on his hips and tipped his head back as if to examine the canopy of leaves overhead. When he looked at her there was a look of grim determination in his eyes. "I came to offer you a job."

"What?" she asked, wondering if she could possibly have heard correctly.

"A job," he repeated. "I have one if you want it."

"You heard about Rose firing me?"

"Yeah."

"I don't want your charity," she said, her chin rising along with the heat in her eyes.

"And I'm not offering you any. I have a legitimate job proposition."

"I don't have any office skills, other than interior design and a bit of art."

"You don't need any office skills."

Her frown deepened, and the cynicism she'd gained

through the years surfaced. "What are you going to do then? Chase me around the desk?"

To her surprise, a dull red crept into Cal's lean cheeks. "Of course not! The job isn't at the sheriff's office. It's at the house." She saw him take a deep breath before he blurted, "I need a baby-sitter for Beau and Claudia."

"Baby-sitter?" Stunned by the offer, Amber didn't know if she should grovel in gratefulness or turn around and storm into the house.

"I'm in a bind with summer coming up," Cal said. "I can't leave them alone all day."

"Of course not," she agreed, "but—"

"They're good kids. Claudia is no problem. None whatsoever. They really need a woman's touch. She's growing up, and—"

"Why me?" she interrupted. "I haven't baby-sat since I was fourteen," she said, still bewildered by the proposition.

"Like I said, I heard you were out of a job."

It was Amber's turn to be embarrassed. "Ah. The Vanity grapevine again." She grew thoughtful for a moment, than asked, "Do you mind telling me what happened to their mother?"

"You haven't heard *that* through the grapevine?"

"I've heard the gossip. I'd like to hear the truth."

"The truth is pretty much as the rumors have it. Georgina was pregnant when she and Dean married, and when he died she got a lot of money. She decided life was passing her by and she was tired of the responsibility of the kids. She wanted to go places and see things. So she left them with me for the weekend and took off. Never came back. No one in her family showed any interest in taking them, so I did. I understand she's found herself a new husband along the way."

"She hasn't contacted the kids since she left?"

"No."

Amber lifted her shoulders in an uncomprehending shrug. "She just left Beau and Claudia with you without saying anything to them? Without letting anyone know she was leaving for good?"

Cal nodded. "Though I heard a week or two ago that she does plan to come back so her family can meet her new husband."

"Do you think she'll stay? Will she want to see the kids?"

"Who knows?"

"What if she wants them back?"

"Over my dead body." The expression in his eyes told her he wasn't fooling. Amber would hate to be in opposition to Cal Simmons in any matter—especially one as important to him as his niece and nephew.

"The job is more than baby-sitting," he said, taking her silence for consideration. "You'd be my housekeeper— you know—keep the house clean, do the laundry, cook the meals..."

"I know what a housekeeper is. I grew up with a series of them," she said, disturbed by the thought of anyone abandoning sweet little Claudia, who had absolutely no self-confidence. An image of Beau nudged aside the vision of his sister. Beau with his belligerent attitude and the chip on his shoulder. She gave an inward shudder.

While she was lost in thought, Cal turned away abruptly. She grabbed his arm. The flesh beneath her hand was warm and firm. "Where are you going? I haven't turned you down yet."

He shook his head and again focused his attention on the cattle across the way. "You don't have to. This was a stupid idea." He cut a self-deprecating gaze to her. "I forgot you're Amber Campion. You aren't a housekeeper. You *have* housekeepers.''

''Make that past tense,'' she said, her lips twisting in a parody of a smile. She took a deep breath. ''So let me get this straight. I cook, clean, keep up with the kids. All the wifely duties without the fringe benefits—or the snoring.''

Cal's gaze drifted from her face downward. Amber crossed her arms over her breasts in an instinctive gesture. He nodded.

''What's the pay?'' she asked, more confused than angry.

''Pay?''

''Yeah. You do plan to pay me, don't you?''

''Of course I'd pay you, but surely you aren't seriously considering this asinine proposal.''

''Cal, darlin','' she drawled. ''At this point, I'd seriously consider a proposal from the devil himself if he made me an offer. What's the pay?''

''Room and board and two hundred a week.''

''Two hundred a week! That won't even keep me in nail polish and lipstick.''

Rapidly becoming familiar with her sarcasm, he figured she'd made the exaggerated statement as much for shock value as dismay. He felt a flash of guilt for a moment but stood his ground. On his salary, it was the best he could do.

He nodded. ''Two hundred. Less taxes. But remember, you won't have any rent, utilities or food to buy.'' Her willingness to at least consider his offer bolstered Cal's determination. ''For all intents and purposes you'll be your own boss.''

''Hmm. I'd have my own room?''

''Yeah. The guy who owned the house before me converted the laundry room into a bedroom for his mother-in-law and moved the washer and dryer out to the storage building. I've been using the room for extra storage.''

"I'll be sleeping in the laundry room?''

"It was a fairly large room,'' he said. "As laundry rooms go.''

"When would I start? I can't wait until school's out.''

"Anytime. Tomorrow, if you want. I thought starting someone before school lets out would give them time to get settled with the house before the kids become a full-time responsibility.''

"Sounds logical.'' She shook her head. "I can't *believe* I'm really considering this asinine offer,'' she said, recanting his earlier statement.

"But you are? Because if you aren't I need to contact a couple of other people.''

"Oh, yeah. I am.'' She thought she saw a glimmer of jubilation in his eyes, but she couldn't be sure.

"When can you let me know?''

Play it cool, Amber. Don't sound as desperate as you are. "Let me sleep on it,'' she told him. "I had a couple of things over in Thibodaux I wanted to check on in the morning. I'll stop by your office after lunch and tell you one way or the other.''

"Great.''

Cal walked back to the cruiser, uncertain which was crazier—his offering Amber the job to begin with or trying to talk her out of taking it once he had. When she'd mentioned doing the work of the wife without the fringe benefits, he'd been unable to keep from looking at the softness of her unbound breasts beneath the opaque fabric of her T-shirt. Once again, she'd made him acutely and uncomfortably aware of the length of his self-imposed celibacy. He thought of her being under his roof, sleeping just down the hallway. Coming out of her bedroom, her short blond hair mussed from sleep, her curvaceous body clad in something that would drive him crazy.

Crazy. That's exactly what he was. Crazy for even contemplating hiring her. Crazy for thinking they could inhabit the same space without some sort of explosion igniting between them. Cal shook his head. He still couldn't believe he'd done it. Or that she was thinking it over. He crossed his fingers and hoped he hadn't sounded too nonchalant when he'd lied about contacting some other people.

After Cal left, Amber sat on the steps until darkness and the arrival of a cloud of mosquitoes forced her inside. Her feelings vacillated between surprise that Cal had offered her a job to embarrassment that he apparently knew about the seriousness of her financial situation. Why would he even consider her as an employee after the way she'd treated him in school? Was it a way to get back at her? Make her eat crow, so to speak?

Don't be ridiculous. That was ages ago. Cal didn't get to be sheriff or gain the respect of everyone by harboring petty feelings of revenge. Their past was just that. They were both adults.

Adults, yeah. Another of the things that was bothering her. She'd grown up, but so had Cal. And nicely, too. No one could deny that he'd become a very attractive man. She'd be naive not to consider the consequences of their living under the same roof. She wished she'd never made the comment about doing all the wifely things without the snoring or the fringe benefits. It had triggered a realization in Cal that had been evident by the heat reflected in his brown eyes. If the awareness zinging through her whenever he came within three feet of her was any indication, she had a feeling that the fringe benefits might be excellent.

Which presented a problem. There were bound to be times they'd be faced with uncomfortable situations. Like Cal wandering through the house shirtless. Or bumping into him as she came from the shower.

''Don't let your imagination run away with you, Amber. It may never happen,'' she said aloud.

But it could, which would make a potentially impossible situation. If she took the job—and she was leaning toward just that—it would be up to her to see that their employer-employee relationship stayed just that. She couldn't afford to let the unaccountable fact that Cal Simmons made her heart rate accelerate come between her and a paycheck.

The money was almost an insult, she thought, going over his offer for the dozenth time. But still, not all that much less than she'd have brought home from the dollar store—if she'd managed to get in a full week's work. And she had to remember that room and board was worth a lot. In truth, if it weren't for the fact that it was Cal offering her the position, she'd jump at it.

What about Beau?

She groaned and dropped her head into her hands. Beau. The fly in an otherwise nicely scented ointment. She recalled the way he'd talked back to her at Hannah's birthday party the previous year. Remembered the challenge in his eyes. Was she up to dealing with Beau on a daily basis? The little beast was a handful, and that was a fact. She'd been a handful, too, but Gwen had never given up on her, and she'd turned out all right…after a while.

She'd been little more than a toddler when her dad had married Kim's mother, but Gerald and her own mother had already spoiled her terribly. She'd demanded instant gratification.

As she grew older, it was inevitable that she'd hear the rumors about her mother being with another man when the car accident had taken her life, something Amber had taken very personally. Hadn't she and Gerald been good enough for her mother? What had they been lacking that she'd had to look for her happiness and pleasure with someone else? The self-destructive behavior she'd adopted hadn't been so much a rebellion against her stepmother and her father, but rather a punishment she'd meted out to herself, for not being good enough.

Knowing the story behind Claudia and Beau's mother's leaving made putting herself in their shoes a little easier. Possibly, the Simmons kids were experiencing the same feelings of rejection she herself had once felt. Claudia had responded by pulling into herself. Beau reacted with belligerence and unacceptable behavior. Would understanding the reasons behind their actions make handling them easier?

It couldn't hurt, she thought, rising and heading for the minuscule bedroom. She flicked on the light and looked around. Surely the bedroom-cum-laundry room was bigger than this. Heck, she'd be moving up in the world.

So you're going to take the job?

"I don't have much choice," she said aloud. The positions she'd mentioned in Thibodaux were nonexistent. Cal had caught her in a very vulnerable, very needy moment.

It's more than that, Amber, and you know it.

Yes, it was. Though she didn't want to examine the reasoning too closely, she knew that part of her desire to take a job caring for two children whose mother had abandoned them was to try to assuage the guilt she felt every single day over giving up her own child. Knowing it was impossible. Knowing she had no choice but to try.

* * *

Cal made certain he was in his office all afternoon the following day. No way was he going to miss Amber when she came in. He'd told the kids she was considering the position, which seemed to make Claudia happy—at first. Later, she'd sunk into the doldrums, and nothing he said or did could bring her out. Beau had responded to the news by rolling his eyes and drawling his customary "Whatever."

They'd cleaned house like demons all evening and into the night, dusting, mopping, vacuuming and clearing out the room that would be Amber's if she took the job. Finally, at ten o'clock, Beau's complaining had become too much, and Cal sent both kids to bed with a hug of thanks.

Alone, he'd stood in the small room and tried to look at it through Amber's eyes. It was small, no doubt about it. He'd fitted it with one of Beau's twin beds and an extra bureau that he'd unearthed from his own walk-in closet. A plain Shaker-style table stood next to the bed, and a small slipper chair done in a rose-patterned chintz that had belonged to his mother sat in one corner. There was nothing but a recently washed miniblind at the window. There wasn't a bedspread on the bed. Somehow, he didn't think Amber would appreciate Ninja Turtles. Unable to find anything else suitable, he'd opted to cover the bed with solid navy-blue sheets.

He'd stood there, his hands on his hips, shaking his head. He must have been out of his mind to think that Amber Campion could ever be satisfied with this room...this house. The sentiment hadn't gone away, even some fifteen hours later. His doubts were growing with each passing minute. Where was she? He asked himself, glancing at his watch.

As if on cue, Jimmy Rowell poked his head through the door and said, "Hey, boss, your baby-sitter—" he waggled his eyebrows and gave Cal a salacious grin "—is here."

"Stuff it, Jimmy," Cal grumbled, rising and rounding the desk. "My interest in the lady is purely professional."

"Yeah, yeah, yeah," Rowell said. "Hey, I see you polished your shoes."

Cal felt his face growing red, but before he could reply Rowell closed the door between them. In a matter of seconds, Amber was knocking.

Hoping against hope, Cal opened the door for her. Immediately, his senses were awash in her perfume, a floral scent that reminded him of sunny days and hot sultry nights. She was wearing a sleeveless, scoop-necked bright plaid cotton dress that accentuated the shapely length of her legs.

Fighting the overwhelming desire to nuzzle her neck and see if that were the source of the scent, he cleared his throat, motioned her to a chair and took the one behind the desk.

"Is it still hot outside?" he asked.

"It's pretty warm," she said with a smile.

"Would you like something to drink? We have a soda machine."

"No, thanks."

Out of small talk—never one of his gifts—and anxious to hear her answer, Cal blurted, "Well? What did you decide?"

Amber frowned. "I don't have any experience with kids."

"Hey," Cal said. "You've been one."

"Yeah," she said with a droll smile. "There is that." She paused uncomfortably. "I'm sure you've heard about the problems I've been having holding a job around here."

"I have. And not even you could be that big of a problem."

"Thanks." Her mouth slanted wryly. "I think."

Cal realized he'd made a colossal blunder. "What I meant was that I've found that people are seldom all the world perceives them to be. Like Beau."

He saw Amber grimace.

Now why did you have to go and bring up Beau?

"Beau can be a really sweet, caring boy," he told her, hoping the stock statement was enough by way of damage control.

"You don't have to give me the hard sell, Cal," Amber said. "Beau and I probably have more in common than either of us knows." She took a deep breath and met his gaze squarely. "I'm not sure I can do you a good job, but I need to work. I accept the offer."

Chapter Four

The lack of reaction on Cal's face made Amber wonder if he'd heard her. Finally, he said, "You will?"

"Yes." She sighed. *Against my better judgment.*

A wide smile lit up Cal's face, bringing the dimple in his right cheek to play, along with the gathering of an attractive collection of lines at the corners of his light brown eyes. Amber's heart took a little nosedive.

His smile faded. "You won't change your mind?"

"Not if you promise not to fire me for something like having a flat tire."

Cal stood and thrust out a hand. "Deal."

Almost reluctantly, Amber placed her hand in his. Warm. Strong. Callused. She experienced a fleeting image of that hand cradling her cheek, his thumb drifting over her mouth, scraping her teeth. The effect on her breathing was startling and immediate. The air in the room seemed to disappear. She became acutely aware of the inherent danger that accompanied the humble position of baby-sitter.

Darn it, Cal! Why did you have to grow up to be so good-looking? And why have you come into my life when I'm my most vulnerable? She only hoped she wouldn't be sorry. That none of them would be sorry.

"Deal," she repeated, and pulled her hand from his.

"Would you like to go out to the house to meet the kids and look things over?" His lethal smile reappeared.

"That would be nice," Amber said primly, getting to her feet.

Cal opened the door for her, and she preceded him to the outer office, where he introduced her to Jimmy Rowell.

"I remember Jimmy," Amber said. "How've you been?"

"Just fine, Amber. And you?"

"Great." It was a lie, and they both knew it, but at least she'd done as she'd been taught. Never, Gwen had often told her, let other people know things weren't as well as they might be. No one wanted to hear your troubles, and putting up a good front often made a world of the difference not only in how others perceived you, but in your own feelings of self-worth. Sort of a healthy self-delusion.

"Amber will be taking care of Claudia and Beau."

"Good," Rowell said in a hearty voice.

"If she calls for any reason, I want you to contact me immediately."

"Sure thing, boss."

"I'm taking her out to meet the kids," Cal told his dispatcher. "We won't be long."

"I'll be here." Rowell's smile was as wide as his nod was enthusiastic.

Amber left, wondering what the heck was wrong with Jimmy Rowell.

* * *

Neither Amber nor Cal spoke much on the first leg of the drive to his home in the country. Finally, he shifted his gaze from the road. She saw a glimmer of concern in his eyes. "Don't let Beau intimidate you. Or manipulate you. He's a master at both."

Amber remembered that from Hannah's party the previous year. "Don't worry. I don't scare easily and I've had a lot of experience with manipulating men."

"David Perkins?" he asked.

"I wasn't thinking of David or men who manipulate. I meant that I was quite the little manipulator myself as a kid. I know how it works."

Instead of the snide comment she halfway expected him to make about her youth, he only smiled. "Takes one to know one, huh?"

"Exactly."

"You'll love Claudia. She's a sweetheart, but I confess that I'm at a loss as to what to do..." Cal paused, as if he were trying to find the right words. "I'm not sure what to do for her, how to deal with her. I feel as if she needs something I'm not giving her. I feel...I don't know... inadequate."

"Ah. Inadequate. Not an easy emotion for a guy who's used to solving problems, I'll bet," she said.

"No."

"If it's any consolation, you aren't alone. From what I've read, inadequacy, fear and anger seem to be natural feelings for parents when kids hit their teen years."

"I'm not her parent, which, I think, is also part of the problem."

"I'm sure it is," Amber said. She didn't miss the way his mouth tightened. Cal was no doubt thinking of Georgina and how she'd abandoned her children. Amber attempted to squelch a familiar pang of guilt by saying, "She seems very shy."

"She is. I think Georgina's leaving them the way she did had an impact on them both that none of us fully understand."

The sorrow inside Amber grew. Was her son or daughter angry, like Beau, or was he or she like Claudia, lacking self-worth, nurturing the idea that there was something wrong with them because the mother who had given them life had handed them over to strangers?

"Are you okay?"

Amber turned toward Cal, who'd taken his eyes from the road and was regarding her with some concern.

"Fine," she lied, forcing a smile. "Who's with the kids today?"

"Beau went to the batting cages with a friend this morning." Cal grinned. "The boy's dad just happens to have played college ball at LSU. Beau should be back home by now."

"He plays Little League?"

"Catcher," Cal said with a nod. "And a darn good one. And he's got an arm on him you wouldn't believe."

The pride in Cal's voice was unmistakable. "What about Claudia?"

"Claudia is old enough and dependable enough that I can trust her by herself. She isn't the kind of kid who gets into mischief." Cal turned on the turn signal, and in seconds the tires were crunching along the rock driveway.

The house was built of cedar with a Cajun-style roofline that protected the porch spanning the front of the house. Wisteria clambered up one of the porch supports and crawled across the shingled roof, dripping clusters of grapelike blooms. Flower beds were scattered around the yard, and blossoms that Amber couldn't identify turned their brightly colored faces to the sun, their heads bobbing in tune to the melody of the soft breeze that tugged at the hem of her short skirt.

"It's charming," she said, as Cal cut the car's engine.

"It needs some fixing up," he said, opening his door, "but there never seems to be enough time."

Amber opened her own car door. "I imagine you're on call day and night."

"Pretty much."

They exited the car together. Cal stepped aside for Amber to precede him up the brick sidewalk. At the door, he reached around her to turn the knob, brushing against her. Once again, she was stunned by the effect of his nearness. Swinging the door inward, he called, "Hey, kids! We're here!"

Amber stepped into a large room that boasted a rock fireplace, hardwood floors and various wildlife trophies hanging on the walls. Her first impression was of size and light and raw masculinity. Her second was that, while the room was spotlessly clean, it was in dire need of some sprucing up. The floors needed refinishing, the sofa was worn, the drapes dated. She could well imagine that with caring for his niece and nephew and keeping a watch over the citizens of the parish, Cal lacked both time and inclination to tackle decorating in the evenings.

"Claudia! Beau!"

The children came into the room from a hallway that Amber guessed led to their bedrooms. Other than needing a haircut, Beau looked quite presentable in khaki shorts and a T-shirt. Amber assumed that Claudia wore shorts beneath her oversize T-shirt. Her hair was slicked back in a ponytail that emphasized her high forehead. The dark circles beneath her eyes accentuated an unhealthy pallor. By the expressions on their faces, they might have been headed for the gallows instead of having to meet a new baby-sitter. Both studiously avoided Amber's gaze.

Cal crossed to Claudia and gave her a hug, then tipped her face back so he could look at her. "Feeling any better?"

She nodded and, after giving her another hug, he turned to Beau and riffled his hair. "How'd you do?"

Beau backed away from his uncle's touch and slanted a glance at Amber before giving a shrug. "Fine. Mr. Steve says I need a new bat."

Cal raked a hand through his short hair. "We just bought one last year."

Beau shrugged. "Mr. Steve says I need a longer one."

"He's grown a foot since last spring," Amber said.

Cal turned toward her, as if he were surprised to see her. "I'm sorry," he said with a shake of his head. "I haven't introduced you, but I was worried about Claudia. She had an asthma attack last night."

Asthma. Amber stifled the urge to groan. She'd forgotten that Claudia suffered from asthma. She didn't know a thing about the condition, except that it could be dangerous.

Before she could ask how serious Claudia's problem was, Cal said, "This is Amber Campion, Beau. She's agreed to look after the house and keep an eye on the two of you for the summer. Claudia, you remember Amber, don't you?"

Claudia nodded.

"I remember her, too," Beau said, his voice flat, matter of fact. "She's the one who threatened to have you cuff me and haul me off to jail."

Of course he'd remember that! Amber struggled for something to say...some explanation. All she could think of was, "I'm sorry about that, Beau, but that was a particularly unruly bunch, and I haven't had a lot of experience with kids. I was at my wit's end.''

The sudden gleam in his eyes told her she'd made a mistake. She'd admitted to having a weakness, given him something to use against her.

Beau turned to his uncle. ''If she doesn't have any experience with kids, how come you hired her to take care of us?''

Cal wasn't stupid. The animosity radiating from his nephew was palpable. He pinned Beau with a hard stare. ''Let's just say you're gaining a reputation Beau and leave it at that.''

Beau lifted his chin in a defiant gesture, but Amber thought she saw a hint of red in his cheeks. ''I don't give a rat's a—'' he caught himself ''—butt what people think of me.''

''Well, I do.'' He turned to Amber. ''Let me show you around.''

Amber's view of the rest of the house was the same as her opinion of the living room—that of a man with more things on his mind than whether or not the curtains matched the bedspread. Claudia's room boasted Little Mermaid linens and curtains, and Beau's had Ninja Turtles. She imagined they'd both outgrown their fascination with those particular characters long ago, a sentiment Cal expressed with a sigh.

''Originally, Claudia's bedroom was the master bedroom, and this room—'' he indicated a small room with a television, worn sofa and computer ''—was the third bedroom. The former owner was an electrician who used it for an office because it was so small. He built a master bedroom and bath off the back of the house.''

He led her back down the hallway to the kitchen and dining area, which also needed a major overhaul, and pushed open a door at the back of the dining room. "This is the master bedroom."

Amber stepped through the doorway, more curious than she would have believed to take a look at the place where Cal slept. She couldn't help gasping when she stepped through the door of the room. A Victorian bed of cherry wood—with an intricately carved headboard that soared to within inches of the ceiling—dominated the room. A matching mirrored dresser that was as wide as the bed resided on the opposite wall.

Though she'd never been an antiques buff, Amber had grown up with antiques, and Gwen had done her best to instill the importance of recognizing, respecting and pre-serving the past in both Kim and Amber. Until this mo-ment, Amber had no idea the lessons had stuck. "Good grief!" she said, crossing the room to take a closer look.

Misunderstanding, Cal shrugged. "It's a little feminine for my taste, but it's been in the family since the turn of the century. My grandfather, father and my brother and I were all conceived in that bed. Claudia and Beau, too, I guess. As the older son, it went to Dean when our parents died. After Dean was killed, Georgina told me to come get the monstrosity. I'm just grateful she didn't want to keep it."

Amber's face radiated with a smile of genuine delight. "It's exquisite," she said, running her fingers over the details of a carved flower petal.

"You know, Amber, you should do that more often."

"What?"

"Smile. It lights up your whole face."

Uncomfortable with the intensity in his eyes, she gave a short, humorless laugh. "I smile."

"Yeah. You hand out a lot of those little sarcastic quirks of your lips. But you seldom smile with your whole face.

With your mouth and your eyes…the way I remember you smiling when we were growing up.''

Amber straightened. ''There hasn't been much to smile about lately.''

''I know things have been hard for you since you came back, but hang in there. Sometimes it takes the people of Vanity a while to wake up to the truth about a person or situation, but they generally do.''

''And what do you think is the truth about me?'' she asked, wishing immediately that she hadn't.

''That the hard-nosed, smart-mouthed woman is a cover-up.''

''A cover-up for what?''

He gave a slow shake of his head. ''I'm not sure yet.''

Amber let out a pent-up breath slowly. How had their conversation taken such a personal turn? She didn't like the vulnerable way his observations made her feel. ''Tell me about Claudia's asthma.''

It took Cal a moment to adjust to the conversational shift. ''I didn't mean to keep it a secret. She's had it for years. The spells are triggered by allergies. She had a really bad bout a few months ago. So bad she had to be hospitalized for a night. We have to keep Adrenalin in the house now. She had a pretty rough spell last night. She'd gone home with a friend who has a cat.''

Amber looked alarmed. ''I don't know anything about taking care of someone with asthma,'' she said. ''Especially when it's bad enough to require hospitalization.''

''It rarely comes to that. When Claudia has an attack, she knows what to do. She can usually get things under control herself.''

''You sound as if you think I can do this.''

''If I didn't think you could handle it, I wouldn't have asked you to take the job.'' Amber met his steady gaze for several seconds. He was either telling the truth or a great poker player. He swept an arm toward the door. "Would you like to see your room?"

"The laundry room?" she asked, tossing him one of those mocking smiles.

"The *former* laundry room." She preceded him from the bedroom and headed in the direction he pointed. "It's small, and I didn't have much to fix it up with, but I figured you'd want to put your own things in anyway."

He was right. The room was small and sparsely furnished but immaculate. Still, it was bigger than her bedroom in the travel trailer. Things were looking up.

"There's a half bath as you come in from the carport, but to shower, you'll have to use one of our bathrooms."

Shower in Cal's bathroom? The very thought of it sent a frisson of something delicious scampering down her spine. Showering in Beau's bathroom brought a feeling of horror. She could imagine frogs or fish—or worse—in Beau's tub.

"I'll see if Claudia minds if I share with her. She's less apt to object to 'girl things' lying around than Beau. Or you," Amber tacked on. Cal didn't respond to that.

"The main thing is that I want you to feel at home," he told her. "You'll be responsible for laundry, and for keeping things clean and neat—"

"Yeah, yeah. You told me all this," she interrupted. "The stand-in wife without bedroom privileges." Amber had to forcibly stop herself from cringing. Whenever she got around Cal it seemed as if the first thing she did was open her mouth and insert her foot. If she kept it up, he'd think she was interested in him, and just because she'd had a couple of fluttery feelings in her stomach when he got too close certainly didn't mean she'd fallen for him.

"That makes twice you've mentioned sex not being part

of the deal," Cal said, cutting off her thoughts. He crossed his arms over his broad chest, leaned against the door frame and regarded her with a taunting gleam in his eyes. "If that's a problem, we can probably work something out."

She lifted an eyebrow in a surely-you-jest gesture and said, "Dream on, Sheriff."

"No doubt I will, Ms. Campion."

Even though the smiling admission was no doubt just another taunt, it brought a visual image to mind that warmed her blood and her cheeks. Drat the man, anyway! He knew exactly how to get to her.

"So when can I move in?"

"You're taking the job?" he asked.

"It looks that way."

Cal shrugged. "I guess you can move in whenever you want. Tomorrow, if you like. If you need some help, I can take off a couple of hours early."

"That's okay. I don't have any furniture. Just clothes and personal items. I can load them in the car."

"I'll have an extra key made first thing in the morning. You can stop by the station and pick it up. The kids will be in school, so you can feel free to poke around and find things."

"Find things?"

"Yeah, like pots and pans, things like that."

"I may as well warn you, I'm not much of a cook." She offered him an apologetic smile. "Actually, I don't do much besides TV dinners and takeout. But I'm sure I can learn," she tacked on when he frowned. "If you can read a recipe, you can cook—right?"

"Right," Cal echoed. But he didn't look convinced.

That night, after a dinner of fried catfish, hush puppies, French fries and cole slaw from the grocery deli, Cal sat at his computer staring at the screen. The thriller he'd been working on in his spare time—the one that had at least enough merit an agent wanted to see the completed manuscript—was as dead in his mind as the corpse the protagonist had just discovered in the water. He couldn't concentrate, couldn't think of anything but the fact that Amber Campion was moving in.

What the heck had he done? She had no experience with kids, couldn't cook, and the minute she got within ten feet of him his temperature began to rise. Not only that, but when he told the kids she'd accepted the job, they'd reacted with about as much enthusiasm as if he'd told them he was bringing home a deadly virus.

"I don't want her here," Beau had said earlier that evening. "She won't fit in, and she'll be going through all my stuff."

"She'll be keeping your room clean, not delving into your deepest darkest hiding places." Cal pinned his nephew with a stern look. "Which, by the way shouldn't have anything in them you'd feel uncomfortable having someone see. Like *Babes* magazines."

Beau rolled his eyes.

"She's here to do things like cooking, cleaning, shopping and watching after you kids when you get home from school. This summer, I'll see to it you have plenty to do. Amber can take you to all your activities. I'm not always available, and you know I can't leave you alone to fend for yourselves."

"Why her?" Beau asked.

"Because, Beau," Cal told him with a look of supreme long suffering. "I looked high and low and there wasn't another soul in town willing to take you on for the money I could afford to pay. I don't want to hurt your feelings, but I wasn't kidding when I said your reputation has preceded you. Your attitude stinks, and your behavior isn't any better. If you don't straighten up, there won't be a mother in Vanity who'll let her son play with you. And despite your tough-guy act, I don't think you want that."

Beau made no reply, and Cal looked at Claudia. "You don't seem too happy about the situation. I thought you liked Amber."

"She's okay." Claudia gazed at Cal with troubled eyes. "What if she can't take it? What if we give her a chance, and we think everything's going along okay, and she just up and leaves one day?"

There was a lot Cal didn't know about bringing up kids, but he was smart enough to realize what was at the root of the question. Claudia was afraid of getting attached to Amber and then having her leave the way her mother had done. He knew there was nothing he could do to guarantee that she wouldn't. All he could do was be honest as possible about the situation.

"Good point. I can't honestly see Amber being here forever. She's young and pretty and may find someone, fall in love and get married. Or I might. She's smart, so she may find a better paying job. But I don't think Amber is the kind of person who'd leave without giving us some warning." Cal realized as he said the words, he meant them.

"I know this will be different for us," he'd told them. "And it may be difficult. I know Amber will get on our nerves sometimes, and in our space. We will hers, too. All I'm asking, guys, is for you to give her a chance, okay?"

Claudia and Beau had looked at him and nodded. What else could they do?

"Let me get this straight," Gerald said when Amber drove to Lafourche Farm to break the news to him.

"You're going to live at Cal Simmons's place and baby-sit his niece and nephew."

Amber nodded. "Baby-sit, do the cooking, cleaning, that sort of thing. But the main thing is to be there for the kids."

Gerald shook his head, his disbelief clear. "Do you have any idea how ornery Beau Simmons is?"

"I have a general idea."

"He's trouble with a capital *T*," Gerald said.

"Thanks so much for the encouragement," Amber drawled. She reached into her purse for her cigarettes, realized she was supposed to be quitting and sighed.

"I don't mean to discourage you, I just wonder if you have any real idea what you're getting into."

"I know I get room and board free, which means that's two less things I won't have to eke out of my meager salary."

Gerald leaned forward, his expression earnest. "Honey, you're smart. Talented. You can do better than being a live-in nanny."

"Maybe I should be able to, but obviously, Daddy, I can't," she said. She reached out and patted his knee. "Don't fret so. It's only until something better comes along, and Cal really needs someone. There's something about being needed, you know?" She sighed. "I only hope I won't let them down."

"Amber?"

"Sir?"

"Is there something going on between you and Cal Simmons?"

Afraid to admit to the impact the sheriff had on her, Amber reverted to form. She winked and grinned. "Not yet."

* * *

Giving up on his novel, Cal punched in Dudley's number at the rehab. The answer he got was, "Joe's mule barn."

"Dudley?" Cal asked, even though it was one of Dudley's favorite greetings.

"And who else would it be?" Dudley asked, his tone testy.

"What's the matter with you?"

"What's the matter is that they informed me this afternoon that I'm definitely being detained here until school is out. That's the bad news. The good news is that I'll be there to keep an eye on the kids for the summer."

"I'm glad you'll be home, buddy, but I called to tell you I hired Amber Campion this afternoon."

"Hired her? You didn't even tell me you'd approached her about the job."

"I know. It was a last-ditch measure when none of the ladies on our list would say yes. It's mutually beneficial. She needs the job as much as I needed someone to look after the kids. I'm glad you'll be around, though, in case she needs some support."

"Support?" The old man chuckled. "I'd rather hang out with Beau—you know? Peeking through the keyhole as Ms. Campion bathes."

"We don't have keyholes, Dud."

"Oh, that's right. Well, he's a smart lad. I'm sure he'll figure out something."

"No doubt."

"How's the novel coming?"

"I couldn't seem to get anything going tonight."

"Hmm." The simple sound held a wealth of meaning, all of it smug and knowing.

"What's that supposed to mean?" Cal snapped.

"It means, hmm."

"I wasn't thinking about Amber Campion."

"Liar. Tell me, Caleb. Is she as hot as the rumormongers claim?"

Cal thought of her long tanned legs and the swell of her full breasts beneath the worn T-shirt. Of the way his heart started thundering in his chest whenever he got a whiff of her perfume. "Times two," he said grudgingly.

"Hmm," Dudley said.

After Amber and her father shared a dinner of roast beef with carrots and potatoes, Amber called her landlord to tell him she'd be moving. Since she was paid up through the end of the month, there was no problem. He could find another renter and pocket a little extra money for the month.

Because her phone had been disconnected, she hadn't spoken to Kim in a while, so she dialed her sister in Kentucky to catch up on the news. According to Kim, spring on the Kentucky Thoroughbred farm was gorgeous, Hannah was enjoying preschool three mornings a week, and the baby was fine, the sweetest thing this side of heaven. Drew was more than fine. Fabulous, in fact. Wonderful. Perfect.

While Amber was thrilled that her sister's life was going so well, she couldn't help feeling a little down as she related the news of her new job.

Kim's reply was, "You're going to do *what?*"

"Go to work for Cal Simmons as a live-in baby-sitter and housekeeper."

Amber went into round two with her sister, her conversation with Kim almost verbatim to the one Amber had had with their father.

"You could work there at the farm for Dad," Kim suggested. "Sort of be his social secretary and run the house for him the way I used to do."

"I'm not taking anything from Dad," Amber said. "I've taken enough. I have to make it on my own, Kim—one way or the other. Besides, when he and Maria get married, she'll take care of things for him."

"What about coming out here and staying with us? I'm sure you could find something more up your alley in Lexington or Louisville."

"Thanks, but no thanks. I've told Cal I'll take the job, and I will. Trying to corral Beau Simmons will be a challenge, but Claudia… I don't know, Kim, she really gets to me. She's so lost and insecure. She really needs a woman in her life."

"I'm sure they all do."

Amber gave a short laugh. "Maybe. Funny how you see things differently as an adult. For all that I resented Gwen and the fact that she expected so much from me, I look back now and see how hard it would have been to grow up without her. She was always there for me, even when I rejected her help and her advice. I was so…ungrateful." A tremulous breath escaped her. "I'm just sorry I never had the chance to tell her." Amber heard the thickness caused by unshed tears in her voice.

"I'm sure she knew," Kim said, her voice shaky, too.

"So anyway," Amber said, injecting an upbeat tone in an attempt to shake off the mood, "I figure it's payback time. I'm certainly not Gwen, but I can try to make life easier for Beau and Claudia. And even Cal. Maybe if I have some cookies straight out of the oven for them when they get home from school, they won't care that they're slice-and-bake instead of homemade."

"You've come a long way, baby," Kim teased.

"Yeah, I have," Amber said, and there was pride in her voice. "But I still have a way to go."

"So basically, you'll be doing all the things for Cal a wife would do."

Amber laughed. "Not everything."

"No?"

If Cal had been listening to the conversation, he'd have thought Kim's answer sounded suspiciously like "Hmm."

Chapter Five

"Hey, Sleeping Beauty, rise and shine."

The gruffly spoken words had no place in the delicious dream where Amber lay sleeping beneath the big tree down by the pond behind Cal's house, and Cal was kissing her. She moaned in protest and burrowed deeper beneath the covers.

"Come on, Amber, wake up. It's time to fix the kids something for breakfast."

Amber, who was sprawled on her stomach, raised the pillow and thrust her head beneath it.

"I hope you have clothes on under that sheet, because I'm half a second away from hauling your pretty behind out of that bed and sticking you in a cold shower."

Definitely not part of the dream.

It was Cal, threatening to drag her out of bed! With another groan, this one of dismay, Amber flopped to her back and draped her forearm over her eyes. She peeked out at Cal, who stood at the side of her bed poking his uniform shirt into his pants with an enviable economy of motion. He was freshly showered and shaved, and there was a look of exasperation on his face as he stared down at her.

"Don't look at me."

"What?"

"I don't have on any makeup," she mumbled. "I look horrible without makeup."

"Women!" he grumbled, just loud enough that she heard it. He grabbed her foot and shook it. "Come on. Get up. The kids will miss the bus if they don't get a move on."

Kids! Beau and Claudia. Full wakefulness came with a rush. Amber forgot about her face. It was her first day on her new job, and she'd overslept! Her eyes flew open, and she threw back the covers, giving Cal a momentary flash of tanned thigh and gently rounded derriere sheathed in silky peach-hued panties.

"Oh my gosh!" she groaned, going from zero to Mach 2 in the matter of seconds. She took a couple of steps, grinding her fists into her eyes. "I can't believe I overslept! I couldn't find my alarm clock, and I didn't sleep very well—the bed, I guess. Are the kids up? Why didn't you wake me earlier? What—"

As she tried to brush past him, Cal grabbed her upper arm. "Whoa! Slow down."

Forcibly stopped in her tracks, Amber turned, angling her head to look up at him. "Don't get your panties in a wad," he told her. "I'm not Rose Milford. I won't fire you because you overslept your first morning on the job."

"Oh." All the tension she'd felt on waking seeped out of her body, making her suddenly, acutely aware of Cal's,

which was so near. She closed her eyes for a brief second.
Dear, sweet heaven, he smelled so good....

"The kids are up, getting dressed. There's cereal in the
pantry, or they can have breakfast bars if they want. Beau
will want chocolate milk. Tell him no dice. It's orange
juice or plain milk. I'd stay and help, but there's a crisis,
and I have to go into the station early."

She shook her head and gave a wave toward the door.
"No problem. Go on. I'll manage."

Cal turned to go, then turned back, almost knocking her
over she was so close behind him. He grabbed her shoulders to steady her. "What?" she asked, an alarmed look
in her eyes.

"I just wanted to tell you you're wrong."

She frowned. "Wrong about what? You may as well
know up front that I don't function too well until I get
some caffeine in my system."

Cal grinned. "Me either. You're dead wrong about how
you look without makeup." The laughter left his eyes. He
reached out and touched the crest of her cheekbone with
the tips of his fingers. "You don't look horrible. You're
beautiful just the way you are. All the cosmetics are just
gilding for the lily."

The comment and his choice of words, reminiscent of
the poetry he'd once written for her, did more for her than
a gallon of caffeine.

"You always did have a way with words, Sheriff," she
told him.

Before he could reply, Claudia called, "Uncle Cal! Did
you put that load of clothes in the dryer last night?"

Whatever it was that had been building between them
vanished like an object behind a magician's puff of smoke.

"Yeah, honey, I did," he called back. "Whadda ya
need?"

"Underwear."

"They should be there."

"Hey, Uncle Cal!" Beau bellowed from the kitchen, which was closest to Amber's room. "Somebody drank all the milk."

A stricken look crossed Amber's face. "Oops!" She lifted one shoulder in an apologetic little shrug. "I couldn't sleep. I got up and had some milk and cookies."

"No problem," Cal said. He disappeared through the door, yelling, "Man cannot live on cereal alone, buddy. Have a Pop-Tart or something."

Fighting a sinking feeling, Amber squared her shoulders and started after him. He poked his head through the door and smiled the smile that made her heart do crazy things. "Welcome to the zoo."

Cal left soon after telling Beau to eat a Pop-Tart. Instead, Beau had taken a chicken potpie from the freezer and stuck it in the microwave, giving Amber a look that dared her to say anything about his choice of breakfast food.

Not up for a verbal sparring with the boy, who obviously had a chip on his shoulder ninety-nine percent of the time, and feeling that eating *something* was more important than nothing, Amber smiled at him and asked him if he'd nuke one for her while she checked on Claudia.

He didn't answer. Instead of pressing the matter, she crossed the room and smoothed an errant strand of his hair as she passed, "You need a haircut." He jerked away from her touch, the way he had from Cal's.

When she returned from Claudia's room a few minutes later, Beau was sitting at the table wolfing down his breakfast. A steaming potpie sat in the middle of a paper plate across the table from him. "Thanks, Beau," she said, sitting down and reaching for the fork he'd placed beside the plate.

He mumbled something that might have been, ''you're welcome,'' but it was hard to say because his mouth was full of food.

''It isn't polite to talk with food in your mouth,'' she said.

His reply was to stick out a tongueful of chewed potpie for her inspection.

Wonderful! Instead of jerking him up and tanning his hide the way she would have liked, Amber rested her forearms on the table and leaned forward. ''I don't react the way most girls do to gross, Beau, and trust me, I can outgross you any day. But I won't because I'm the adult here.''

She smiled at him, a smile as cold as a winter's day. ''If you plan on making my life here a living hell, just remember that I'm the one who reports to your uncle.''

''So if I do something I shouldn't, you're gonna tattle on me?'' He shoved a big forkful of food into his mouth.

''*Au contraire.* I'm not going to tattle, but I am going to tell Cal the truth *if* he asks me about your behavior. And don't take such big bites.''

Beau thrust another gargantuan forkful into his mouth. ''And I'm going to tell him you have me waiting on you hand and foot and that you called me contrary.''

Without a word, Amber got up and rounded the table. Beau looked up at her, his mouth and eyes wide, clearly fearful of what she was going to do. She tapped his chin with a gentle fist. ''Chew with your mouth closed, please.'' Then she snatched up his plate from the table, crossed the kitchen and dumped it into the trash.

For one priceless moment, Beau was speechless. Then

his face turned red, and he cried. "You threw away my breakfast!"

"Well, I'll be," she said in mock wonder. "The kid is really smarter than he acts. Yeah, I threw away your breakfast, and if you deliberately do something I ask you not to just to see how far I can be pushed, I'll do it again. Or worse."

"You can't lay a hand on me."

She regarded her manicured hand, thoughtfully. "Why would I want to chance breaking a nail?" She gave a mirthless laugh, "Trust me, there are a lot of punishments worse than spankings." Amber crossed her arms over her breasts and leaned against the cabinet. "The truth is, Beau, I'm trying to quit smoking and I'm a little short on patience, so let's just lay out the ground rules so we'll both know where we stand."

Beau glared at her.

She held up a single finger. "First, I'm in charge while your uncle Cal is away. I'm not a mean person. I *like* things nice and pleasant. I'd really like everyone to get along. I'll do my part, if you will. If you won't—" She shrugged. "Understand?"

He mumbled something.

"Did you say something?"

"I said, yeah."

"What?"

"I said yeah, I understand." he said louder, scraping back his chair and standing up.

"Yeah, I understand," she repeated, then shook her head. "No, Beau, I don't believe you do."

Beau scowled and snapped to attention, his arms rigid at his sides, anger his eyes. "Yes, ma'am," he said, sketching her a little salute. "I understand, ma'am."

"Excellent," she cooed. "You may go now." He turned

to leave, and she called his name. He turned and fixed her with that familiar glare.

"I just wanted to tell you that new table rules are that we chew with our mouths closed, and we do not talk with food in our mouths. We may forget now and then, but generally, that's the way things are done. Got it?"

"Got it. Ma'am."

"By the way, Beau," she said. "*Au contraire* doesn't mean you're contrary, though you are. It means on the contrary. And your doing something for someone, like you fixing the potpie for me when I was busy is called being considerate of someone. I appreciate it. Thanks."

Beau just scowled and left the room.

When Beau and Claudia got on their separate school buses some forty minutes later, Amber sat down on the porch swing, took a deep breath and thought again about her confrontation with Beau. Had she handled the situation in the right way? She didn't know, but she did know that she'd gained the little brat's full attention. She doubted he'd try her in those particular areas again. At least not for a while.

She sighed and pulled open the front door. It was time to get on with it. She'd finish putting her things away, then check the to-do list Cal had left for her. He'd mentioned that he'd left some cash for the electric bill, and she knew for certain that a trip to the grocery store was inevitable. They were out of milk.

"*Welcome to the zoo.*" Zoo, ha! A zoo was tame compared to the Simmons house in the mornings, she thought. Lord, she needed a cigarette!

Amber emptied all her boxes, stowing her things in the chest of drawers and the minuscule closet that had been built into one corner of the room. She was about to head to Claudia's bathroom for a shower when she recalled seeing some exercise equipment in Cal's room. She hadn't done any sort of exercise in ages. In L.A. she was used to going to the gym and working with a trainer, but there hadn't been any money for that since she'd moved to Vanity, and even if she'd have had the money, there was no gym. Surely, Cal wouldn't mind if she used his equipment while he was gone.

Thirty minutes later, Amber wiped the perspiration from her face with the hem of her T-shirt. It was absolutely amazing how out of shape a person could get in so short a time. She was about to head to the shower, when the stack of books sitting on a desk in the corner of the room caught her eye again. As it had earlier, curiosity grabbed her. You could learn a lot about a person by checking out his reading material. Suppressing a twinge of guilt, she headed toward the desk.

To her surprise there was a book on poisons, another on serial killers and several on law. Amber frowned. Was he researching something that had to do with his job? She put one of the law books down and picked up a yellow legal pad. It was filled with doodling and notes.

Go back to chapter five and put in the info about Sam's conversation with Claire. Is Sam coming across as too tough for potential women readers? Spice up his sex life—the waitress at the café, maybe?

Comprehension dawned with the suddenness of the proverbial flash of light. Cal was writing a book! Either a medical or legal thriller, if his choice of research material was any clue. Why hadn't he said anything?

Get real, Amber. Why should he confide in you. It isn't

as if you're bosom buddies. Had she heard anyone else mention it? Kim or her husband, Drew? No. Cal was a private person. He'd kept the fact that he wrote poetry a secret during high school because he was afraid of what his football friends might say, so it made sense that he was keeping his novel writing a secret for the same reasons.

The phone rang, and she jumped as if she'd been caught with her hand in someone's piggy bank. It was Cal, wondering how her morning was going.

"Good," she said, thinking that his voice sounded sexy over the phone. "I'm getting ready to take a shower and go into town. Oh! I used your exercise equipment. I hope you don't mind."

"Not at all."

She hesitated telling him she'd found out about his book, but Cal must have sensed she was holding something back. "What is it?" he asked.

"Uh, I was…checking out your reading material, and I couldn't help seeing that you're writing a book."

"You didn't read it did you?" he barked.

"No!"

"Well, don't!"

Amber felt as if she'd been slapped. "I'd never do something like that without asking you first. It would be an invasion of privacy."

"I'm sorry." She heard the contrition in his voice. "I didn't mean to come down on you so hard. It's just that I'm not sure I'm ready for anyone to see it. Writing a book is sort of like baring your soul, you know?"

"I think so. But when you are ready, I'd love to read it. Thrillers are my favorite."

"Really?" She heard the disbelief in his voice. "I'd have had you pegged for all that glitz and glamour stuff."

"Not me. Give me a good psychological thriller and I'm a happy woman."

"I'll remember that. Oh—gotta go," Cal said. "My other line is blinking. I just wanted to check in and see if you were still there."

Amber laughed. "So far nothing's come up I can't handle."

"Great. See you at dinner."

They hung up, and Amber stared at the receiver. Cal, a writer. Trying to imagine him at the computer in his spare time, trying to eke out a novel between his work and caring for Beau and Claudia wasn't as hard for her as it might be for some other people who knew him. As she'd told him earlier, he'd always had a way with words.

The poems he'd penned for her in high school—mostly free verse—had been beautifully crafted, evoking images that had stirred her, even then. They had shown unusual sensitivity, and an insight into the human condition far beyond that of the other sixteen-year-old boys she knew—or the eighteen-year-olds for that matter.

There was one short one she could still recite from memory, one her own actions had sparked. Because she knew he was carrying a torch for her, she, in her patronizing, superior way, had picked a branch laden with lilac blossoms and handed it to him as he was about to go onto the track field one spring day.

"Here," she'd said, thrusting it at him. "For luck. Remember me when they bloom next April."

The next day, she'd found the poem and a perfect red rose in her locker.

The lilacs bloomed in April, just like you said they
would. I filled a milk glass basket with them, and
every time I caught a whiff of their perfume, I thought
of you.

Even now, the words had the power to touch her—or maybe it was regret that made her vision cloudy. She realized with a sense of sorrow that she'd never told him that she liked the poems, never said thanks. Instead, when one of her friends had caught her reading that particular poem, Amber had crumpled the piece of paper and tossed it carelessly to the bottom of her locker.

No one had seen her rummaging around for it at the end of the day. No one had seen her smooth the wrinkled paper and tuck it into her purse. No one knew she'd stuck it in a locked cedar box that Gwen had given her for her twelfth birthday. The box held all her important things: a snapshot of her biological mother, the love letters from her boyfriends, a locket Gerald had given her when she was ten, the corsage she'd worn at her eighth grade graduation and the diary she wrote in daily. She'd put all Cal's poems in there as well. Now, as she set Cal's notes aside and left his room, she found herself wondering for the first time in years where the box was.

An hour later, she was headed for Vanity, a grocery list and a wad of money stuffed into her small handbag. Cal had written down the items he knew they needed and told her to pick up whatever she thought she might like to fix for the rest of the week.

Amber had jotted down some dinner ideas for several days, hoping Cal was telling the truth when he'd told her the only things the kids wouldn't eat were liver and cabbage. Then she'd called her dad's cook and asked what she needed to prepare the meats and what vegetables would complement them.

She felt a little conspicuous as she went into the grocery

store, as if everyone in town was whispering behind her back. Things like how she'd gotten fired from so many jobs and who she was working for now. Why had Cal hired her, for cryin' out loud? And how long would it be before he sent her packing?

Ignoring the stares she received from the checkers and the other customers, Amber got her buggy and started down the aisle. It took her a while to find everything, and when she did, she compared prices, trying to shop for the better value. She certainly didn't want to blow this job.

Still, by the time she was finished, her buggy was full. When the checker rang up the total, it was staggering. She counted out the money Cal had given her for the groceries and was fifty dollars short. She had no choice but to use part of the money for the electric bill to pay for the groceries. She'd tell Cal what had happened when he got in that evening. He could give her some more money and she'd drive in and pay the bill the next day. No problem, since she was sure he'd be thrilled to have a decent, home-cooked meal on the table.

She was driving home when an armchair and matching ottoman sitting in front of a ''junktique'' store caught her eye. She loved finding old things with potential, buying them at bargain prices, finding a special place or use for them and making them into serviceable objects again. Even from a distance, she could see that the chair was larger than most, perfect for a man of Cal's size. With some new plaid fabric, it would be a perfect addition to Cal's living room, as she pictured the renovations in her mind's eye. Amber braked and pulled into the parking lot.

''Nice, iddn't it?'' the woman who ran the place said around a wad of tobacco. ''And it's still sturdy. Harve got it at an estate sale the other day.''

Amber took out the cushion and checked the springs.

All okay. She and the woman tilted the chair to its back and checked out the underside. Other than being worn and dirty, the chair and ottoman were indeed a buy at seventy-five dollars—which, unfortunately, Amber wouldn't have until payday.

Reading the expression on Amber's face, the old woman said, "If you want it, you'd best get it. It won't be here long."

Amber chewed on the inside of her lip and stared contemplatively at the chair. In L.A., even at a much higher price, it would be snapped up in a heartbeat. Even in Vanity, with the traffic that went up and down the highway, it would probably be gone by the time she got paid.

"Can you deliver it?" she asked.

The old woman spat out a stream of tobacco juice. "Well, Harve don't usually deliver, but I suppose he would fer a price. Where's it goin'?"

"Out on the Bakerstown Road. Sheriff Simmons's house."

A shrewd expression crept into the old woman's rheumy blue eyes. She smiled, showing tobacco-stained teeth. "So you're the sheriff's new dolly. Folks been wonderin' what you look like."

Amber had to clench her jaw to keep her mouth from falling open. She injected a note of pleasantry into her voice and said, "I'm sorry, but you've been misinformed. I'm not the sheriff's girlfriend. He hired me to look after his house and the children."

The elderly woman cackled, the same sound Amber had always imagined a Halloween witch would make. "Pull the other one, honey," she wheezed when she stopped to draw a breath. "It's got bells on it."

Thoroughly incensed, Amber turned to leave. She

wasn't taking insults, and she wasn't putting up with being the brunt of local gossip, chair or no chair!

"Don't you want the chair?" the woman called after her.

Amber turned. "I'll give fifty dollars for it. Delivered."

"Sorry. Can't do it."

Amber started for the car.

"Make it sixty-five, and you got a deal," the woman screeched.

Amber turned and lifted her chin. "Sixty. Delivered."

"Done."

Amber pulled the sixty dollars—another portion of the electric money—from her purse and handed it to the woman, insisting on a receipt. Surely Cal wouldn't object since she'd repay the money for the chair from her paycheck. She climbed into the car, shaking her head at her own stupidity. *How can you expect to make it if you use your money buying things for Cal?* He was paying her peanuts, certainly not enough to splurge by buying something for *him.*

"It's only this once," she said aloud. And maybe since she'd bought the chair for his house, Cal would see fit to reimburse her. If not, she'd at least have the pleasure of seeing him enjoy it.

When Claudia stepped through the front door, she was greeted with the scent of baking cookies and roasting meat. "What smells so good?" she asked, slinging her backpack onto the table.

The question surprised Amber, who had expected more of the silent treatment. "Chocolate chip cookies and a roast," she said, sliding a fresh-from-the-oven platter of golden-brown cookies across the table. "Have some while they're warm. There's milk in the fridge."

Amber sliced more cookies while Claudia filled a glass with milk and got a saucer from the cabinet.

"How was your day?" Amber asked, as she slid the cookie sheet into the oven.

"Okay."

"What grade are you in?"

"Seventh."

Amber nodded. "That's what I thought. One more year of junior high. Do you have a boyfriend?"

"Are you kidding?" Claudia asked, plucking two of the largest cookies from the platter. "Boys like pretty girls. Not nerds like me who stay at home and read all the time."

"They call you a nerd?" Amber asked.

"Not to my face." She forced a smile that looked more like a grimace. "It's okay. Most of them are a bunch of phonies, anyway. I have some friends. Real friends. And I'd rather have the ones who are genuine. Know what I mean?"

"Yes," Amber said, amazed at Claudia's maturity. She knew that as a teenager herself, she'd have been one of the girls putting Claudia down because she didn't have the in look, no matter what her feelings for the girl might have been. Just as she'd blown Cal off because he ran with a different crowd. The realization that she'd been a snob, or at least had let her peers influence and manipulate her reactions to people, brought a sense of shame.

"You may not see it, but you're really a very pretty girl," she said, wanting to make amends for the past and not certain that she could. "You just aren't making the most of what you have."

Claudia took a swallow of milk, dabbed her mouth with a paper napkin and asked, "What do you mean?"

"A lot of girls go through a chubby period at your age. You're nice and thin."

"Try beanpole," Claudia said, reaching for another cookie. "I barely fill out a training bra."

Amber couldn't help smiling, though she thought it a sad commentary on the American life-style that so many women measured their self-worth by their bra size. "The boobs will come, I promise. As I recall, your mom was well-endowed in that department. I'll bet you a chocolate milk shake that within two years you'll be happy with your bra size."

"I don't bet," Claudia said. Her face had clouded at the mention of her mother. "Besides, if I did, I doubt you'd be around to collect—or pay up."

And there it was in a nutshell, Amber thought. The thing she knew had influenced Claudia's and Beau's lives. The fear or assumption that, because their mother had deserted them others would, too. "I may not be working for Cal in a couple of years, Claudia, but I'll be around. I've come back to Vanity to stay. I've been off to college, and I've lived the big-city life. It had its moments, but I've learned that it's important to be near family and friends."

"Even though it's hard for you? When I told the kids at school you'd moved in to look after us, some of them said you couldn't find a job."

"Well, they're partly right. I couldn't find a job doing what I was trained to do, but I did find several jobs before this one." She sat down across the table from Claudia and touched her thin hand. "There are all kinds of prejudices, Claudia. Against poor people, plain people, people who aren't smart. But strangely enough, there are plenty of prejudices against people who have moral standards, people who are beautiful and people who have money, too."

"Really?"

"Really. The people who fired me had a preconceived notion about what I was like because they knew my father has money. They thought I'd be spoiled. Maybe I was, but I was also taught by my stepmother that any honest work is honorable and that when you work for someone you give it everything you have.''

''That wasn't fair!'' Claudia said.

''No, it wasn't. But life isn't always fair, honey. Things happen, and we just pick up and go on the best we can. As my brother-in-law would say, you play the hand you're dealt.'' Amber smiled. ''Now you were dealt a pretty good hand when it comes to looks. You have a clear complexion. Your eyes are beautiful and your eyelashes are to die for.''

''They are? They're so pale I can hardly see them.''

''But they're long. Maybe your uncle Cal wouldn't mind if you started using some light cosmetics. You're getting close to thirteen, aren't you?''

''Twelve and a half.''

''Close enough to start with a little.''

''There's an end-of-school dance coming up,'' Claudia confessed with a tentative eagerness. ''I'd like to go even though the only person who'll ask me to dance is Bobby Townsend, and he's as nerdy as I am.''

Amber laughed. ''Nerdy is as nerdy does. Is he cute?''

Claudia thought about that for a few seconds. When she spoke, there was a note of surprise in her voice. ''Yeah, he is. Sort of.''

''Why is he a nerd?''

Claudia shrugged. ''I don't know. He's real smart. He helps tutor kids sometimes. He's sort of shy and he's really interested in computers. Not just messing around on them the way most of us do, but how they really work.'' She shrugged again. ''I guess he's a nerd because everyone says he is.''

''Just because he's smart doesn't mean he has to be a

nerd. And just because he's shy, doesn't mean he can't work at overcoming that shyness,'' Amber told Claudia. ''He might be an interesting guy if everyone would give him a shot, just as I might be a good employee if I had a shot.''

Claudia thought about that a moment. ''Uncle Cal is doing what you said, isn't he?'' she said after a moment.

''What's that?''

''Playing the hand he was dealt. It isn't fair that he had to take responsibility for us just because our mother didn't want us, but he did.''

''Oh, Claudia!'' Amber said, feeling as if she might start crying at the pain she saw in the young girl's eyes. ''Just because your mother left, doesn't mean she didn't want you. Sometimes things happen in our lives, and we're thrown off track. We don't know who we are, or we aren't sure how to handle things. Sometimes grown-ups forget what's truly important. Maybe that's what happened with your mom. Maybe she's just trying to sort things out in her mind.''

The resentment in Claudia's eyes told Amber she'd wasted her breath trying to make up for Georgina Simmons.

''Uncle Cal will give you a fair shot,'' Claudia said, instead.

''I know he will. And you and Beau need to remember that he took responsibility for you because he loves you and wants the best for you, not because he had to.''

Once she was alone Amber couldn't get her conversation with Claudia out of her mind. The twelve-year-old was far more mature than Amber herself had been at that age, and Claudia had a very adult grasp of the situation she, her brother and her uncle had been forced into. Their talk had also given Amber a clearer picture of her employer. Even though she'd known him to be a good and decent man for taking in his niece and nephew, Claudia had given Amber new insight as to how taking on that responsibility must have changed his life.

Cal was a good-looking, sexy, very available man, as her body reminded her every time they shared the same space. At the very least, taking on custody of Claudia and Beau had to have curtailed his social life—if it hadn't put it to a complete end—which was a shame.

A man like Cal deserved the best of everything, Amber thought, surprising herself with that thought. And that best included a woman to share his life. She was further surprised to realize that the thought of another woman in the house, sharing the everyday things she was now sharing with him and the kids, left her feeling threatened...and a tad angry. She refused to answer the question that popped into her mind. Why?

Chapter Six

Amber borrowed Claudia's alarm clock to make sure she got up on time her second day at the Simmons'. Other than oversleeping, she considered her first day a success. Harve had delivered the chair as promised, and it sat in the shed out back, waiting for the local upholsterer to give a bid for recovering it. The cookies had been one of the better ideas of her lifetime. Beau had descended on them like a ravenous wolf, remembering to say his yes ma'ams, pleases and thank-yous.

Dinner—the roast and vegetables she'd put into the oven earlier in the afternoon—had turned out so well, she felt as if she'd been cooking for years. Everyone had raved about the meal, and they had all pitched in to help clean up the kitchen. Amber was especially thrilled by the expression of satisfaction she'd seen in Cal's eyes. She had gone to bed, pleased with her accomplishments, certain that she'd made inroads with Beau and equally sure she'd gotten closer to Claudia. She vowed her second day would be even better.

She'd set the alarm early enough that she'd have time to hop in the shower and put on a little makeup before facing the day—and Cal.

The moment the alarm rang the following morning, she slapped the Off button and leaped from the bed, even though it was barely light outside. She'd laid out a pair of clean shorts and a T-shirt the night before, so there'd be no time-consuming search for misplaced clothing.

Ten minutes later, she left the bathroom. Her hair, which was more in need of something than ever, was moussed into the tousled look that suited her so well, and a light application of makeup helped fortify her for the day. She longed for that first cigarette of the morning, which seemed to be the one she needed the most, even though she'd been doling them out at three a day. Unfortunately, she'd misplaced her last pack somewhere, so maybe she'd just quit cold turkey. Still, she realized her craving wasn't as intense as it had been a week ago.

She woke both the kids—Beau first, then Claudia, then back to Beau's room again. Only when he was sitting on the edge of the bed in his boxer shorts did she feel comfortable starting breakfast.

Amber entered the kitchen to the aroma of freshly brewed Colombian coffee she'd purchased the day before to replace the generic brand she'd seen in Cal's pantry. If anyone had asked, she'd have said that automatic timers on coffeepots were one of the greatest inventions of the century. She poured herself a mugful, inhaled the bouquet like a wine connoisseur and took a healthy swig. Ah. Nectar of the gods. If she could only find her cigarettes!

Putting the cup aside, she set about assembling the things she needed for the sausage-and-pancakes breakfast she'd planned. She located the cutting board, sliced the roll of sausage into thick patties and put them on the electric griddle to fry. Next, she mixed a batch of pancake batter according to the instructions on the side of the box. When the sausage looked nicely browned, she put it on a pretty platter she found in the cupboard and poured out three nice-size pancakes.

"I can't find my gym shorts!" Claudia wailed from the doorway. She was already dressed in jeans and a T-shirt and had pulled her hair back into its customary ponytail. "I forgot them yesterday and couldn't dress out. Mrs. Macy gave me a zero for the day."

"I put them in your chest of drawers."

"I can't find them."

With a sigh, Amber started for Claudia's room. As she passed Beau's she saw that he'd flopped back across the bed and was sound asleep, with his knees dangling over and his toes brushing the floor.

"Beau!" she screeched. "Get up! You're going to be late for the bus." She flew into the room, grabbed him by the shoulders and hauled him into a sitting position.

"I'm up!" Beau grumbled, trying to push her away.

She dragged him to his feet. "Stand up!"

He gave her a typical, belligerent Beau stare, but due to the fact that his too-long hair was tousled and his sleep-puffed eyes were little more than slits, the look lost some of its sting.

She went to the chest and drew out some jeans and a shirt. "If you aren't dressed by the time I come back, I'm stripping you and marching you into a nice cold shower," she said, threatening him the way Cal had her the morning before.

That woke him up. He was reaching for his clothes before she completed the sentence. Smiling with satisfaction,

Amber left the room. Claudia held up the gym shorts as she stepped through the doorway.

"Found them."

"Good." Amber started to leave.

"Amber."

"Yes."

"About the dance." Claudia fidgeted, wadding the shorts into a ball and clutching them to her chest. "Do you think you'd have time to take me shopping for a dress? Uncle Cal said it would be okay."

The uncertainty in her eyes broke Amber's heart. "Of course I'll have time."

"Thanks." She shifted her weight from one foot to the other. "Would you mind if I have some girls over for a sort of end-of-school slumber party afterward?"

A memory of the slumber parties she and Kim had had when they were young flashed through Amber's mind. The makeup and hair fixing. Listening to music. Gossiping. The giggling and talking about boys.

"If you don't want to, I understand," Claudia said. "It's just that I've never had a slumber party before. Uncle Cal was always afraid he'd get called out for something in the middle of the night."

Encouraged by Claudia's desire to socialize more, and wondering at the sudden frown that marred her face, Amber said, "A slumber party sounds like fun. We'll get together after school this evening and figure out a plan."

To Amber's surprise, Claudia's reaction was to wrinkle her pert nose in disgust. "Is something burning?"

Amber sniffed the air. "My pancakes!" she moaned, sprinting from the room. In the kitchen, a black cloud rose from the griddle and spiraled through the sunlight that streamed through the window. Amber muttered a mild curse.

"Something's burning!" Cal yelled from his room.

"No kidding!" Amber murmured. She picked up the egg turner and called back, "No problem. It's all taken care of."

Scooping up the charred pancakes, she dumped them into the trash, then poured out three more. The trio was nicely browned when Claudia—dressed and ready for school—came into the kitchen.

"Just in time," Amber said, putting the perfect pancakes onto a plate.

Claudia vanished into the pantry and came out carrying a loaf of bread. "Other than cereal, I can't take sweet stuff for breakfast," she said, setting the bread and the platter of sausage on the table. "It makes me feel queasy. I'll just put a couple of pieces of sausage on some bread."

The satisfaction Amber had felt on getting up in time to fix a nourishing breakfast vanished like the last of the acrid smoke being sucked out of the kitchen by the vent fan. "Oh."

Seeing the disappointment on Amber's face, Claudia said, "Beau loves pancakes, though. He should be here in just a minute."

Claudia fixed her sausage sandwich and took a bite, which—to Amber's horror—she promptly spit onto her plate. Wiping her mouth, she cast an apologetic look in Amber's direction. "I'm sorry," she said, completely mortified by her actions. "But it's raw in the middle. Mom always said pork had to be cooked real done."

Overcoming her surprise and her own chagrin, Amber went to the table and used a fork to cut into one of the patties. Claudia was right. Though the thick slice of meat looked done on the outside, the inside was still pink.

"Put a paper towel on top and pop the platter in the

microwave for a couple of minutes,'' Cal said, buckling on his gun and holster.

Embarrassed that she hadn't done better, Amber picked up the platter and did as Cal suggested.

"Do you want some pancakes?'' she asked Cal.

"I'm not much for sweets early in the morning,'' he said, an apology in his eyes.

"Oh.'' She set the timer and leaned back against the sink, the high spirits she'd felt on waking sagging beneath the blow of her failed breakfast.

Cal rounded the table, reached out and lifted her chin, forcing her to meet the smile in his golden-brown eyes. "Cheer up. It's not the end of the world.''

Amber forced a wobbly smile of her own. Cal's faded and something else entered his eyes. Something that made her very aware of how close they were standing, how big and masculine he was. His thumb drifted over the curve of her chin.

The microwave beeped. Cal cleared his throat, stepped away from her and busied himself pouring a cup of coffee. Amber opened the door of the microwave. The paper towel had shifted and the sausage had popped grease all over the interior. She sighed and set the platter on the table. What was it Gwen used to say about a woman's work never being done?

Following Claudia's example, Cal put a couple of pieces of the fully cooked sausage on some bread and wrapped it in a paper towel. "I gotta go,'' he said, an uncomfortable expression in his eyes. "I'm going to be late.''

He was halfway to the door when she called his name.

"Yeah?''

"Is it okay if I rearrange things?''

"Like furniture and stuff?''

"Yes. And pictures. And the living room could really

use a coat of paint." Sensing his hesitation, she added, "I have a degree in interior design. It's what I worked at in California—when I wasn't working in art galleries. And I'm a very good painter."

He frowned. "Will it be expensive? I don't have a lot of extra money since I hired you."

"I'll use cheap paint. It shouldn't take over three gallons."

Cal shrugged. "Why not? This place has needed some sprucing up for a long time. Do whatever you want, as long as the cost doesn't get out of hand. I've got an account down at the lumber yard. You can charge the paint there."

Amber smiled. "Thanks. You won't be sorry."

"Sure." Cal said goodbye and hugged Beau, who had sauntered into the room.

As Amber expected, he pulled free of Cal and said, "Are those mine?"

"Yes!" Amber and Claudia and Cal said in unison.

"Wow!" Beau said, sitting down in front of the pancakes and helping himself to several pieces of sausage. "Pancakes *and* sausage! My favorite."

Amber watched in amazement, as he devoured the pancakes and asked for more. As ego balms went, it wasn't bad. Later, she would look on the disastrous breakfast as the high point of her day.

The first thing Amber did toward renovating the living room was to roll up the braided rug and drag it outside onto the porch. It was a major undertaking—and she longed for Cal's brawn—but the colors were all wrong with her new vision of the room, and it was in the way of her moving the furniture. She took down all the drapes, which dated the room. She also took down the blinds, which, surprisingly, were real wood and a nice mahogany color. She cleaned them with a damp cloth and polished them with lemon oil. They'd be fine by themselves.

Next, she masked off the door and window frames and took all the pictures and Cal's various trophies off the walls. Cal—the very thought of him filled her with a fluttery sensation. The warmth in his eyes, the gentleness of his touch. The disturbing way her heart raced whenever he came into the room. She groaned. *Forget him.* But it was easier said than done. The silence in the room made it too easy for thoughts of him to formulate.

Amber was shoving the sofa, whose legs were sitting on pads made from washcloths, across the floor when the phone rang. Pushing a lock of damp hair away from her face, she picked up the cordless phone and punched the on button.

"Simmons residence."

"Is this Amber Campion?" The feminine voice had an unfriendly edge.

"Yes, it is."

"This is Miss Marx, the principal at the elementary school."

Before Amber had time to make the connection that Miss Marx was Karla Marx, the straitlaced spinster who'd once taught her geometry, the principal rushed on. "It's my understanding that you're in charge of the Simmons children. Is that correct?"

Every sense went on sudden alert. "Yes," Amber replied warily.

"Then I need you to come and pick up Beau. He's been suspended for two days."

"Suspended! What did he do?"

"We found some cigarettes in his backpack."

So that's where her cigarettes had gone!

"Perhaps you aren't aware of it, but we have a zero tolerance for substance abuse, weapons and disrespectful attitudes at this school, Ms. Campion."

"Substance abuse!" she cried. "We're talking cigarettes, here, Miss Marx—not hard drugs."

"Be that as it may, you need to come and get Beau. Or I can call Sheriff Simmons, if you prefer."

"No!" Amber said quickly. Beau and Claudia were in her charge; she'd deal with it. Besides, she was sure Cal wouldn't look favorably on the fact that it was her cigarettes Beau had lifted. "There's no need to bother him. I'll be there in fifteen minutes."

True to her word, a disheveled Amber arrived at the school in the allotted time. Beau was waiting on a chair near the front office and, to his credit, looked properly penitent, which was a good thing, considering Amber had murder on her mind.

Miss Marx, who came out at the receptionist's request, hadn't changed much. With a rare spurt of uncharitableness, Amber thought the former teacher's mustache made her look more like Groucho than Karla. The principal made her sign Beau out, instructed her that he could return to school on Friday and suggested she try to find out his "source."

"I'll do that." Amber replied sweetly. Taking Beau's upper arm in a firm grip, she said, "Come on Beau, let's go."

Amber managed to control her anger until they got to the car. "What on earth were you thinking?" she cried once they were inside and the engine was turned on.

"I don't know," he said with a sullen shrug.

Amber pulled onto the street, slanting him an exasperated look. "This is a bit more serious than copping an attitude and talking back. There's no way I can keep your being suspended from Cal, even if I were so inclined, which I'm not.''

''I never asked you not to tell,'' Beau said in his own defense.

''I know you didn't.'' Aggravation marked her sigh. ''Why did you take my cigarettes, Beau? You know smoking is bad for you.''

''You smoke.''

Darn! Hoist by her own petard. ''Yes, I do. But in case you haven't noticed, I'm trying to quit. The operative word here is *trying*. It's a bad habit, one that's very hard to break.''

Beau had nothing to say to this.

''You wanted to look cool in front of your friends, didn't you?''

The question was met with another shrug.

''Well, it isn't cool, and because you've been suspended, you'll have to face the music. I have no idea what your uncle will do for your punishment, but you're not going to lie around and play video games while you're at home.''

Beau turned to look at her. ''What *am* I going to do?''

Amber pinned him with a hard look. ''Whatever I darn well say.''

''Yes, Ma'am,'' Beau said with another of those little salutes.

When they got home, Amber instructed Beau to put on some old clothes and check back with her. She found a note from the upholsterer on the back door. The man said he'd looked at the chair and quoted her a price that made her gasp. He might as well be wearing a mask and toting a gun, she thought, in a state of semishock. It would take the greatest part of her salary to pay to have the chair redone, and when she took out the sixty dollars to put back what she'd used of the electric money…

That train of thought came to an abrupt halt. She'd forgotten to tell Cal she'd overspent on the groceries and bought the chair. Remembering his concern earlier that morning about the cost of the paint, she felt a qualm about her purchase. She'd thought of asking Cal to reimburse her for the chair, but on second thought, maybe she'd just tell him about the groceries.

She couldn't expect him to pay for her indulgence, even if it was for him. Whatever it took, she'd have to work this out herself. If she waited until the end of the week to pay the electric bill, she might have to pay a late charge, but Cal wouldn't know she'd used his money to buy a chair.

Amber sighed. Most of what she wanted to do to Cal's house would have to wait. She wasn't daddy's little girl who got her every wish anymore. She didn't have unlimited resources. She'd have to take out a little from her paychecks every week until she saved enough to have the chair reupholstered. It was the responsible thing to do, and the Lord only knew she was doing her darndest to become responsible.

Why the heck didn't Cal have a gas grill? Amber thought several hours later. She was tired to the bone. Her back ached from moving the rug and the heavy furniture. The ladder had almost tipped over, spilling half a bucket of paint on the pegged hardwood. Thank God it was water-based, and there was no carpet on the floor. It had been mess enough as it was. Every bit had to be mopped up on her hands and knees, requiring several buckets of hot water. She'd broken off a nail to the quick and hit her elbow on the wall trying to divert the disaster.

Now the darn charcoal wouldn't light, and Beau had a Little League game at seven. Cal had called earlier with an emergency and told her that if he didn't make it home in time, she'd have to take Beau to his game. It must be some sort of conspiracy.

Thirty minutes and almost a bottle of lighter fluid later, she finally had the charcoal going. Because time had slipped away from her, she'd forgotten to thaw the chicken, so she'd changed the evening menu to hamburgers, baked beans from a can and chips. She'd forgotten to buy hamburger buns, but she found some for hot dogs in the pantry, which would just have to do. There'd better not be any complaints, she thought, as she rolled the ground beef into long cylinders to fit the buns.

Once the hamburgers were situated on the grill, she closed the top and looked out across the yard. Beau, who'd spent the day straightening the shed, pulling weeds from the sad-looking flower beds and picking up sticks so he could mow the lawn the next day, was poking at something with a stick. Probably a bug, she thought in disgust. Some boy thing.

"Beau!" He looked up at the sound of her voice. "You can call it a day. Go on in and take a bath. Dinner will be ready in a little while."

"Okay."

Amber went inside and prepared the rest of the meal, got the vegetables ready and took a mental inventory to make sure she had everything ready. She didn't need another culinary disaster. Not when she was trying to convince Cal she could handle the job.

Glancing at the clock, she decided she'd have plenty of time to clean up before the burgers were ready. She longed for a long, leisurely soak in the tub, but there wasn't time if she wanted to put that color treatment on her hair. Besides, Claudia and Beau had both bathtubs tied up. It would have to be a quick shower...in Cal's bathroom.

Amber chewed on her lower lip. He'd told her it was okay to use his facilities, but there was something so private about sharing a bathroom. But it was her only course of action if she wanted to get cleaned up before dinner. With a sigh, she grabbed the hair color and some bath gel and headed for Cal's room.

Like the rest of the house, it needed lots of help to reach its potential. Still, she felt a sense of pride to see the bed made, everything in its place, and the furniture gleaming with polish, and realize she was the one responsible for the room's transformation.

She took one of the oversize gray towels from the linen closet, laid it on the seat of the commode and stripped, while making minuscule adjustments to the hot and cold faucets and reading the instructions on the back of the hair color box.

She'd decided to go back to her natural color. Though everyone said she looked good as a blonde, it was expensive to keep up, and, right now her financial situation didn't warrant an expenditure that wasn't absolutely necessary.

Satisfied with the water temperature, she stepped inside and closed the door. Immediately, she felt as if she were in a cocoon, shut off from the cares of her day. The scent of Cal's soap, something masculine and peppery, assaulted her senses.

Don't think about him.

But it was hard not to think about him with the scent she'd come to associate with him enveloping her. The image of him in the shower flashed into her mind—water beading on his broad shoulders. Soap bubbles running in tiny rivers through the dark hair of his chest and down his flat stomach....

"Stop it!" she said aloud. In an attempt to escape the erotic thoughts that had taken hold of her senses, she ducked beneath the cool spray and soaked her hair. She squirted the shampoo-in hair color onto her head and brought it to a sudsy froth. Then she dumped some of the feminine, floral fragrance she'd received on her birthday onto her washcloth and, closing her eyes, she began to work the lather over her body.

Without warning, Cal crashed her thoughts again. She recalled the way he looked when he left every morning—well scrubbed, pressed and so ruggedly good-looking he took her breath away. When he came home, he was usually rumpled, tousled and tired, but no less attractive.

She sighed. As short as her time here had been, she felt as if she belonged here with Claudia, Beau and Cal. When he left every morning saying he'd see them at dinner, she half expected him to press a quick kiss to her lips, the way he might if they were a real married couple....

Unable to fight her feelings any longer, she leaned against the tiles and allowed an image of him joining her in the shower to drift into her mind. The washcloth lingered over her breasts, suddenly sensitive and aching, an ache that, though it was unwanted, spread lower and deeper. An ache that was becoming more bothersome the more time she spent in the company of Sheriff Cal Simmons.

The cloth fell to the shower floor, but Amber was too caught up in her fantasy to retrieve it.

Would Cal use a cloth to soap her body, or would he use his hands to slick the bubbles over her breasts and stomach and thighs? Her hands moved over her body slowly, imagining they were Cal's.

She tipped her head back, her hair color forgotten. Sharp droplets of water pelted her face, her throat, her breasts. Would he kiss her while the water pummeled them, their flesh overly sensitized by the longing and need coursing through them? Would he press her to the tiles with the weight of his body so that she could feel the intrinsic differences in their physical makeup, so that she would have no doubts to either his masculinity or her femininity?

The telephone beside Cal's bed rang, jerking her from her erotic fantasy and plunging her back to reality. Her eyes flew open. Claudia would get the phone. It was probably for her, anyway. Meanwhile, there was hair color waiting to be washed out. Meat on the barbecue grill. Cal coming home any minute. The confrontation with Cal and Beau that would no doubt come before bedtime.

Amber Campion, this is your life.

Yeah. It was her life, and despite the problems she was facing, she liked it. For the first time in a long time, she was content.

When Cal left the station, he was hot, hungry and tired. He'd missed lunch and spent part of the afternoon with the volunteer fire department trying to get a three-year-old out of an abandoned, hand-dug well. Thankfully, the well was relatively shallow, and the child had suffered nothing more than fear of darkness and a broken leg. Cal knew just how serious the scenario might have been.

He just wanted to go home, hug both the kids and tell them how much he loved them. Then he wanted to take a nice hot shower and enjoy another home-cooked meal that he hadn't had to prepare himself. He wanted to enjoy that meal sitting across the table from a gorgeous woman. It was an image that held immense appeal. The only thing that might make it more appealing was if, after Claudia and Beau had gone to bed, he and Amber could do the same....

Don't even go there. The woman may be pretty, talented and smart, but she broke your heart once.

Yeah, and while he'd never forgotten, the real sting of his heartbreak had lasted all of two months, until cute little Margie Parsons had caught his eye. His teenage heart hadn't been too badly scarred at all.

But he wasn't a teenager anymore, and he was smart enough to know that letting his grown-up heart become emotionally entangled with the grown-up Amber Campion was the way to disaster. This time, his heart wouldn't be so quick to recover.

As he pulled into the drive, he saw that someone had been busy in the flower beds. There wasn't a weed to be seen. The limb that had blown down during the last storm had been dragged to a place near the woods where it lay across a pile of sticks and smaller branches. Somebody had been working, he thought, as he got out of the cruiser and started up the gravel walkway. When he opened the door, it was to a scene of chaos and the odor of paint.

Nothing was where it should be. Furniture had been pulled away from the walls and was covered with drop cloths. The dark paneling had had the grooves filled in and were now the color of toffee. Amber had started doing something to give the walls the look of leather that echoed the texture of the darker leather couch he'd splurged on the year before. As leery as he'd been when he left that morning, he had to admit that what she'd done looked good. Really good.

He checked on Claudia, who was sitting in the middle of her bed cross-legged style, reading a book.

"How was your day?"

"Good," she said. "How was yours?"

"It could have been better."

"You look hot and tired."

"I am. A three-year-old boy fell into a shallow well. I gave the firemen a hand."

Claudia's eyes grew wide. "Is he okay?"

"He'll be fine, and I'll be fine once I get some of this grime off." He blew her a kiss. "See you at supper."

When Cal spoke to Beau, he wouldn't meet his gaze. Cal's suspected his nephew had gotten into some sort of trouble, but whatever it was could wait until he'd showered and had dinner. The evening was shaping up to be too good to ruin by a confrontation with Beau.

"Did you do the yard work?"

"Yes sir."

"Good job. Thanks." Smiling at the boy, Cal started down the hallway to his room, intent on having a shower. The phone rang as he stepped through the doorway. He jogged across the room and plucked up the cordless receiver. Some part of his brain noted that water was running.

"Sheriff Simmons," he said, sinking wearily onto the edge of the bed.

"Good evening, Caleb. Dudley Milsap here."

"Oh, hi, Dud. How's it goin'?"

"Superbly, thank you," Dudley said. "I called to let you know that the powers that be say that if I improve as much next week as I have this one, they're going to spring me from this joint a week from Friday."

"That's great!" Cal crossed his right ankle over his left knee and tugged off his boot, then reversed the position and rid himself of the other one. He cocked his head to the side. There was definitely water running in his bathroom.

"Too bad you already hired Amber," Dudley said as Cal headed toward the sound. "If you could have held out a little longer, I could have taken up the slack."

Cal barely heard. The sight that greeted him as he stepped through the doorway halted his footsteps and his breath as well as all rational thought. Amber had been using his shower. The small room was filled with the delicate scent of something light, floral and deliciously feminine. Amber herself stood not five feet from him, her wet hair—no longer blond—slicked away from her face, her eyes wide. She clutched an oversize towel in front of her to hide her nudity.

"What in the hell have you done to your hair?" Cal asked.

"What do you mean, what have I done to my hair?" Dudley asked.

Amber placed a palm against her wet head. "I put it back to my natural color. I hope it's okay that I used your shower," she tacked on. "Claudia and Beau had the other two bathrooms tied up."

"I wouldn't have said it if I didn't mean it," Cal told her, his gaze fastened on the full-length mirror that hung on the wall behind her. She had no idea that the mirror's placement gave him an unobstructed view of her smooth back, small waist and shapely derriere.

"Wouldn't have said what?" Dudley asked.

"I liked you as a blonde," Cal said into the mouthpiece, though his attention was definitely focused elsewhere. He hadn't even heard Dudley's question.

"So did I, but being a blonde is too expensive to keep up. What are you staring at?"

"Nothing."

"Liar." Amber glanced over her shoulder, saw what held Cal so entranced and, muttering something very unladylike under her breath, whipped the edge of the towel around her back in another valiant attempt to guard her modesty.

"I didn't mean to, uh, stare—"

"Stare at what?" Dudley asked in exasperation.

"—but, uh, it was hard not to, when the view was just...there."

"View? What view? Cal, you aren't making any sense." Dudley's voice held a note of concern.

Amber's smile was as brittle as her voice. "Oh, that's understandable. You're a man. And since men have a notoriously low smut threshold, I'll forgive you. Let's just forget it, all right?"

"I don't think I can," Cal said, shaking his head.

"Can what?" Dudley asked. "Cal, is someone there? Should I call back?"

"Forget what I saw."

Seeing the blatant desire in his eyes, Amber took an involuntary step backward. "Cal..."

"What did you see?" Dudley asked.

Hardly aware that he was answering, Cal replied, "Amber getting out of my shower."

"Uh-oh," Dudley said. "Uh, why don't I call back later, when you aren't so...busy?"

"Yeah. Do that." Cal turned off the phone, set it on the vanity and took a step toward Amber.

Amber saw the determination in his eyes. She clutched the towel tighter with her left hand and held her right out, as if she hoped to keep him at arms' length. "Cal," she said, her voice little more than a whisper. "Don't."

"You're wasting your breath," he replied, the huskiness

in his voice reflecting the same desire that gave his tawny eyes a slumberous, sexy look.

She knew she didn't stand a chance, not when her heart was pounding and her lips were already tingling in anticipation. His arms were much longer than hers. His hands closed over her bare shoulders and drew her close, pulling her lower body intimately against his.

Their gazes collided, startled blue to golden-brown. Amber realized suddenly that she'd known it would come to this, even as she'd convinced herself she felt nothing for him. It was the moment she'd dreaded…longed for. Dreamed of.

With her arms imprisoned between them, there was nothing she could do to stop him even if she wanted to, which, of course, she didn't. Every sense was on alert. She saw the darker brown, shattered-glass pattern in the irises of his eyes. She felt every nub of the terry cloth towel against her sensitive flesh. He lowered his head toward her, and she closed her eyes to block out the intensity of the heat she saw in his. She skimmed her tongue over her lips in a gesture that betrayed her tenseness and heard a noise that sounded like the contented growl of a big cat sough from Cal's lips. The touch of his mouth brought a moan from her that sounded like capitulation.

Which, of course, it was. She was drowning in sensation—the thunder of blood racing through her veins, the erotic probe of his tongue that conveyed the sweet tang and scent of peppermint. His lips moved from hers to her throat, and she arched her neck to accommodate the trail of kisses he strung downward to the hollow of her throat and back up to her ear. The hand that wasn't holding the towel clutched at the front of his shirt.

''You smell good.'' The words weren't so much spoken as breathed into her ear. Weren't so much heard as absorbed. She knew she was treading thin ice, dangerous ground, setting herself up for a fall, but with Cal's arms around her, his body pressed so closely to hers, and his breathing a sweet litany in her ear, she couldn't find it in herself to care. Cal's kisses…his touch…the man himself were different in a way she couldn't have explained to save her life.…

"Uncle Cal!" Beau shouted from the bedroom.

Cal tensed, and Amber tore free of his grasp, anxious to put some distance between them before Beau caught them in a compromising situation.

"What is it?" Cal bellowed over his shoulder, his gaze fastened on hers.

"The barbecue grill's on fire!"

Cal swore. Amber gasped. She'd forgotten about their dinner! She watched him close his eyes as if he were counting to ten. Then he heaved a sigh and opened his eyes again, spearing her with a decisive look and pointing a finger at her.

"Later," he said and left her standing there, her shell of boldness shattered around her.

The tension in the small room vanished along with Cal. The breath Amber had been holding gushed from her lips in a soft sigh. Her heart was beating ninety to nothing, her mouth was dry, and her legs felt weak. Oh, yeah, she was definitely playing with fire, here. Gathering the towel around her and tucking it tightly across her breasts, she almost ran to her room.

She slipped into her private domain, closed the door and leaned against it, as if doing something so simple would block out not only Cal but the memory of the heat in his eyes when he'd said "Later."

Amber gave a delicate shiver. The single word was as much a promise as it was a threat. She placed her palms against her hot cheeks. What was she going to do? She needed this job. But the simple truth was that she'd gone and done the unthinkable, the forbidden, the—positively most stupid thing she'd ever done!

She'd gone and fallen in love with Cal Simmons.

She groaned and paced the small room on shaky legs. How could she have let it happen? Cal might want her, and it was clear that he did, but with her track record, he would never love her, or believe she was capable of that emotion. Unfortunately, she wanted more than a fling at this stage of her life.

Feeling as if her legs still might give way, Amber raked aside the clean clothes she'd laid out and forgotten to take to the bathroom.

Her fingertips encountered something silky and cold that moved beneath her touch. Some sixth sense told her it was a snake even before she saw it slither back into hiding under her clothes.

She screamed.

Chapter Seven

Unmindful of the puddle of water gathering at his feet, Cal and his nephew stared down at the drenched and smoking remains of his dinner, trying to identify the charred remains of whatever critter had been sacrificed at the altar of the demanding barbecue god.

"What is it?" Beau asked.

"Darned if I know," Cal replied.

The scream that came from the heart of the house sent the hair at the back of his neck standing on end. *Amber!* Something was wrong with Amber! He shoved the water hose at Beau.

"Shut the water off!" he yelled, sprinting toward the house with a speed he'd seldom reached since his college football days. He went through the back door so hard that it slammed against the wall with a deafening thud. Thank God no one had been headed outside, he thought. They'd have been flattened.

Cal hurried down the short hall that led to Amber's room and thrust open the door. She was standing in the middle of the small space, still wrapped in the gray towel, her hands pressed against her mouth, staring at the small pile of clothes on her bed as if it were a monster from some horror flick.

"Amber?" The sound of his voice caused her to react like some toy whose switch had just been turned on. Pivoting on the ball of her bare foot, she launched herself at him. He staggered back as her arms wound around his neck. Involuntarily, his arms closed around her.

She burrowed deeper into his embrace and buried her face against his neck. Her total yielding made him forget about the crisis that had brought him running. As he had been moments before, he was intensely aware of the fact that the body pressed to his was bare beneath the towel, of her wet hair brushing his chin. He couldn't have stopped himself from nuzzling her hair with his nose if his life depended on it. As he expected, she smelled as delicious as she felt. The whimper that escaped her brought his mind back to the business at hand.

"What's wrong?"

"Snake," she said in a whisper, as if saying the word aloud might disturb the creature in some way.

"Snake? Where?" He tried to pull free, but she refused to let go of her stranglehold of his neck except to point toward the bed. "Did it bite you?"

Her hair brushed his chin as she shook her head. "If it had, I wouldn't be standing here," she murmured against his throat. "I'd be dead of fright."

"Are you sure it's a snake?"

"I'm sure," she said, nodding. "When I got back here, my legs were shaking, and I was going to move the clothes over so I could sit down.'' She shivered and tried to get even closer. ''I touched it.''

''What kind of snake is it?''

Irritation loosened her grip on him enough so she could lean back and look up. ''How would I know?'' she asked in a disgusted tone. ''It's a snake, so it's a bad one.''

Cal's hand moved up and down her back in a comforting gesture. The fluffiness of the towel felt coarse compared to the silkiness of her skin. ''Okay, calm down,'' he said, doing his best to focus on the current situation. ''It's just that I can't imagine how a snake could get into the house.''

''I can.'' Her voice held a certainty that was reflected in her eyes.

''You can? How?''

''Ask your precious nephew.''

''You think Beau did it?'' he asked.

Amber shrugged, and the towel might have given way if she hadn't been standing so close to him. ''He had motive, means and opportunity.''

''But why?''

Amber glanced over her shoulder, then back up at him. ''Can we talk about this later? Like after you get rid of the dratted thing?''

''Sure. Stay right here.'' Cal put his hands on her shoulder to move her away, but she held on tight.

''Don't leave me!''

''I'll be right back,'' he said in a soothing voice. ''I'm going to get the hoe.''

''The hoe!'' she shrilled. ''Why are you going to get the hoe?''

''Would you rather I use my revolver?''

The irritation in her eyes died as understanding dawned. She let go of him and stepped away. ''I'm coming with you.''

"No. You stay here and make sure the snake doesn't crawl away."

If possible, her face paled even more. She swallowed hard and gave a curt nod.

"I'll be back in a jiffy," he told her again, unable to keep himself from running a knuckle along the sweet curving line of her jaw. "If it tries to come off the bed, just get out of its way."

She nodded. He turned to go, and her fingers clutched at his arm. "What?"

"Hurry."

The fear in her eyes tore at his heart. He had never seen her afraid—not even when she was facing David Perkins and his gun. Without thinking beyond the need to offer her some sort of reassurance, he bent and pressed a quick, hard kiss to her lips. "I'll be right back."

Claudia was coming inside with the hoe in hand as he reached the back door. "How did you know I needed this?"

"I came to see what was wrong and heard Amber telling you about the snake," Claudia said. "I went out to try and find the hoe. Beau already had it handy."

Cal didn't miss the significance of that statement or the fact that his nephew was nowhere to be seen. "Quick thinking," he said. *Too quick.* He'd take care of Beau later. Cal took the garden implement with a smile of thanks, and he and Claudia started back toward Amber's room. She hadn't moved an inch.

"Still there?"

"Me or the snake?" Amber asked with a hint of her usual dry humor. Cal chuckled.

"This is no laughing matter."

"I know. Go out into the hall with Claudia," he told her.

Amber couldn't get out of the small space fast enough. Claudia slipped her hand into Amber's and gave it a comforting squeeze. Touched by the gesture, Amber squeezed back. From the relative safety of the hallway, they watched as Cal used the hoe handle to lift first Amber's shirt, then shorts and underwear from the bed, revealing a small, darkish snake with yellow stripes running its length.

Cal let out his breath with an audible sigh. To Amber's horror, he leaned the hoe on the bed and picked up the small reptile. Both she and Claudia shrieked.

"It's just a ribbon snake," he told them. "It isn't poisonous."

"Well, that certainly makes me feel loads better," Amber told him.

He held the writhing snake out for their inspection. "It's pretty, isn't it?"

Claudia backed away, her palms facing outward. "I'm getting out of here." She turned and left Cal and Amber standing in the hallway.

Feeling suddenly vulnerable and more than a little embarrassed over her reaction to such a small, harmless snake, Amber raised her chin. "A snake pretty? I don't think so."

Cal made a *tsking* sound. "And I thought you liked animals."

"I do like animals. I loathe snakes."

He laughed. "Why don't I take this little critter outside where he belongs while you get dressed? Then we'll see what we can rustle up for supper."

A stricken look passed over Amber's face. "The hamburgers burned?"

"Is *that* what they were?"

Amber's face turned a pretty pink. One shoulder rose in a small shrug. "We didn't have any hamburger buns," she explained, "so I just sort of…rolled the ground beef into hot dog shape."

"Good thinking. But they're charred beyond redemption."

"I'm sorry."

"No problem." He raked her with a hot gaze that grew even hotter. "You'd better get some clothes on. Much more of you parading around in front of me half-naked and dinner will be a couple of hours late."

Amber's mouth fell open. She hadn't expected Cal to openly admit to his desire. Habit caused Amber to seek refuge in cool haughtiness, even though she was burning up inside. "That wasn't part of our agreement, Sheriff."

Cal countered with a mocking smile. "Believe me, Ms. Campion, I know that." Without another word, he turned and walked down the hallway, leaving Amber alone with the chaos of her thoughts, the memory of his kiss and a wildly beating heart.

For dinner, Cal substituted smoked-turkey sandwiches for the burgers, claiming they went just fine with the beans and chips. Beau came to the table dressed for his ball game. To her knowledge Cal hadn't taken Beau to task for what he'd done, and Amber wondered why.

Beau had nothing to say during the meal, unless he was asked a direct question. He did say his ma'ams and sirs and pleases and thank-yous, and he chewed with his mouth closed, casting Amber mocking glances when Cal wasn't looking. Amber observed his pseudo-penitent attitude with a heavy heart. She didn't stand a chance of lasting long around here if it came to who could do the better job of buttering up Cal. Blood was thicker than water. A curious sense of sadness swamped her.

As soon as dinner was finished, Cal instructed Beau to

get his bat bag. Cal had showered and changed into khaki shorts and a plum-hued plaid golf shirt. His legs were tanned and well muscled and dusted with golden-brown hair. If Amber had thought he was handsome in his sheriff's garb, he was even more so in his civilian clothes. He looked like any proud father taking his son to a ball game.

"I hate to leave the cleaning up for you," he said, as she gathered the plates. "But Beau needs to be there early for practice."

"It's okay," she said without looking at him. "There isn't much to do, thanks to paper plates."

"Do you want to go watch the game?"

"Not this evening," she said smiling without meeting his gaze. "I'm pretty tired from painting and all the excitement." It wasn't exactly a lie. She was tired, but not that tired. Still, there was no way she could go sit next to Cal during a ball game. She couldn't take any more close contact with him at the moment. She was already suffering from sensory overload, and a feeling of dejection she couldn't explain.

"I'll stay and help Claudia with her science project."

"Maybe another time," Cal said.

She glanced at him and saw that he was frowning.

"You do like baseball, don't you?"

Amber braced herself to meet his gaze. Thankfully, she suffered only a minor jolt to her nervous system. "I don't know. I never played, and I didn't have any friends who did. I like football, though."

Cal's grin was fleeting but no less devastating for its brevity. "Well, that's definitely a plus."

Up went her chin. "What are you doing, Cal? Making a list of my positive and negative attributes?"

"And if I am?" he countered.

"I'd ask why."

He hesitated, but only for a moment. ''I'd say that any good employer does that, even if he or she isn't aware of it.''

''Oh.'' For some reason, the answer only added to Amber's growing sense of doom. She carried the stack of plates into the kitchen. When she got back, the room was empty. Hearing the sound of Cal's sports-utility vehicle starting up, she went to the window and watched them leave, feeling strangely left out.

''I could have cleaned up the kitchen if you wanted to go,'' Claudia said from behind Amber.

Amber turned and smiled, pushing away the doldrums. ''I didn't. Not really. How's the science project coming along?''

''I'm just finishing up a little lettering on the poster. I shouldn't be but an hour or so.'' She paused. ''I hate to bother you, but did you ask Uncle Cal about having the slumber party after the dance?''

''I did,'' Amber said, her spirits lifting a bit. ''He said fine, as long as I was here to supervise.''

Claudia's face lit up. ''Really? That's great! When I finish with this darned science project, I'm going to go in and make some invitations on the computer. I'll make a list of the snacks we should buy, too. Can we order pizza?''

''I'm sure that will be fine.''

If possible, Claudia's smile grew even wider.

''How many girls were you thinking of inviting?'' Amber asked, hoping the numbers wouldn't be too unmanageable but loath to ask Claudia to keep her guests to a limit. The child was so excited, she seemed about to explode.

''About six, I think. Is that too many?''

''Perfect.''

''Do you think we can go look for me a dress after

school tomorrow? The dance is just a little over a week away, and you know it may be hard finding something I like.''

Amber smiled. ''Claudia, darlin', your new baby-sitter may be a slouch in the cooking department and child-development skills, but she's an expert when it comes to shopping.''

Claudia giggled, and Amber thought of Georgina and how much she was missing. *You're not the person to be throwing stones, Ms. Campion.* Her own foolishness had cost her plenty, but she hoped that by being here at a time when Claudia—and even Beau—needed someone, she could partially atone for her mistakes.

''Thanks, for everything, Amber.''

''No problem.''

''Well, I'd better get back to work,'' Claudia said with a sigh.

''Tell you what. You work on your science project, and I'll whip up a batch of Rice Krispies treats.''

''You can make Rice Krispies treats?''

''It's one of my most prized accomplishments,'' Amber said with a smile. ''I figure my sister and I made a jillion batches growing up.''

''They had Rice Krispies treats back then?'' Claudia asked in disbelief.

''Yep,'' Amber said with a wry grin. ''Even back in the stone ages.''

''You know what I mean.''

''Yeah, Claudia, I do. So go get to work.'' Claudia started to leave the room. ''Claudia.''

''Ma'am?''

''Is Beau any good as a ball player?''

''As much as I hate to admit it, he's great.''

Amber nodded. She'd figured as much.

* * *

A week passed, and Amber managed to struggle through without any major catastrophes. She was amazed at how much planning went into getting the simplest meal on the table. She was learning, though, and finding that she actually liked planning meals and cooking. Maybe because it challenged her creativity.

Gwen would be proud of her, she thought. Kim was. According to Kim, Drew was still a nonbeliever who said he'd trust she could cook when he saw it with his own eyes. Amber had retaliated by inviting them for the Fourth of July. She'd do a brisket. Drew said he'd take her up on that. Since it wasn't within her rights to ask her company to Cal's home, they'd eat at Lafourche Farm.

Amber felt she was fully accepted by Claudia. There was nothing like a shopping spree or two and a couple of chocolate milk shakes to ensure feminine bonding. They'd found the perfect dress and shoes, and Claudia was scheduled to have her hair cut and styled the day of the dance, which was the following day. The snacks had been purchased, and Amber had promised to help the girls do makeovers as part of the slumber party fun.

Though Cal hadn't confronted Beau about his actions until after the ball game, fitting punishment had been meted out. Beau had been grounded until after school was out for putting the snake in Amber's bed, which he claimed he'd done to get back at Amber for making him work in the yard and for getting on to him about his manners.

Amber wasn't sure about his punishment for his taking her cigarettes and the subsequent suspension from school, but if the greenish look on his face and Cal's comment—"He won't be trying that again for a while"—was anything to go by, she suspected Beau's penance involved doing just what he'd planned to do with the pilfered cigarettes—only in excess.

The living room was finished, though it could use just the right picture here and there and a couple more pieces of furniture—like the chair she planned to have recovered. The pleasure in Cal's eyes confirmed his verbal acknowledgment that he liked what she'd done. While Amber was satisfied, the living room's new look only made the neglect in the rest of the house more noticeable. She'd decided that her next project was to strip the dark varnish off the kitchen cabinets.

Tomorrow would be a big day. Not only was it Friday, the end-of-school dance and the night of the slumber party, Dudley was coming home. Cal had asked Amber if she'd do one of her pot roasts, since roast was Dudley's favorite and her last one had been such a success. Pleased that Cal had asked her, she'd agreed, hoping she was as lucky this time as she had been the first time. Pleased that she had pleased him, even in a small way.

Life was as good as it had been in a long while, Amber thought the following afternoon, as she made a mental inventory of things she needed to do. The six girls would come home with Claudia after the dance. Amber had reserved several movies she thought might be suitable for young girls and bought some inexpensive beauty products for the facials and makeovers.

She'd filled the pantry with all sorts of snacks, and the pizza was set to be delivered at eleven. All that was left to do was pick up Claudia from school to have her hair done and drive into town to pick up the rental movies.

Beau and Cal would spend the evening keeping Dudley company on his first night home, where they would eat the pot roast. They'd come home at bedtime. Amber only hoped they could sleep with girls giggling and shrieking in the background.

She was taking her keys from the hook near the back door when she saw a strange man walk across the yard. Frowning, she went outside, passing by the hall mirror as she did. She caught a glimpse of her reflection and automatically reached up to touch her newly cut and newly bleached hair.

Throughout the week, Cal had kept commenting on how he liked her better as a blonde. Probably, she thought, because she'd started putting in blond highlights during high school and it was the only way he'd ever known her. She'd called around for some prices, done some figuring and come to the conclusion that the money she'd save by not smoking would more than pay to have her roots touched up as needed.

With the confidence women gain from a new hairdo, Amber felt as if she could tackle not only the party and Dudley's arrival, but anything Beau could dish out, too. She could certainly take care of a trespasser!

To her surprise, the stranger in the yard was Joe Bob Milford, husband of her former employer at the dollar store. Joe Bob's shirt bore the insignia of the electric co-op. A queasy feeling settled in the pit of Amber's stomach.

"Oh, it's you," Amber said. "I didn't know you worked for the electric company."

"Well, you do now," Joe Bob said, swaggering to within a couple of feet of her. She took a step back. She didn't like strangers in her space, and besides, Joe Bob reeked of some cheap men's cologne. She knew the day's growth of stubble was supposed to be sexy, and on some men, including Cal, it was. Joe Bob just looked unkempt.

"You're lookin' *real* good, Amber. I like your hair."

"Thanks. Are you here to read the meter?" she asked hopefully, though her heart of hearts told her Joe Bob was there for an entirely different reason.

"Nope, sugar. The customer does that. I'm here to shut off the electricity."

The squeamish feeling inside her coalesced into a knot of nausea so intense she pressed a palm to her stomach. She hadn't paid the electric bill Cal had asked her to pay on her first day of work. As she'd promised herself, she'd replaced the money she'd used to buy the chair, putting the cash in an envelope as soon as she cashed her first paycheck, which had been a week ago today.

Unfortunately, in all the hubbub of settling in and redecorating, she'd forgotten to tell Cal about overspending at the grocery store and how she'd had to use some of the money for the electric bill to pay for the groceries. Excuses aside, she hadn't done what she was supposed to do. Cal would be furious. He might fire her. The churning in her stomach intensified.

"What's the matter? Is the sheriff too tired these days to walk down the street to pay the bill?" Joe Bob chuckled and raked her body with a look that made his meaning obvious.

Slimy weasel! Amber suppressed the inclination to smack him. That wouldn't help her cause. Her mind worked furiously. Cal hadn't paid her yet today, but if she used the money she'd returned and the money Cal had given her for the beauty shop and the party, she could pay the bill. That would put her short, but as much as she hated to, she could always borrow the money from her dad. Maybe that wouldn't be necessary. Maybe she could talk Joe Bob into taking partial payment.

She forced a smile. "Actually paying the bill was my job. It's just that I've been so busy settling in, I forgot. Can I pay you for part of it today and bring the rest in on Monday morning?"

"No can do, sugar. It's a two-month bill."

"Two months!"

Joe Bob nodded. "Sheriff sent in the new reading more than two weeks ago." He rubbed his cheek as if he were thinking over the options then took a step closer and reached out to trail his knuckles down her cheek. "Don't fret, pretty girl. I'm sure we can work out something."

Amber's stomach roiled, but she forced herself not to back away—or slug him. "Why, Joe Bob!" she asked in mock surprise. "Are you suggesting what I think you are?"

He offered her what he thought was a sexy smile and a negligent shrug.

"What would Rose say?" Amber asked.

"I won't tell Rose, if you don't tell the sheriff," he said. "And believe me, you won't want to…afterward. If you get my drift."

The egotistical slimeball! "Exactly what do you have in mind?" she asked.

"How 'bout if you come up with all of the past-due amount and be real nice to me I give you a little more time on the other…say till the middle of next week. What do you say?"

"I say that smacks of blackmail and sexual harassment."

"Beggars can't be choosers, sugar."

"You'd know all about that, I'm sure," Amber quipped. His frown told her the comment had gone over his head. She glanced at her watch. She needed to hurry. Claudia would be waiting. "Look, I have an appointment. I was just walking out the door when you drove up. Let me get the money, and we'll work out the details."

"Sure 'nough, sugar."

Amber could have sworn he puffed out his chest, savoring his victory already...a legend in his own mind, as the current popular phrase went.

Fuming, Amber left the disgusting excuse for a man and went inside. She found her purse, took the money she needed from what Cal had given her earlier and added it to the envelope she'd stuck in her lingerie drawer.

Joe Bob was standing where she'd left him, filling out a receipt book. She offered him a phony smile and waved the envelope. "Here you go. Right down to the eighty-seven cents."

"There's a late charge," he told her. "Did you include it?"

Amber ground her teeth together. "How much?" she gritted, stifling the urge to scream. When he told her the amount, she counted out the extra money and thrust it at him. "Here's your darned late fee." She glanced at her watch again. "Look, can you hurry with that receipt. I've got to go."

Joe Bob handed her the small receipt, which she folded in half and stuck in her bag. "Catch you later," she told him, and, turning, started for her car.

She'd taken no more than three steps when Joe Bob grabbed her arm and hauled her around. The strap of her purse slid off her shoulder and the open bag tumbled to the ground, spilling the contents at her feet. Amber was more concerned with the obstinate gleam in his eyes. "When?" His fingers dug into the flesh of her upper arm.

"When what?" she asked, trying to pull free.

He jerked her closer and leaned so close his mouth was just inches from hers. "When are you gonna pay up?"

"When hell freezes over, Joe Bob, that's when."

His mouth twisted, and his grip tightened. "A deal's a deal."

Amber laughed, a sound with no true mirth. "Yeah, but

some of us deal better than others.'' She knew she should leave well enough alone, but some uncontrollable impulse prompted her to add, ''You didn't really think I'd sleep with you, did you, Joe Bob? When I'm living with Cal Simmons?''

He let go of her arm as if it had suddenly grown too hot to hold on to. As she'd hoped it would, the implied threat of messing with the sheriff's woman made Joe Bob back off. As she backed away, it crossed her mind that Cal might not like being used that way, but since Joe Bob assumed she was carrying on with Cal, why shouldn't she play that trump card? He would never know, and it *had* made Joe Bob turn her loose.

He glared at her and called her a name.

Amber massaged her aching flesh. ''I outgrew name calling in the sixth grade, Joe Bob. Why don't you grow up and act like a man instead of a sex-crazed teenager? There's more to being a man than making conquests, and I'm sure Rose would be a lot happier if she wasn't worrying about whose bed you were trying to get into.''

''My marriage is none of your business,'' he snarled.

''On the contrary. Your flirting cost me a job. If you're smarter than you look, you'll get in your little white truck and drive away. If you don't argue with me, I won't even mention this little episode to the sheriff.''

''Maybe I'll mention it to him myself.''

''You do whatever you think you have to, big guy. Now get out of my way, so I can pick up my things.''

Joe Bob glanced down at the jumble of items that had fallen from her purse, crossed his arms over his chest and took a giant sideways step forward, putting him right in her face. His smile gave her the creeps. ''Make me.''

Amber stared into his malevolent dark gaze for several seconds and determined that he had no intention of moving until he was darn good and ready. The man was certifiable, she thought, as her bravado faded and trepidation began to set in. She stooped and began to grab tubes, pens, keys, loose change and a half-dozen store receipts as fast as she could. Afraid to get too close to him, she let some loose dollar bills, a few pieces of change and a tube of her favorite lipstick lay where they were, between Joe Bob's spread feet.

Without another word or a backward glance, she crossed the yard to her car. Inside, with all the doors locked, she gripped the steering wheel to steady her shaking hands and drew a deep, relieved breath. Then she started the engine and backed down the driveway. As she pulled away from the house, she checked the rearview mirror. Joe Bob had squatted down to take something from the ground, like a vulture picking at the last remains.

"Jerk," Amber said aloud. She tried to banish the incident from her mind and concentrate on Claudia and her big night. There was nothing to do but ask her dad for the cash until Cal paid her. Gerald would understand.

Amber took Claudia to the hairdresser and, after deciding on just the right style, announced that she'd be back in an hour or so. She had some errands to run.

"Don't forget the movies," Claudia said.

"I won't, worry wart," Amber said with a smile. "You're in good hands. Just relax and think happy thoughts."

"I'll try."

Amber left her young charge and started down the highway that led to her dad's place, reliving every sickening moment of her confrontation with Joe Bob Milford. She was almost to Lafourche Farm when she turned around and headed back to town. She wouldn't ask her dad for the money. Couldn't. Not even for two days. Not even for an emergency. Not even for Claudia. This was just another disaster in a long line of disasters she'd suffered since she'd come back to Louisiana. She'd worked her way through the others; she could figure out how to get through this one.

With a sigh, she held up her left arm. The diamond tennis bracelet her father had bought for her twinkled in the sunlight. She loved the bracelet, had hung onto it through all the tough times she'd encountered, both here and in L.A. But it was only a piece of jewelry, and she didn't want to have to worry about Joe Bob coming out again next week.

Cal hadn't given her money for the new electric bill yet, probably because he didn't think there was a problem since she was supposed to have paid the *other* one. With Dudley coming home and Claudia's dance and party, she didn't want to bother him with the mix-up tonight. No, she'd just go to the pawn shop, hock her bracelet and take care of the electric bill herself, which, she told herself, was what a mature, responsible person would do.

Ten minutes later, she stood staring at the owner of the pawn shop in horror. "You'll give me *what* for it?"

"Six hundred."

"But it's worth at least six thousand."

The man shrugged and probed at his teeth with a toothpick. "This is a pawn shop lady, not an estate sale. Take it or leave it."

Amber touched the gleaming stones and raised a resolute gaze to his. "I'll take it."

Five minutes later, she was in the electric co-op office, explaining to the young woman in charge about Joe Bob coming out to turn off the electricity, how she'd let it slip by her and how she'd paid him cash for the delinquent bill.

"He said that would keep the service on until the middle of the week," Amber said. "I could come in with the other money then." She smiled at the woman, little more than a girl. "I managed to get the cash for the other bill, so I thought I'd just come in and get the account current."

"No problem," the girl said. "Do you have your receipt?"

"Sure," Amber said, and began rummaging around in her purse. Unable to locate the piece of paper, she dumped the contents onto the counter. The receipt was nowhere to be found. A flash of memory surfaced: Joe Bob refusing to move so she could pick up her things, of his stooping over to pick up something from the ground. The jerk had seen the receipt, stepped on it and picked it up after she left. She had no proof that she'd paid the past-due bill!

He'd probably have a high old time on the money she'd given him, knowing that when she went in to pay the bill the following week, she'd have no proof of what passed between them. Nothing but her word. Amber shook her head in despair. She had to hand it to him. It was a brilliant revenge for having turned him down. "I can't seem to find my receipt."

"Maybe you took it inside after you paid," the co-op clerk said, willing to give her the benefit of the doubt.

"No." Amber shook her head. "I was getting ready to leave. Joe Bob and I had our little confrontation outside."

The woman's face took on a stricken look. "Joe Bob Milford?"

Their eyes met for several seconds. Amber couldn't read the woman's expression. Afraid she'd said too much—after all, she didn't want the whole town to know Joe Bob had made a pass at her—Amber said simply, "Yes."

"I'm sorry, but I can't give you credit for a cash payment without a receipt. If you want to get the account current, you'll have to pay both months."

Amber knew there was no use railing against the rules. No use insisting she'd already paid one bill. She had no choice but to cough up the money again, unless she wanted to confess to Cal that she'd been lax in her duties and that she'd used an imaginary affair with him to fend off Joe Bob Milford's advances.

"I understand. If I find the receipt, or if Joe Bob confirms that I paid, you'll give me a refund, right?"

"We'll be glad to."

"Fine." Amber counted out the correct amount and took the receipt for two months' payment, sticking it into the purse's zippered compartment. First thing Monday morning, she'd give good old Joe Bob a call and tell him he'd better hand over her receipt.

Chapter Eight

Stifling the urge to go to the dollar store and tell Rose exactly what a loser she was married to, Amber went instead to the video store and picked up the movies for that night. By the time she finished there, it was time to pick up Claudia.

She must have been waiting for Amber, because as soon as the door opened, Claudia was hurrying toward her, a big grin on her face.

"You look fantastic!" Amber said and meant every word. Claudia's thick hair had been thinned and cropped to shoulder length and turned under around her face. Wispy bangs hid her high forehead. At Amber's instruction, the beautician lightened the hair around Claudia's face, giving it a sun-kissed look. The most miraculous part wasn't the new hairdo. It was the glimmer of happiness in Claudia's eyes.

"Thanks," she said fervently.

"Thank Gloria," Amber said, waving a hand toward the smiling beauty operator. "I take it you like it."

"I love it. Do you think Uncle Cal will?"

"Yes and no," Amber told her with a smile. "Yes, because you like it and it makes you look so pretty. And no because it makes you look so pretty and now he's going to have to worry about all the boys who are going to start calling."

"He doesn't have to worry about that."

"We'll see."

Amber went to pay the hairdresser, who told her she'd explained to Claudia how to blow-dry her new hairdo. Amber bought her a new hairbrush, a couple of clips to get her hair up off her neck if she got tired of wearing it down and some new earrings, because tonight was a special night. She bought herself a new tube of red lipstick to celebrate her own new hairdo.

Smiling, they left the shop, arm in arm.

When they got home, they were greeted by the mouth-watering scent of the pot roast. Expecting a call from one of her friends, Claudia checked the phone messages while Amber checked the meat. It was done to perfection.

"There's something wrong with the answering machine," Claudia said, entering the kitchen with a frown in her eyes.

"What do you think it could be?" Amber asked, turning the oven to the lowest setting to keep the meat warm.

"I don't know."

"Why don't you go ahead and call Pammie? I'll check the answering machine as soon as I run to the bathroom."

While she was in the half bath, she heard him and Cal come in. She heard the door to Beau's bedroom close and heard Cal whistling as he went to the other end of the house. It was one of those special moments of normalcy that warmed her heart. It felt right to be there sharing Claudia's excitement over her first big dance, hearing Beau banging around in his room and knowing from the short time she'd been there that Cal was headed straight for the shower. If only it could be this way forever....

But there was no guarantee that her job would last until next month, much less forever. Life had ups and downs, as her afternoon had proved. She'd just have to make the most of the moment. Wanting to look her best for Cal, she took the new tube of lipstick from her pocket and brightened her lips, then fluffed her own new hairdo.

A few seconds later, Amber was examining the answering machine when Cal strode into the room.

She spoke without looking up. "Hi." Good grief! Was that squeaky voice hers? She hadn't been this nervous around a member of the opposite sex since she was Claudia's age. But she was quickly learning that loving Cal was forcing her to experience a whole gamut of emotions she'd forgotten...or never felt at all.

"Did you have any trouble with the water earlier?"

Amber looked up and saw Cal standing a few feet away wearing nothing but a towel slung low around his hips. It crossed her mind that he was a very beautiful man—all hard muscle, bronze flesh and gold-tipped hair—before the ability to think at all disappeared in the thunder of her wildly beating heart. It was all she could do to meet his questioning gaze, harder still to speak through a mouth that was suddenly dust dry.

"It was working fine before I left. Do you think it could be fire ants again?" Cal lived outside the city limits and a deep well serviced the house. Like everything else, it was getting old and worn, and recently they'd been troubled twice with fire ants getting on the points and fouling the electricity.

"Probably," Cal said in disgust. "Why this evening of all evenings?"

"My TV won't work," Beau said, his complaint preceding him and Claudia into the living room.

"My CD player isn't working either," she said.

Frowning, Cal turned and flipped on the light switch. Nothing.

A chilly sense of foreboding made Amber's blood run cold.

"Maybe there's a power outage somewhere," Claudia suggested.

"Maybe," Cal agreed, but he didn't look convinced. "Let me get some clothes on, and I'll see if I can figure out what's going on. Beau run out to the meter and see if it's turning."

Amber's heart didn't sink as much as it crashed inside her chest. She knew she could save Beau the trouble. It was Joe Bob. He hadn't given her until the middle of the week to come up with the other money. He had taken her money and her receipt and turned off the electricity anyway. For spite. Because she'd turned him down and bruised his inflated ego.

She must have spoken his name out loud because Cal turned to look at her. "You did pay the electric bill, didn't you?"

"Yes." Amber had no intention of explaining what had happened in front of the kids. She didn't want to ruin Claudia's evening by arguing with Cal.

Beau came running back into the room. "It looks as if there's a lock of some kind on it."

Cal swore softly. Then he planted his hands on his hips and pinned Amber with an angry glare. "Do you mind explaining why the electricity has been cut off if you paid the bill?''

''Joe Bob.''

''How am I going to get ready for the dance with no electricity?'' Claudia wailed. ''And my friends! What will they say?''

Cal gave Claudia a tight smile. ''You'll get ready if I have to take you to Dudley's. And the electricity will be back on by the time you get home from the dance, I promise.'' He turned to Amber. ''Joe Bob?''

Amber nodded and glanced at the children. ''Do you mind if we discuss this privately?''

Cal regarded her for a moment, then looked at his niece and nephew and jerked his head toward the hallway. They left the room without a word. Cal folded his arms across his chest. His bare, hair-dusted chest. ''Well?''

She blew out a jittery breath. ''It's a little hard to concentrate with you—'' she waved her hand in a vague gesture ''—running around half-dressed.''

''Get over it,'' he said. ''And explain to me how you can pay a bill and still have the service cut off.''

Amber felt a sudden rush of sympathy for the suspects who were forced to undergo an interrogation by Cal. The man was brutal in his determination to get at the truth. She sighed again. ''Joe Bob came by earlier today to turn off the electricity. That's when I remembered that I hadn't paid the bill that first day you asked me to.''

''Ah.''

Amber curbed the urge to walk out the door and let him figure it out for himself. Instead, she continued. ''I spent more on groceries than what you'd given me that first day, so I had to use some of the electric money. I was going to tell you and ask you for some to replace it the next day, but I forgot that evening and things were pretty chaotic the next morning when I ruined breakfast.''

"And you've forgotten every day since?"

Amber gave a shaky laugh. "Well, you have to admit that life around here can be a little wild. The next day was when the barbecue grill caught on fire and Beau got suspended from school." She lifted one shoulder in a shrug.

"You look a little guilty. What else haven't you told me?"

Amber knew there was no use trying to hide it. "I used some of the money to buy a chair."

"You did what?"

"Don't make it sound like a federal crime!" she cried. "I bought it for you."

The anger in his eyes subsided a bit. "For me?"

Amber nodded. "I saw it at a junk store. Except for needing recovering, it was perfect for the living room, and it was oversize, so it would fit you better. I had no idea the electric bill was late. I was going to put the money back when I got paid last Friday, which I did. It's been in an envelope in my drawer. But I kept forgetting to ask you for the money I'd used for the groceries. And this week has been so hectic with the party and everything...."

"So you didn't pay the bill," he said in a voice that was all the more menacing in its quietness.

Her own guilt and self-disgust exploded into anger. "I did pay the bill!" she cried, as furious as he'd been earlier. "As a matter of fact, I paid the darn thing twice!"

"Then why the hell don't we have any electricity?" The angry question thundered throughout the room.

"Because I wouldn't sleep with Joe Bob Milford!" she cried. "And don't you dare yell at me!"

Cal blinked; his anger vanished. "What did you say?" Again the quiet deadliness of his voice was far more frightening than his blatant fury. Amber told him about her confrontation with Joe Bob: that he said two months of electrical use was due, how he'd propositioned her, how she'd pretended to go along to buy some time and how, once she had the receipt in hand, she'd told him exactly what she thought of him, his slimy deal and his high opinion of himself. Cal didn't interrupt her during the telling of the story, but a muscle in his jaw jumped repeatedly.

"We just got the second month's bill. It isn't overdue yet."

"I know. But I didn't find that out till later. I didn't want to be beholden to the jerk, so after I took Claudia to the hairdresser's, I went to pay the second month."

Cal extended his arms, palms out. "Whoa! Back up. How did you pay Joe Bob the first time?"

"With the money I'd put back to repay you for the chair and part of Claudia's beauty shop and video money," Amber supplied promptly and without a qualm. She'd done her best. Let him do his worst.

The angry gleam leaped back into Cal's eyes. He started to say something but clamped his mouth shut. Amber could almost see him doing a mental countdown to ten. When he spoke, he sounded almost normal. "If you used that money the first time, how did you manage to pay for a second month?"

She gave him a haughty look. "I liquidated an asset."

"I beg your pardon."

Anger surged through her again. She hadn't wanted to admit what she'd done. "I pawned something I'd been hanging on to in case of a true monetary emergency, okay?" she snapped.

She dropped her head and regarded the nails of her right hand for several seconds. They weren't long and painted anymore. The ones that hadn't been broken to the quick were cut to a more manageable length and bare of color.

She raised her limpid gaze to Cal's. "I figured this was that emergency. My inability to handle the responsibility you entrusted me with got me into the mess, so I should be the one to figure out how to get out of it. Besides, it didn't just affect me. It affected Claudia."

Cal was silent. Finally, he shook his head. "I'm trying to work through this. After you found out we didn't owe a second bill, why did you have to pay the other bill again?"

"I couldn't find my receipt." The memory of Joe Bob's ugly anger made her shiver. "I guess it fell out when I dropped my purse."

"And why did you drop your purse?"

She closed her eyes and expelled a soft, resigned breath. "Joe Bob grabbed my arm."

"He actually put his hands on you?" Cal yelled.

"It's no big deal. I'm used to men making moves on me. And I'm used to putting them in their place." She met his steady gaze head on. "I may as well tell you all of it."

He scowled. "There's more?"

"I implied there was more going on between us than there is." She wouldn't meet his eyes, but she felt the intensity of his gaze. "I thought it might deter Joe Bob...knowing he'd have to answer to the sheriff if he messed with his woman."

"And did it?"

"I guess so. He let go of my arm."

"Quick thinking. He didn't try anything else did he?"

"No. But he was mad, and I was getting pretty nervous. I just wanted to get out of there. When I started gathering up the things that had spilled out of my purse, he wouldn't move. So I left some money and a tube of lipstick on the ground. I saw him picking up something as I pulled out of the driveway. He must have been standing on the receipt. It's the only thing I can think that might have happened to it.''

''That's quite a tale.''

''It's the truth.''

Without a hint as to whether or not he believed her, Cal turned and headed in the direction of his room. Amber sat where she was, her hands knotted in her lap, trembling with the aftermath of the ordeal, sick at heart because she'd inadvertently ruined Claudia's big night and let Cal down. She'd let everyone down because of her impulsiveness and her inability to handle the duties entrusted to her. She may as well pack her stuff first thing in the morning. Cal was probably calling someone to take her place at that very moment. She was hardly aware of the two tears that slid down her cheeks.

''Amber?''

The sound of Claudia's voice brought her head up. She swiped at her eyes, even as she thought how pretty Claudia looked with her new hairdo, and, with a sharp pang of poignancy, she realized just how attached she'd become to the child in the two weeks she'd been working for Cal.

''Don't worry about a thing,'' Claudia said. ''Uncle Cal will take care of getting the electricity turned back on. And he'll take care of that nasty old Joe Bob, too!''

''You were listening?'' Amber asked.

Claudia nodded. ''I know we shouldn't have, but—''

''It's okay. I just didn't want you and Beau hearing what a mess I'd made of things.''

''Everyone makes mistakes,'' Claudia said with a wisdom beyond her years. ''That's what Uncle Cal says. He told us that the main thing is to learn from them.''

Amber felt the sting of fresh tears. "Your uncle Cal is a pretty smart guy."

"Here." Claudia dug around in the pocket of her shorts and pulled out something. "Hold out your hands."

"What?"

Claudia grinned impishly. "Just hold out your hands."

Amber did as she was told. Claudia dumped some loose change, a solitary earring and a tube of lipstick onto Amber's outstretched palms. "I found it outside, right where you told Uncle Cal you were."

"Thank you, Claudia."

"Sure." Moving awkwardly, she stepped closer and pressed a kiss to Amber's cheek. "Thanks for taking me for a haircut and for doing the sleepover and everything."

Amber blinked furiously to hold back the tears. She couldn't speak, so she squeezed Claudia's hand. "And don't worry about what you said about you and Uncle Cal...you know.... Some boy at school already said something to Beau about it, so it isn't like you said anything that people don't already think is true." She squeezed Amber's hand again and bolted from the room.

Amber's mouth dropped open in surprise. Once again, the Vanity grapevine had been hard at work. She might have known a few people would assume the worst, but for kids at school to be gossiping about her relationship with Cal was too much.

Amber felt a twinge of sorrow realizing that this job, too, would be short-lived. She didn't want the children to think there was anything inappropriate going on between her and Cal. And she didn't want them to be so accepting—the way Claudia seemed to be—even if there was.

"It's all taken care of," Cal said, striding into the room, still appealing even though he was fully clothed. "The electricity will be back on within the hour, so Claudia should have plenty of time to get ready for the dance.'' He turned toward the hall and bellowed, ''Beau! Let's go!''

Cal handed Amber a key. ''This is the key to Dudley's house. Can you take the food over there while I'm gone? Maybe put it in his oven to keep warm?''

''Sure.''

''And check the phone messages, please.''

Amber nodded and Beau came into the room at a dead run. ''I'm ready!''

''We shouldn't be but an hour or so,'' Cal said. ''I'll take care of Joe Bob after we get Dudley settled in.''

Amber felt a frisson of alarm. ''What are you going to do?''

''Get your money and your receipt.''

''So you *do* believe me?''

Cal smiled at her, a smile that showed her a flash of white teeth and brought a teasing glint to his eyes. The bottom seemed to drop out from under her heart. ''Yeah, I believe you. You spun too wild and complicated a story for it not to be the truth.''

The man from the co-op arrived within fifteen minutes, did something to the meter, announced they were back in business and apologized profusely. Amber thanked him and went inside to check the phone messages. There was a message from Georgina that brought a chill to Amber's heart.

''Hi, kiddos! This is your mama.'' The voice was smooth, confident, just as Amber remembered Georgina Simmons being, despite her humble background. ''I just wanted to let you know that I'll be in town Monday through Friday of next week, so let's plan to spend some time together, okay? My new husband, Nick, and I will be looking for a big ol' house, so we can all be together again real soon." There were kissing sounds followed by, "Love you. See you soon. Bye."

Amber let the last message play without really hearing it. Georgina's timing couldn't be worse, Amber thought. Cal would be furious that his sister-in-law had even called much less thought he'd consent to her spending time with the kids. She thought about his response when she'd asked him a couple of weeks ago if he thought Georgina would want the kids back.

"Over my dead body."

She knew Cal had applied for and received legal guardianship of his niece and nephew. He adored them and wouldn't give them up without a fight. "Lotsa luck, Georgie," she murmured, but deep in her heart, she felt that same troubling flash of feeling, almost a foreshadowing that her days as nanny for the Simmons kids was drawing to an end. She'd have to start thinking about what her next move would be, but not tonight. Tonight was Claudia's night, and Amber refused to let anything ruin it for her.

After setting up for dinner at Dudley's house, she went back to Cal's and helped Claudia finish dressing. The twelve-year-old was waiting impatiently at the front window when Cal's vehicle pulled into the driveway and he, Beau and Dudley got out. With a little squeal of excitement, she scampered back down the hall so that she could make her grand entrance. Amber would be driving Claudia to the dance, since Cal would be helping Dudley, but Cal wanted to see his niece in all her finery and take some pictures for the family album.

Amber, who'd changed into a short sleeveless dress of vibrant red, met the trio at the door. Since she remembered Dudley from her childhood, when he and his wife occasionally attended a social function at Lafourche Farm, in-

troductions weren't necessary. Gentleman that he was, he
took her proffered hand. Flirt that he'd always be, he carried her hand to his lips brushed her knuckles with the
whisper of a kiss. Then he winked at her.

"Amber, my dear. You're looking wonderful—as always. The years have been kind."

Amber smiled in genuine pleasure. He was such a
rogue! She hadn't seen him since her college days, but
other than the arthritis, he'd aged well, like the fine wines
he was known to favor. She'd always thought he epito-
mized the word *distinguished* and had always appreciated
his blunt ways and often dry humor. Even as a child, she'd
recognized the remnants of the drop-dead handsomeness
of his youth, even though he'd have been at least fifty back
then.

"Why thank you, Dudley," she replied. "I might say
the same about you."

He laughed in delight and patted her cheek. "You always did know the right thing to say."

Amber smiled again and let her gaze move from his to
Cal's. "I left dinner in the warming oven, and there's a
pitcher of iced tea in the refrigerator. You guys should be
all set."

"Thanks."

"And where is our party girl?" Dudley asked. "I can't
wait to see her."

As if she'd been waiting for her cue, Claudia stepped
out of the hallway into the living room. The dance was a
dress-up occasion—probably so the parents and teachers
could see the students in something besides tennis shoes
and blue jeans. With Amber's assistance, Claudia had chosen a short white dress with an equally short lace jacket.
A drop necklace and chunky heels completed the ensem-
ble. Amber had applied soft pink lipstick to Claudia's lips,

feathered the lightest stroke of color across her cheekbones and darkened her eyelashes. With the new hairdo that framed her face, even that slightest enhancement of her features was enough to draw attention to the promise of beauty.

Cal was silent. Beau breathed a stunned, "Wow!" Dudley said, "My stars and bars. She looks like an angel."

"I don't want to look like an angel," Claudia said. I want to look *hot*. Uncle Cal, what do you think?" She did a pirouette for his approval.

"Well, to paraphrase Garth Brooks, I'm way too young to feel so damned old." He looked at Amber. "I'm not sure if I should thank you, strangle you or fire you."

"Uncle Cal!"

"That means he likes the way you look, Claudia, but as the person responsible for your welfare, he's feeling threatened by the hordes of young men he knows will be gathering around you."

Claudia blinked. "It does?"

Amber smiled. "Men speak an entirely different language than women. It's a wonder they manage to communicate enough to propagate the species. I'll have to teach you some time. But not now." She glanced at her watch. "Right now we have to get some pictures before you leave. Cal, will you do the honors?"

"Sure thing."

Cal snapped several shots of Claudia and took one of her and Amber with their arms around each other. Finally, Amber announced that the carriage was waiting to take the princess to the ball, adding, "You should be fashionably late if we leave right now."

Claudia's face seemed to freeze at the thought of actually walking into a group of her peers.

Amber reached out and tipped up Claudia's chin. She

smiled into the child's worried eyes. "No frowns. You'll make wrinkles. Smile. You'll be fine."

"Listen to Amber," Dudley said. "Do as she says and you'll be the hit of the dance."

"Okay." Claudia took a deep breath. "I can do this. I can do this," she chanted in a low voice, as if the words were a mantra to give her protection. After a moment, she squared her shoulders and looked at Amber. "Let's go."

An hour and a half later, Amber was making certain that everything was ready for Claudia and her friends when she saw the light on in the shed. She headed down there to investigate.

The approaching darkness cooled the air and softened the edges of the day. The scent of tea roses mingled with the smell of fresh-cut hay from the neighboring field. Fireflies blinked in the gathering darkness, sending out messages only their peers could decipher. A whippoorwill sang his sad song, and from a distance, an owl gave a mournful call.

As she drew closer to the shed, she could see someone moving around inside. She caught a flash of blue, the same color as the shirt Cal had been wearing. What was he doing? she wondered. He was supposed to be with Dudley and Beau. She paused outside the door, her palms sweaty at the thought of facing him.

"Come on in."

She jumped at the sound of his voice. She hadn't known he was aware of her presence. Taking the same advice she'd given Claudia, Amber took a deep breath and crossed the threshold. Cal was sitting in the chair she'd bought him.

"What are you doing in here?" she asked, moving into

the room, which, thanks to Beau, was now straightened and swept.

"I just got back from the Milfords'."

Amber's heart gave a little leap.

"I wanted to see the chair that caused such a problem," he told her, resting his forearms on the chair arms. "You're right. It's a good fit. What did you have in mind for upholstery?"

"Plaid," Amber said distractedly, not caring one whit about the chair at that moment. "What did Joe Bob say?"

"I got your money and your receipt." Cal stood, reached into his jeans pocket and pulled out the items. He took her hand and pressed them into it.

"He just handed it over?"

"Not exactly. I told him what you said. He tried to tell me you were lying about paying, that you were the one trying to trade sex for the bill, until I told him you'd been to the co-op to pay the other one. I also told him that the girl who worked there said he'd made moves on her, too. He didn't have any recourse then but to come clean."

"The sorry little weasel," Amber said.

"I told him that if he so much as looked toward the house when he drives by, I'd see to it he loses his job. I don't think he'll give you any more trouble."

"Thank you."

"Sure." He looked as uncomfortable as she'd felt a few moments before. "And I'm sorry I accused you without gathering the facts first."

"It's okay."

They stood in an awkward growing silence where Amber imagined she could hear the thudding of her own heart.

Cal plunged his hands into his pockets. "I've been thinking about what you said earlier. It has been a hectic two weeks, and I've thrown a lot at you. In retrospect, you've done a great job settling in.''

Amber was so surprised by the praise she couldn't think of anything to say.

''And I appreciate you making dinner for Dudley. It was delicious. He was especially impressed that you went to the trouble to fix up the table.''

''Thank my stepmother,'' Amber told him. ''Gwen was always big on taking everyday happenings and making them special—an A on a test, winning a blue ribbon on field day, whatever. She claimed it was as important to celebrate the little things as the big ones.'' Amber's eyes grew moist. What a tragedy that she hadn't recognized what a gem she had in Gwen until after she died.

''That's a great way to live life.'' He smiled at her. ''And speaking of big things, you've really gone all out to make tonight a special one for Claudia. I've never seen her as excited as she is about this slumber party. And she looked so pretty I got a little nervous thinking about the next few years.''

''She's easy to be good to,'' Amber told him. ''All she needs is a little self-confidence, and she'll blossom into a lovely young woman.''

''Well, tonight looked like a great start.'' His face darkened. ''Sometimes I'd like to strangle Georgina for what she did to those kids.''

''Oh, I forgot!'' Amber blurted, remembering suddenly. ''She called.''

''Georgina?''

''Yes. You told me to check the answering machine, and there was a message from her.''

''What did she say?''

''That she'd be in town Monday for a few days and wants to see the kids. That she and her new husband would be looking for a house, so they could all be together again.''

Cal raked a hand over his face. "I'd heard she was coming back but I wasn't sure she'd have the guts to face me." He swore under his breath. "If she starts something, it will just mess up their minds even more."

"Can she do it? Can she get the kids back?"

"Not without a fight. I'm their legal guardian, and she abandoned them. None of her family offered to take them."

The words pricked the sore spot of guilt in Amber's heart. "I'm sure she didn't realize how her leaving would affect Beau and Claudia."

"There's leaving and there's leaving," Cal said flatly. "She could have talked to them first, but she didn't care. All she was worried about was herself. How life was passing her by and how she had to get out of here before she smothered."

"She actually told you that?" Amber asked, aghast.

"Yeah, she did."

"She and Dean got married so young," Amber said. "Maybe it was just growing pains. Maybe she'll come back and be the best mother the kids could ever hope for."

"Why are you defending her?" Cal asked, frowning.

"I'm not defending her," Amber said, wondering if he could pick up on the guilt she felt. "I'm just playing devil's advocate. There are always two sides to a story. Gwen always told me and Kim that we shouldn't judge, that a person deserved the benefit of the doubt."

Cal regarded her solemnly for a moment. She could see him struggling with his anger. "I'm trying not to judge Georgina. But I was taught that you know a tree by its fruit. Georgina's fruit has been pain and sorrow, and I love those kids too much to sit around and watch her destroy them a second time.''

Amber's shoulders lifted in a shrug. "I can't argue with that.''

"You've been more of a mother to Claudia and Beau the past two weeks than Georgina was the two years before Dean died.'' Amber's surprise must have shown. "Oh, yeah, she was showing signs of discontent long before he crashed his plane. As a matter of fact, they'd had a big fight the morning he died. He called me all upset because she'd told him she wanted a divorce.''

"I didn't know,'' she said, moving closer in an instinctive gesture.

"How could you?'' He turned and went to the window, staring out into the gathering gloaming while Amber struggled to find words to fill the emptiness. "Dean never should have gone up that morning,'' Cal said, almost to himself. "It was suicide.''

Amber sucked in a shocked breath, and Cal turned. "Not actual suicide. Dean would never have done anything like that. But crop dusting is dangerous work that demands total concentration. His mind was probably on the fight with Georgina instead of where the power lines were located.''

Amber didn't say anything. There were no words to temper Cal's pain, or his anger. It was something he'd have to deal with in his own way, his own time. Still, she understood so much more now, both of his bitterness toward his sister-in-law and his fierce protectiveness for his niece and nephew.

Suddenly, unexpectedly, he reached out and touched her hair, an expression of bemusement on his face. "I just realized you did something to your hair. I knew something was different, but I guess I was too upset earlier to realize what it was."

"I went back blond."

"It suits you." His fingertips feathered over the barely noticeable scar, along her cheekbone, around her ear and down the curve of her jaw, coming to rest on her chin.

Amber couldn't have moved if her life depended on it. She knew what was coming, knew she should stop him. It would only complicate a situation already rife with the potential for disaster. But sensing that he needed some sort of physical contact to soothe his pain, needing to know that pain was eased more than she needed her next breath, she didn't tell him to stop, didn't step away. Instead, breathless, she waited for his next move.

Cal tipped her head back and circled her throat with his big hand. His thumb caressed the hollow below her ear. "Why haven't you ever gotten married?" he asked instead of kissing her as she expected.

The question came as such a surprise she never thought to lie. "No one ever asked me. Besides, I'm not good marriage material."

"Says who?"

She shrugged. "It's just something a person knows about himself."

"It might have been true once, but you've changed. Anyone with two eyes can see it." Sliding his hand up to cup her cheek, he moved his thumb and gently brushed it over the fullness of her lower lip, the way she'd often imagined him doing. "I want to kiss you again."

"I know," she told him on a soft suspiration.

"It would be a really stupid thing to do."

"Yes," she said. "It would."

"It would only make the situation here more complicated than it already is."

She nodded, her gaze locked with his.

"Stop me."

"I can't."

He lowered his head and covered her parted lips with his. The kiss was gentle, almost exploratory, its very nature urging Amber to give in return. She felt a jolt to her system as the tip of his tongue touched hers, briefly, tentatively. Her reply was a soft groan.

Taking the sound for acquiescence, Cal slid his arms around her. Amber's went around his neck, and she gave him back kiss for mind-drugging kiss. He was an excellent kisser, expertly using his lips and tongue to kindle the passion that had lain dormant for so long.

Then, somehow, they were in the chair, Amber on Cal's lap while his hands....oh, his hands.... Like a virtuoso whose skill wrought the sound of laughter and tears from wood and strings, the skill of his touch that roamed from thigh to hip to breast, roused a dichotomy of emotions, from the evoking of long-repressed desire to the provoking of a tenuous hope. A feeling of completeness filled her, yet she knew she would never be filled until she and Cal were one in every way....

"Hey, Uncle Cal!" The sound of Beau's voice shattered the perfectness of the moment, drenching their desire as effectively as a bucket of cold water. Knowing it would be disastrous for Beau to see what was happening between them, Amber pulled herself from Cal's embrace and managed to struggle to her feet just seconds before Beau stuck his head in the door. The boy seemed to have a knack for interrupting them at the most inopportune moments. But then, maybe she should be thankful that he did, she thought, as his cool, deliberate gaze moved from her to

Cal. The too-adult look in his eyes told her he knew he'd interrupted something.

"What is it, Beau?"

"The station called. You've got an emergency."

Chapter Nine

It was nearing midnight, and the seven girls showed little sign of slowing down. And as sleepy as Amber was, she knew the tangle of her thoughts wouldn't let her rest. So, while the girls watched TV, ate popcorn and did makeovers, Amber sat in the kitchen drinking coffee, eating ice cream and brooding over what had happened between her and Cal.

As he'd said, it was stupid. Incredibly stupid. Why had she let him kiss her, again? How could they ever go back to a comfortable, employer-employee relationship when every time she looked at him, she'd remember the way his mouth felt against hers, the way her heart raced beneath his palm.

She should leave. Amber buried her face in her hands. But how could she walk away from Cal and the children when she felt as if she were home for the first time in years? How could she leave sweet, unassertive Claudia, so timid, so needy of a woman in her life?

How could she leave Beau, who reminded Amber of herself in so many ways? Beau, who needed—what? To know he was worthy of unconditional love? Most certainly. But more than that, Amber wanted to help him overcome his anger and resentment and to be secure in the knowledge that he wouldn't be abandoned, no matter how he behaved.

And how could she leave Cal when she loved him more every day, when her days didn't really begin until she saw his smile in the morning?

On the other hand, to let what happened between them continue, develop into more—which every feminine instinct told her it inevitably would—was unthinkable. As much as she yearned for Cal, she couldn't allow them to set a bad example for the children. She had no choice but to start planning what she'd do when she left the Simmons household.

But what? It was an irrefutable fact that she couldn't find and keep a job in Vanity or, obviously, the surrounding towns. Maybe she'd just strike out and do something on her own.

Like what?

Good question. What could she do that would earn her a decent living, that would leave her responsible to no one but herself and the bank? She recalled Cal's comments about the living room and what she'd done at Dudley's. She'd been trained to be an interior decorator by one of the best schools in the country. She liked to shop, but now had a limited budget. She loved to find bargains, like the chair she'd bought for Cal. And she loved mixing the old with the new, finding new uses for old things. She'd been into the shabby chic style long before it became a decorating trend.

So what are you thinking, Amber? Are you really considering setting yourself up as an interior decorator in Vanity, Louisiana?

Why not? Granted, people in small towns didn't have mansions to renovate or decorate—though every town had its few rich movers and shakers—but even in Vanity there were bound to be people who wanted a new look and didn't have a clue as to what to do. There were bound to be women who had limited funds for a quick room face-lift.

Owning a business that combined old and new, that made use of what a person already owned, that didn't require an unlimited amount of money to spend on a decorating project would be just the kind of challenge she loved. It would be fun to see what a statement she could make within parameters. Despite herself, Amber felt a tingle of excitement. And starting a business of her own would keep her mind off how much she'd miss Cal and the kids.

There was only one problem. Seed money. Amber gnawed on her lower lip. She hated to ask her dad after all the "loans" she'd hit him up for in the past, but if she actually worked up a business plan to prove she'd given the venture some thought, he might help her.

"Hey, Ms. Campion!" The greeting brought Amber's head up. Claudia's best friend, Pammie Cavanaugh, who still hadn't gotten rid of her baby fat, stood in the doorway smiling, her arms full of empty cola cans. "Getting sleepy?"

Amber smiled wearily. "A little."

"It's a great party," Pammie said, dumping the cans

into the recycling bin. "The only thing missing is the sheriff."

"The sheriff?"

"Yeah. We all think he's a hunk. Don't you?"

"Oh, yeah," Amber agreed with a smile and a sigh. "He's definitely a hunk."

"And you're so pretty and so sweet. We've been in the bedroom talking about how neat it would be if the two of you got married."

Amber wasn't sure what was most bizarre: the idea of twelve-year-olds planning her future or the ridiculous notion of her and Cal as man and wife. It was one scenario she hadn't allowed herself to contemplate as she considered her alternatives, one she knew could never be, even though the thought of being married to Cal and waking beside him every morning was the sweetest of fantasies.

"Do you girls need anything?" she asked, leaping to her feet and changing the subject. "More cola? Some dip?"

"We're fine, Ms. Campion, thanks. But I just wanted to tell you we all think you're the bomb."

Having no idea what Pammie was talking about, which reinforced the generation gap theory all the more, Amber said simply, "Thanks."

From the bedroom came a round of girlish screams. Amber ignored them. She'd learned early in the evening that screaming could mean anything from their favorite band was singing on the music video channel to someone playing a prank on someone else to general rowdiness.

"Amber!" Claudia's outrage preceded her into the room. "Beau's outside the bathroom window spying on the girls when they get out of the shower."

"What!" All the earlier tender feelings Amber had experienced toward Beau vanished in a heartbeat. Beau was supposed to be at Dudley's until Cal got back. Actually, he should be in bed, asleep. Where he should *not* be was peeking through the windows at naked girls.

"How could he do this to me?" Claudia asked through her tears. "No one will ever want to come back."

"I will," Pammie said, putting a comforting arm around her friend.

"Just calm down," Amber told the tearful Claudia. "I'll take care of Beau." Without another word, she went outside to check around. Sure enough, the ladder that had leaned against the shed earlier was now situated beneath Claudia's bathroom window. Beau, however, was nowhere to be seen.

"Beau," she called into the darkness. "I know you're out here, and I know what you did, so there's no use pretending you're innocent." She was answered by complete silence. Even the hoot owl, possibly the only witness to the crime, had fled the scene.

"Here's the deal," she continued. "You come forward like a man and go inside and apologize to your sister and her friends and I keep quiet about this whole thing. If you don't do that, I'll tell Cal what you did. In light of your recent suspension at school, your smoking and looking at smutty magazines—not to mention the snake incident—I don't think your uncle will take kindly to the news that you've become a Peeping Tom."

There was no noise, no discernible movement in the darkness. Then, from the corner of her eye, Amber caught sight of Beau slipping through the stand of trees, which, along with a vast section of pastureland, separated Cal's house from Dudley's. Mumbling under her breath, thankful she was wearing a pair of sneakers in case she had to give chase, Amber called out to him.

"I see you, Beau! And if you know what's good for you, you'll stop right there."

To her surprise, he did. She jogged over to where he stood leaning against a spindly pine tree, his posture suggesting an insolent defiance. Was there no remorse in him? No innate sense of right or wrong? Or was it that he just didn't care?

She saw so much of her own youthful actions in his. And, looking into the future, she saw that the headlong flight into doing what he wanted when he wanted would only increase his misery and that of those around him. He might grow up to realize his mistakes. She had. But then, there were thousands of kids who never did.

Her anger disappeared beneath a chilling despair and crushing sense of defeat. She might be able to help Claudia, but she didn't have the skill to deal with a child like Beau. She could make him apologize, and she would. But that was the equivalent of putting a bandage on the incision of major surgery. It wouldn't solve whatever it was that caused Beau to do the things he did.

The thought flickered through her mind that somewhere out there she had a child who was in as much pain as Beau. To her horror, she felt tears sliding down her cheeks, heard the sound of a gut-deep sob cut through the stillness of the night. She dropped to her knees and hugged herself tightly as she cried, as if she could keep herself from falling apart if she held on tightly enough. Finally, she raised her head to look at Beau.

His eyes were wide, like those of a deer caught in the headlights of an oncoming car. He looked as if he might turn and bolt at the first opportunity, yet he stood there, rooted by the shock of her tears and the fact that she'd warned him to stop.

"Why?" she managed to choke out. When he didn't

answer, she swiped at her tears and asked again, "Why do you keep doing things you know will get you in trouble?"

In the moonlit darkness, she saw his shoulders move in a shrug.

"Do you like being grounded? Having all the kids at school know you were suspended?"

"No."

"Then why, Beau?" Her voice broke on a sob. "You're worrying your uncle Cal to death, and me, too."

"Why should you worry about me?" he asked. "I'm nothing to you."

"That isn't true, Beau. You may not believe it, but I care about you and Claudia. And more than that, you're my responsibility when Cal is at work, just as you're his responsibility to nurture and guide until you're old enough to leave home. I know you and your sister are hurting because of your mother leaving, but acting the way you do won't change things. And it won't bring her back."

"I don't want her to come back."

The harsh statement shocked Amber. The pain went deeper than she'd imagined. "Are you trying to drive Cal away, too? Is that it?"

"No!" he said, sounding stunned by the idea. "Uncle Cal is all the family we have left."

She didn't understand what he meant. She knew he had an aunt and a grandmother in the area. Evidently, they hadn't cared enough to make themselves part of Claudia's and Beau's lives. Was that why Beau thought Cal was the only one who really cared?

"If he's so important to you, don't you think you should take better care of your relationship with him?"

The question was met with more silence. She felt like a blind person with the weight of the universe resting on her narrow shoulders, groping her way through a maze. She wished it weren't so dark, that she could look into Beau's eyes and see his reactions. She struggled to her feet, praying that she'd say the right thing. Hoping she could get through to him.

"Cal loves you, Beau," she told him in an unsteady voice. "He was your age once, and he understands that some of the things you do are just boy things. But you're old enough to think about how your actions might affect other people. It's the people we love who usually suffer the most from the things we do wrong."

"What do you know about it?" he asked, raising his head to look at her in the darkness. "You're so darn perfect. What did *you* ever do wrong?"

In spite of herself, Amber laughed, a weary-sounding, halfhearted stab at mirth. "Oh, Beau, if you only knew. I was a spoiled brat when I was a little girl. And when I got older and I found out some things my mother did, I retaliated by doing some things that were very wrong. I didn't just hurt myself, I hurt my parents. And along the way a lot of people decided I wasn't a very nice person. I had what you kids would probably call a bad rep."

"Is that why you can't keep a job?" he asked.

She nodded. "I've changed in the last few years, Beau, but a lot of people here in Vanity remember the person I used to be, and they won't give me a chance to prove I'm different now."

He seemed to ponder that for a moment, and Amber continued. "You know, you remind me of myself at your age. If you keep going the way you are, the same thing could happen to you that happened to me, and that would be a shame, because I don't think you're a bad kid at all."

"You don't?" There was disbelief and wonder in his voice.

"No, I don't. I may be wrong, but I think you don't

understand why your mom left, and you feel out of control. I think you do things to prove that you're in control of what's happening to you. At least for the moment.''

She didn't expect an answer and didn't receive one. Not knowing what else to say, drained and depressed beyond words, she said, ''Let's go.''

''Where?''

''To apologize to Claudia and her friends.''

''I can't! They'll yell at me. They hate me.''

''And whose fault is that?'' Amber asked. Then she added. ''We reap what we sow, Beau. We get back what we give. If you apologize, and if you promise you'll think about what I've said, I'll talk to Claudia and ask her not to say anything to Cal about your peeping through the window at the girls.''

''Why would you do that?''

''Because I'd rather see you live up to your potential than make you stay in your room.'' She turned and started back toward the house. ''Coming?'' she called over her shoulder.

''Yeah.''

Pammie met them at the back door. ''Thank goodness!'' she said her voice breathless and filled with panic. ''I was going to come and look for you. Claudia's having an asthma attack, and she can't find her breathing machine.''

Asthma? Breathing machine? Dear God, why now, when Cal was gone? Amber's heart began to beat in double time. Even though she had no idea what to do, she brushed past Pammie and ran down the hall. She heard Claudia's labored breathing even before she got to the bedroom. The sound of her trying to draw in enough oxygen was a wheezing, whistling, frightening sound.

What had Cal told her? That usually Claudia could handle the spells herself. That she kept an inhaler nearby. If that didn't help, she took the breathing treatments—as often as every two hours if necessary. Amber also remembered that Cal had told her about Claudia being hospitalized and that they now kept Adrenalin in the house.

The worst-case scenario meant that a shot would have to be administered if the breathing treatment didn't open up her closed bronchial tubes. Amber suppressed a shudder at the thought of having to give Claudia a shot. She hated needles. They'd have to find the darned nebulizer and pray it worked.

"Did you use your inhaler?" she asked, noting the fear in her voice as she pushed through the gaggle of girls surrounding the bed. Claudia nodded.

"Where's your nebulizer?" Amber asked. Claudia tried to drag in a strictured breath and was overcome by a fit of coughing. "Oh, dear God," Amber said, wringing her hands. It was reaction and prayer all rolled into one.

"Where's your nebulizer, Claudia?" she asked again, knowing that the hysteria in her voice was only frightening the girls—and Claudia—but unable to control it.

"I've got it."

The announcement came from Beau, who came striding into the room carrying Claudia's breathing paraphernalia. The girls moved aside for him, like Moses parting the Red Sea. "Open the windows, Pammie," he commanded. "Get some fresh air in here."

He met Amber's questioning look. "Sometimes she has an allergic reaction to perfumes and hair spray and stuff."

Amber looked at the veritable cosmetics counter on the dresser, things she'd bought so the girls could have fun. "Oh, Claudia!" she said. "You should have told me."

Two tears trickled down Claudia's cheeks. "I wanted to do it," she wheezed.

Amber took Claudia's hand and squeezed it. "I'm sorry."

Claudia nodded, and Amber gave her full concentration to watching Beau as he unwound the tubing, plugged the apparatus into the electric outlet and added the medicine. His movements were steady, sure. Thankfully, he knew exactly what to do.

He glanced at Amber and held up a plastic zipper bag that held part of the breathing apparatus. "You have to keep this sterile."

Amber nodded. Soon the hum of the nebulizer filled the room, and Claudia gratefully breathed in the medication's fine mist. Amber's knees went weak with relief.

In a matter of minutes, Claudia's breathing improved, and by the time the medicine was gone, she was pale but feeling well enough to be embarrassed by the whole ordeal.

"What's going on?" The question came from the doorway where a tired-looking Cal stood, his hands gripping the outer edges of the door frame.

Sparing his uncle the briefest of glances, Beau's gaze slid fleetingly to Amber's before he gave his full attention to unplugging the machine. "Claudia had an asthma attack."

Even as Beau spoke, Amber watched Cal's sharp gaze take in the situation and come to his own conclusion. Concern replaced the weariness in his eyes. He came through the doorway and into the room, bringing a raw vitality and sense of control that gave Amber an overwhelming sense of peace.

He sat down on the edge of the bed and smoothed the hair away from Claudia's face. The tenderness of the gesture was Amber's undoing. Feeling the all-too-familiar prickle of tears, she slipped through the doorway and went to her room.

It was all her fault, she thought, sinking onto the edge of the bed with a groan of dismay. She was simply not cut out for this job. Almost everything she'd done had turned into a disaster, even though she'd been doing her best. The episode with Claudia just reinforced the obvious. It was time to move on.

Both she and Cal had known this wouldn't last forever. It had been a stopgap measure for them both. Dudley's absence had put Cal in a bind, and she'd needed a job, but Dudley was home now, so he could resume the role he'd played in Claudia and Beau's lives before he'd gone to the rehab. Not only had she failed, Amber thought, Cal really didn't need her anymore.

"Amber?"

The sound of his voice was accompanied by a light rapping on the door. Amber grabbed a fresh tissue from the box near her bed and dabbed at her eyes. "Yes?" she said, struggling to sound normal.

"Can I talk to you for a minute?"

Here comes the ax. Well, she thought, getting to her feet, there was no sense prolonging the pain. "Sure." She opened the door.

The light from the kitchen gave partial illumination to the hallway, etching Cal's features into sharp angles and planes. "Why are you sitting in the dark?"

"It's late," she replied, even though it was a poor answer to his question. "Is Claudia okay?"

"She's fine. I think they're all ready to settle in for the rest of the night."

A small sob of relief shuddered through her. "Good."

"You've been crying," he accused. She shrugged. "I know you're blaming yourself for what happened, but—"

"I *am* to blame, Cal," she interrupted, her voice quiet in the semidarkness.

"Claudia knew the risks. She could have told you there was a possibility that she'd suffer an allergic reaction to some of the cosmetics you bought. She chose not to, and she paid the price."

Angry at herself, feeling threatened, and more than a little sorrowful, Amber turned away and strode across the small room. When she'd gone as far as she could, she faced him again.

"*I* should have asked. I'm the adult. Claudia and Beau are in my care when you're away. I should have made it a point to find out all I could about her problem instead of hoping I'd never have to deal with it." Her voice broke, and she raised her chin. "I fell to pieces, Cal. I was less than useless."

Crossing the small room in three long steps, he pulled her into his arms.

Amber didn't have the energy to make more than a token effort at resisting. She wasn't even aware that her arms went around his waist. The only thing that registered in her mind was the strong, steady beating of his heart beneath her ear and the warm strength of his body. "I was so scared."

"I know."

She leaned back to look up at him. "If Beau hadn't been here, if he hadn't known what to do..."

"You'd have gotten through it, somehow."

Yes, she suppose she would have, but at what cost? Would Claudia have been forced into another hospital stay? For a long moment, she let Cal hold her, drawing comfort from his nearness. As calmness overcame her fear, she began to think of him less as a source of strength and more as a man—a man she was in love with. The awareness made her acutely conscious of the desire that grew every time she was near him. She felt the brush of his lips against her temple and knew it was foolishness. She turned her head, blindly seeking his lips with hers. They were warm and seemed to her that the kiss was filled with the same desperation she felt. Needing the very thing she couldn't have, she pressed nearer. When she felt Cal's hand slide up to cup her breast, she gulped, both in pleasure and the realization of where their kisses were leading.

For the second time that night, she recognized the futility of loving him. There was no denying that Cal wanted her, but wanting was a long way from love, and the new-and-improved Amber Campion wasn't willing to settle for anything less. She had to make that clear to him. Gently but firmly, she disengaged herself from his embrace.

To her surprise, he let her go.

She backed up a step to put some distance between them. "Everything I've done since I came to work for you has ended up a disaster," she said. "I'm lousy with the kids. Beau resents me."

"You're not lousy with them, and Beau resents everyone."

"True, but it's pretty clear I'm not the person who can deal with him on a daily basis."

"It's all *I* can do to deal with him on a daily basis," Cal told her.

"I don't mean just *handling* the things he does. I can do that. But I should be able to do more. I should be able to offer him some sort of guidance, to tell him something that will open his eyes, to make a difference."

"Don't you think you're demanding a lot of yourself?" Cal asked. "Don't you think I feel the same way? I'm his legal guardian, a blood relation, and I haven't been able to get through to him."

Unable to argue with that, she said nothing.

"You and Claudia get along," he said. "Since you've been here, she's been happier than I've seen her since Georgina left."

"Which is part of the problem," Amber told him. "Claudia and I do get along, but if I stay, we'll both get more attached to each other, and—"

"You're leaving." It sounded more like an accusation than a statement.

She sighed, raised her head and looked at him in the dim light of the room. "I have to. I am...very attracted to you." *I love you with all my heart.* "I know you're attracted to me, too, but I won't have an affair with you."

"I haven't asked you to."

"I know, but you know as well as I do that it will happen if I stay, and I don't want to be that kind of example for Claudia and Beau."

"What if I promise to keep my hands to myself and think only pure thoughts when you're in the room?" he asked making an attempt at levity.

In spite of herself, she smiled. "I'm not sure I can trust myself to do the same," she said, knowing the admission exposed the depth of her feelings and left her completely defenseless.

"So, are you giving me notice?"

The thought of leaving was like a knife to the heart. "I'm saying I should start looking for something else."

"What do you have in mind?"

"I'm not sure. I've been giving some thought to opening an interior decorating service. I like it, and I think I'm pretty good at it." She gave a small laugh so that he'd never know her heart was breaking. "And I'd be my own boss, so there's no possibility of being fired."

"Where will you get your financing?"

She shrugged. "I thought that if I go about it in a professional way, my dad might lend me the money."

"It sounds as if you've given it a lot of thought."

"Some," she said guardedly.

"What about the kids?"

"Dudley's back."

Cal stood there for a moment, as if he were trying to think of something else to say, knowing, as Amber did, that there was nothing else to say. "It sounds as if you've got it all figured out," he said at last. "So there's nothing I can say." He reached out and touched her still-throbbing lips with a fingertip. "Sweet dreams."

She watched him go, and it was all she could do not to call him back and tell him she loved him. But as strong as the physical attraction might be, she and Cal were too different to forge anything but a fleeting relationship. At least that's what she told herself in an attempt to ease her breaking heart. Moving with slow, wooden steps, she closed her bedroom door.

No doubt she would sleep—eventually. Maybe she would dream. But she suspected that if she did, those dreams would be anything but sweet.

As Cal made his way to his room, his conversation with Amber played and replayed through his mind like a worn-out record. He'd figured it would come to this sooner or later, known that she'd eventually throw in the towel. But he hadn't expected it to be this soon, especially since he thought she was doing a good job.

He knew the ordeal with Claudia must have been scary and that the confrontation with Joe Bob had been disgusting, but Amber was tough, and she wasn't a quitter. *Don't forget the little snake incident.* Oh, yeah. The snake.

You shouldn't have kissed her, buddy. You should have

kept things professional. Businesslike. Cal knew the inner
voice he heard was right, that his lack of control was the
real problem. He'd known Amber Campion was a sexy,
desirable woman when he'd hired her. He'd even taken his
youthful crush into account but figured that was long past,
that he was mature enough to handle any lingering feelings
he might have for her.

He hadn't counted on the impact of the intimacy that
came with sharing a space with someone. Even in the two
short weeks she'd been there, he'd grown accustomed to
finding her there when he got home from work, to seeing
her in his kitchen in the morning when he awoke, to getting into his shower and finding her bath gel on the shelf,
it's lingering, floral scent clinging to the small enclosure
the same way it clung to her skin.

Somehow, she'd gotten *under* his skin. He couldn't recall wanting a woman more. But she was Amber Campion,
spoiled, indulged daughter of one of the state's wealthiest
men. He'd been raised as poor as Job's turkey and had
had to work his rear end off for everything he had. They
had nothing in common. Nothing.

Except the wanting.

"And that doesn't count," he said aloud. It wasn't
enough and never would be. Past experience had taught
him that. Maybe her leaving was for the best. He had to
admire her for taking Beau and Claudia's feelings into consideration. And deep in his heart, he knew she was right.
Cal wasn't sure he could have kept his hands to himself,
even though he'd promised.

Chapter Ten

Amber awoke late the following morning. She hadn't shut an eye until the early morning hours, and the moment her brain began to function, she remembered her conversation with Cal. She climbed out of bed with the enthusiasm of a guilty person waiting for the jury to come back with a verdict. Thank goodness it was Saturday, and she didn't have to get the kids ready for school. With any luck at all, they were still asleep.

She usually had Saturday and Sunday off, but because of the slumber party, she'd agreed to stay until noon. Although Cal tried to keep the weekends free so he could spend time with Claudia and Beau, he was often called to the station for some emergency or another. She'd heard the phone ring earlier, and later, the sound of his car as he drove away. She was grateful for the reprieve, however brief it might be.

She made her way down the hallway to check on the

kids, a purely maternal gesture. Beau slept flat on his back, one arm flung above his head. He was a cute kid, she thought with a bit of surprise, something his behavior had caused her to miss. She moved closer to the bed, so she could look at him without having to deal with rolling eyes, dirty looks or pouts. With his short brown hair and freckles, he might have stepped straight out of a Norman Rockwell painting.

He looked so innocent, she thought, unable to stop herself from reaching out to brush back a lock of hair. He *was* so innocent. It was criminal that he and his sister were the ones to suffer for the lapse in Georgina Simmons's maternal instincts. Impulsively, Amber leaned over and brushed a whisper of a kiss to Beau's forehead, another to his temple. With her heart aching, she left the room, knowing that she'd miss him as much as she'd miss Claudia.

Claudia's room was wall-to-wall sleeping bags with girls sprawled on top. None of them were awake, but one or two shifted restlessly, as if on the brink of wakefulness. Satisfied that everyone was okay and relieved that her duties as chaperon to seven adolescents was almost over, Amber went into the kitchen and poured herself a cup of coffee.

She was finishing her second cup when she realized that Cal's being gone would be a good time to check on the Internet and research asthma and its treatment.

Why bother? You won't be here much longer.

True, but it was her nature to want to find out as much as she could about the problem—just in case. Cal's room was neat, as usual. He'd even made his bed. Amber turned on the computer and began to read everything she could find about asthma.

Thirty minutes later, she'd reached overload. There was no way she could learn everything she should know in such a short time, and she couldn't absorb any more just now. She switched off the computer and was about to leave the room when she noticed the new batch of notes Cal had made about his novel. She picked them up and looked through them, feeling a strange pride that he was tackling such a monumental task.

She wished he'd let her read it. He'd told her he was within a couple of chapters of being finished and said he'd think about letting her have a look when it was done. She only hoped she'd have a chance to read it before she left.

When she returned to the kitchen, Claudia and Pammie were pouring cereal into bowls. Pammie was her usual, cheerful self. Claudia seemed happy but not too energetic.

"How do you feel?" Amber asked, touching Claudia's forehead with the back of her hand.

"Pretty good."

"Great. Is everyone waking up?"

"Starting to."

The phone rang, and Claudia answered it. "That was Uncle Cal," she said a few seconds later. "He's going to be busy for a while. He said that if he isn't back by the time everyone has gone home, for Beau and me to go to Dudley's so you can have the rest of the day off."

A girlish shriek came from the bedroom, accompanied by an angry, "Get out of here, Beau! We're trying to get dressed."

Amber gave a rueful smile. "Works for me."

It was almost noon when Cal returned to the station. He was tired and cranky, partly because he knew Amber's leaving was just a matter of time, partly because almost every weekend something came up to rob him of his time with his niece and nephew. This time it had been a domestic situation that had resulted in a shooting. Thank God the victim was in the hospital in stable condition.

"Is everything quiet around this burg?" he asked the dispatcher as he stepped through the doorway. "Because if it is, I'm going home."

"Everything's quiet but Joe Bob Milford's mouth," Rowell said.

"What's he up to now?"

"Spreading rumors all over town about you and Amber."

Cal swore. "Like what?"

"That the baby-sitting is just a cover-up for the two of you to…you know…." Rowell said, a blush staining his pudgy face.

Cal spread his legs apart, crossed his arms over his chest and said, "Define 'all over town.'"

"Well, I heard it from Punky down at the Fina station when I filled up this morning, and my wife got a call at midmorning from one of the ladies in her circle group who'd heard it from Jewel over at the café."

"Amazing," Cal said with a shake of his head. "Absolutely amazing."

Rowell scratched his head. "Well, now, Cal, you have to admit that it'd be hard for most people to look at Amber Campion and not think there was hanky-panky going on, or that there was something bad wrong with you if there *wasn't*."

"What do you think?" Cal pressed.

"Whoa, now, Sheriff," Rowell said, holding up his hands. "It's not fair for you to put me on the spot this way."

"I'm serious. Do you think there's something going on between me and Amber?"

"I think you'd be a fool not to take advantage of a

situation should it present itself,'' Rowell said. ''And that's the truth. But knowin' you the way I do, I don't figure the two of you are carryin' on in front of the kids.''

''Thanks. I hope you pass your opinion along whenever you hear something.'' He strode past the dispatcher's desk. ''I'm going to pick up some papers from my office, and I'm out of here.''

He had made it as far as his office door when the phone on his desk rang. Fighting the urge to jerk it out of the wall, he snatched up the receiver and barked, ''Sheriff Simmons.''

''Cal, this is Marty Webb,'' came a smooth, masculine voice. ''How in the heck is the world treatin' you?''

Marty Webb was married to Georgina's sister, Leslie. He was also Lafourche parish's most renowned attorney. Cal knew from experience that Marty's good-ol'-boy drawl and aw-shucks manner was just a guise to lure the unsuspecting into the subtle traps conjured up by an exceptional mind. A call from Marty could mean only one thing: Georgina had something serious on her mind.

''I've been better, Marty,'' Cal said truthfully. ''I know you aren't calling to chit-chat, so just spit it out. I've got something pressing at home.''

Marty chuckled. ''No kidding.''

Cal knew what Marty was alluding to, but after a second or two, he decided it might not be to his best advantage to get into a verbal sparring match with his sislter-in-law's attorney—at least not so early in the game. ''Claudia had a bad asthma attack last night. I need to get home and check on her.''

''I understand,'' the lawyer said in what passed for a sympathetic tone. ''How's Beau?''

''Beau's fine. They're both fine.''

''That's good to hear. Leslie and her mom worry about

you having the kids. It's got to be a hardship with you being single and all, and I know your job keeps you away from them a lot.''

If there was one thing Cal hated, it was a hypocrite. Leslie and Marty had only asked Claudia and Beau to do something with them twice in four years, and their grand-mother—who lived just a few miles away—only bothered to contact them on their birthdays and major holidays, when she sent them a token gift. The sudden solicitude and the veiled implication that Cal wasn't doing a good job raised his ire.

''We've managed pretty well, thank you. Look, Marty, let's cut to the chase. I assume you're calling because Georgina hired you to try to get the kids back.''

''Why, uh, no,'' Marty said, clearly caught off guard by Cal taking the offensive. He regained his smooth confidence in a heartbeat. ''Georgie hasn't retained me just yet, but she thought it might be beneficial if I touched base and let you know that she'd appreciate your cooperation.''

''Cooperation in what?''

''She said she left a message on your machine last night saying she was coming to town for a few days the first of the week and wanted to see Claudia and Beau.''

''That's right.''

''She was upset that you didn't return her call.''

Cal could have spit nails. Georgina was upset because no one returned her call. Had she ever considered how her leaving had upset her children?

''No,'' Cal said with the same calm confidence as Marty, ''I didn't. Claudia had a school dance. Amber had planned her a sleepover afterward. Claudia was excited, so I didn't think the timing was right to tell her that the mother who walked out on her on a whim was ready to waltz back into her life.''

"Now you just wait a darn minute, Cal," Marty said, his cool facade slipping a bit. "A man who moves his lover into the house on the pretext of baby-sitting isn't in any position to cast stones."

"I beg your pardon?"

"You heard me," Marty snapped. "And you know how pious old Judge Danvers feels about that sort of thing."

"Is that some sort of threat, Marty?" Cal asked, astonished by the attorney's unexpected loss of professionalism. "If it is, you think about this—Georgina left those kids with no more thought than she left her past-due bills. They haven't gotten over it yet. And if you and Leslie and their Grandma Preston are so damned worried about them and miss them so much, why haven't you come to see them or spent time with them? An even better question might be why one of you didn't step forward and offer to take on the responsibility for them?"

Cal's questions were met with silence. Finally, he said, "Look, despite what happened, I'd never stand between the kids and the rest of their family. I'll be glad to pass on the message that Georgina wants to see them. But if they don't want to see her, I won't force them to."

"She's their mother."

"She should have thought of that four years ago."

"We were hoping we could work this out without it getting ugly, but I can see you're going to be difficult."

"If by ugly you mean legal battles, you can tell my former sister-in-law that if she wants to go to court and fight for the kids, I'm ready, willing and able to take her on—Judge Danvers and all." Without waiting for Marty to answer, Cal slammed the receiver down.

Breathing heavily, he raked a hand through his short hair. He'd just thrown down the gauntlet to the most feared lawyer around. He hoped he hadn't made a mistake.

* * *

As soon as the last girl left, Amber and Claudia started straightening the house. When Beau, who'd been outside, came in and saw what they were doing, he told his sister to go lie down. He'd help Amber clean up.

"You do look peaked," Amber said, touched by the gesture. "Beau and I will take care of this."

Claudia nodded. "Thanks, Beau." She crossed to Amber. "Thank you, too, Amber," she said, surprising her by giving her a big hug. "Even with the asthma attack, it was the best night of my life."

Amber held Claudia's thin body close, fighting the tears that were welling up in her eyes. How could she leave? How could she stay? She pressed a kiss to the top of Claudia's head. "It was my pleasure. Now go get some rest."

Claudia was at the door when Amber called her name. She turned. "I forgot to ask you something."

"Ma'am?" Claudia said, turning.

"Did Bobby Townsend ask you to dance?"

Deep rose filled Claudia's cheeks. "He did, and so did Joey Bartley."

"Who's he?"

"Only the most popular boy in the seventh grade."

"Oh," Amber said with a smile. "Nice going."

When Claudia left the kitchen, Beau gathered up some empty cola cans and put them in the recycling bins, then he sacked up the trash and pulled the drawstring tight. As he worked, he kept sneaking strange, contemplative glances at Amber.

"What is it, Beau?" she asked. "If you're wondering if I told your uncle about what you did last night, the answer is no. I said I wouldn't, and I won't."

"That isn't it," he said.

Amber, who was folding a load of towels paused. "Then what is it?"

"Did you come into my room last night?"

Uh-oh! He'll know that I kissed him, and he'll be so embarrassed. Amber nodded. "I came to check on you, but it was this morning, not last night. Why?"

"Nothing. I just thought it was a dream about my mom. But I don't remember her ever—" He broke off, and his face flamed.

Before Amber could think of anything to say, Beau yanked the plastic trash bag from the can and said, "I'll take this out."

Amber watched him go with a heavy heart. He'd all but admitted that he didn't recall his mother ever coming into his bedroom to watch him sleep, or kiss him simply because she couldn't help herself.

When the house was straight, Amber dropped Claudia and Beau off at Dudley's, told them she'd see them Sunday night and drove into Vanity to see if she could find an empty building that might be suitable for her new venture. Like most small towns, there was an abundance of vacant, crumbling storefronts scattered throughout the small downtown area. She peeked through the windows of all of them, trying to imagine how they would look cleaned up, painted and filled with things to make homes more beautiful. She finally narrowed it down to two buildings and wrote down the telephone numbers. She'd call about them when she got to Lafourche Farm.

Satisfied with her initial scouting mission, she went to the auto-parts store to buy some upholstery cleaner for a spot on her car seat. The man at the register eyed her up and down in a way that made Amber uncomfortable.

"How's the sheriff?" The question was accompanied by a knowing smile and shed considerable amount of light on the man's attitude. He thought there was something going on between her and Cal.

Amber tried to smile. "He's fine, uh—" she looked at the name embroidered on the man's shirt "—Al. I'll tell him you asked about him."

"You do that."

She found the same shrewd gleam in the eyes of the woman manning the desk at the dry cleaners. But instead of asking about Cal, the biddy raised her nose in the air and gave Amber the cold shoulder.

Stopping by Dot's for her weekly milk shake, she noticed three of the waitresses peeking through the glass of the kitchen door and giggling. The knowing looks and raised eyebrows made her uncomfortable. Worse, they made her feel guilty for something she hadn't done. Lord, deliver her from small-town gossip!

Her craving for the milk shake vanished, and she dropped it into a trash can sitting outside the establishment's door as she left. The situation was getting worse by the day. She'd have to put her plan into action as soon as possible, because she couldn't take much more of being grist for the town's gossip mill.

Amber's dad was talking to Maria Antonia when she arrived, and then Maria had to talk to Amber about the upcoming nuptials. It was almost thirty minutes later before Amber found herself alone with her dad.

"I fixed you a glass of raspberry tea," he said, indicating the frosty mug sitting on a wicker table.

"Mmm, thanks." Amber took a sip, pronounced it delicious and swung her feet to the top of a wicker ottoman topped with a brightly hued, floral cushion.

"How was the party?"

"A success until an allergic reaction to some of the cosmetics I bought triggered Claudia's asthma."

"Was it a bad attack?"

Amber nodded. "I was petrified. If Beau hadn't been there, I don't know what I'd have done."

"Beau came to the rescue?" Gerald asked in surprise. "Is he coming around then?"

"Not really." She told her dad about Beau's adventure into voyeurism. Gerald laughed until tears came to his eyes.

"I didn't think it was funny," Amber said in a huffy voice.

"You're paying for your raising, honey," Gerald told her, wiping his eyes on a napkin.

"But it isn't fair!" Amber wailed. "He isn't even my child!" They sat in silence for a few moments. Gerald looked uncomfortable, as if he had something to say and didn't know how to say it, and Amber was searching for a way to tell him that she was going to have to find another job.

"Amber, there's—"

"Daddy, I—"

The spoke simultaneously and laughed together. "Ladies first," Gerald said, making a sweeping gesture with his hand.

"I need to tell you something, but it's really hard for me."

"Just say it, honey. There's nothing you can tell me that will make me think any less of you."

Amber frowned. "This thing at Cal's isn't working out. I'm going to have to find another job," she said, blurting out the truth before she lost her nerve.

"That's it?"

"What were you expecting?" Amber pointed a finger

at him. "And don't hem-haw around. I know there's something on your mind."

"Actually, I thought you might be going to tell me that you and Cal Simmons are having an affair."

Amber's mouth opened to reply but quickly snapped shut. Good grief! The gossip had even spread to her father—thanks, no doubt to Joe Bob Milford. If she ever got her hands on the creep, she'd choke the life from him!

Amber took several deep, calming breaths. What a mess! Everything had been a mess since she'd come to Louisiana. How could she be trying so hard to do right and have so many things go wrong? Maybe it had been a mistake to come back. Maybe California was where she belonged after all. Her warts weren't so noticeable in a place where the population alone provided a certain anonymity.

"Cal and I are *not* having an affair," she began, her voice filled with a weary despair. "But I've gone and done a terrible thing." She lifted her tormented gaze to her father's. "I've fallen in love with him."

Seeing the expression on Gerald's face, she smiled. "I know what you're thinking. I've thought I was in love before, and the man was all wrong. Well, Cal isn't like any man I've ever known, and I'm pretty sure it's the real thing this time."

"Oh, honey!"

"The thing is, Daddy, that I'm afraid that if I stay, the rumors might become fact."

"So...Cal feels the same way about you?"

Amber shook her head. "He wants me. He's made that pretty clear. But wanting isn't love, and it isn't enough. And I don't want to set the wrong example for Claudia and Beau."

"Good girl. Do you have another job in mind?"

She raised an eyebrow. "Are you kidding? With this latest gossip to add to the terrible opinion most of the town had of me, it isn't likely that anyone will hire me. I had an idea for a business of my own, but maybe I should just admit defeat gracefully, tuck my tail and crawl back to California."

Gerald reached out and covered her hand with his. "I can't tell you what to do, honey. You're an adult. But I will say that for purely selfish reasons, I hope you'll stay. I've enjoyed your being here, enjoyed getting to know you again."

Blinking hard, Amber squeezed his hand and tried to smile. "Thanks, Daddy."

"Tell me about your business idea," he said, when she had her emotions under control. "If it's something that sounds feasible, maybe we can work something out."

Cal spent the remainder of the weekend alternately fuming over Georgina's audacity and grieving over the knowledge that Amber's days with them were numbered. He knew he should tell Beau and Claudia, but he thought it might be best to wait until Amber gave him a definite time of departure. There was no use dealing with Claudia's sorrow until it was absolutely necessary, and there was little doubt that his niece would be heartbroken when Amber left.

Knowing he had to face the reality of Georgina's reappearance into their lives, he nonetheless postponed talking to Beau and Claudia until late Sunday afternoon.

Since there was no way to ease into the painful conversation, he'd called them into the kitchen and said simply, "Your mother left a message on the answering machine Friday."

"She did?" Claudia asked, her surprise clear.

Beau got to the point. "What did *she* want?"

"She's coming to town tomorrow. She and her new husband, Nick—your stepfather—will be staying at your grandmother Preston's for a few days while they hunt for a house."

Claudia's eyes widened. "She's moving back?"

"It looks that way," Cal said with a nod. "She'd like to see you both." The statement hovered between them like a dark cloud for several seconds. "But if that makes you uncomfortable, I won't make you go."

Beau leaped to his feet. "Why'd she have to come back and ruin everything?" he yelled. *Ruin what?* Cal wanted to ask, but before he could, Beau said, "I don't want to see her. I hate her."

Even though Cal often felt the same way, he knew he couldn't let his own feelings prejudice Beau. "You don't hate people Beau. You hate what they do. Their actions."

"I'm not going."

"Fine," Cal said. "You don't have to. I know it's a shock that she's come back, but if she moves here, you'll have to see her sometimes, if only on the street. You'll have to deal with it."

Beau crossed his arms over his chest in a frighteningly familiar gesture. Cal could almost see him blocking out the whole conversation. "Whatever."

"Claudia? How do you feel about seeing her?"

"I don't know. More uncomfortable than anything, I think."

"That's understandable." Cal stood. "I'll call her tomorrow and tell her how you feel. We'll go from there."

"Uncle Cal?"

"Yes, Beau?"

"She can't take us away from you, can she?"

It was the question Cal had dreaded. He'd questioned

Dudley at length about his chances of being able to legally keep the kids, and Dudley had told him he thought they were excellent, considering the situation. As he'd told Cal before, it wouldn't hurt if he were married, but on the other hand, Cal had done everything according to the books since Georgina left. And the courts were much more accepting of single parents—even single males—than ever before. The pep talk had boosted Cal's morale, but only a little. Now, faced with answering Beau, he told the truth.

"I'm not sure, Beau. She's your mother. I have legal guardianship, so she can't take you without consent from the court, but they might look more favorably on me if I were married." He shook his head. "It's complicated. I hope it doesn't come down to a legal battle, but if it does I'll fight to keep you, if that's what you want."

"It's what I want," Beau said.

Claudia nodded. "Me, too."

Amber and her dad had spent a fruitful weekend together. She'd told him of her plan and the reasons she thought it would work and showed him the two buildings. Gerald thought she could make a go of it and told her that if she was willing to put together a sound business proposal for start-up costs and a six-month projection of expenditures, he would co-sign a note with her at the bank. It was more than she'd hoped for.

Amber arrived at Cal's late Sunday evening, carrying a box of her high school mementoes. Beau was in the kitchen fixing some microwave popcorn.

"Hi," Amber said, pausing in the doorway of the kitchen, the box propped on her hip.

"Hi," Beau said.

"Where is everyone?"

"Uncle Cal is watching TV and Claudia is in her room, painting her nails," Beau told her. "What's in the box?"

"A snake," Amber said, deadpan.

Beau looked shocked for a second, then a reluctant smile toyed with the corners of his mouth. "You're teasing, right?"

"Right," Amber said. "Actually, it's some stuff from when I was in high school. I thought Claudia might get a kick out of looking through my yearbooks. There are some pictures of your uncle Cal in there."

"She'd probably like to see them. So would I."

"Good." Amber smiled at him, hardly believing that she and Beau were actually carrying on a civilized conversation. "Did you have a good weekend?"

"Pretty good," Beau said. "We went out to eat with Dudley today."

"That sounds nice," Amber said. "My dad took me to dinner on Saturday evening, and we drove to New Orleans to look for pieces for my new—" She stopped abruptly, aware that she was about to say more than she should in front of Beau. "Uh…my new decorating idea," she finished lamely. "We didn't find anything."

"Too bad," Beau said. "Want some popcorn?"

"No thanks," Amber told him, touched by the offer. "I'd better go tell Cal I'm back."

After she took the box to her room, she found Cal in the living room lying in his recliner watching an old western. He looked as miserable as she felt. Amber wanted to tell him everything would be okay, that her leaving was best for all concerned, but it was hard to say the words when, on some level, she really didn't believe them.

"I'm back."

"So I see. Did you have a good weekend?"

"Yes."

"Good." He didn't say anything else, and after a moment she summoned a passable smile. "Well. I guess I'll go...wash my hair or something. See you in the morning."

Beau, who had carried his bag of popcorn into the room, looked from her to his uncle and back again. He was a smart boy, Amber thought. He could sense the tension between her and Cal. She sighed. The next few weeks until she could get her plan into action promised to be long ones.

Cal was in the middle of a typical Monday morning when Miss Marx from Beau's school called. His first thought was to wonder why she hadn't called Amber. The second was that whatever deed Beau had done was so serious, the principal had gone straight to the top.

"Hello, Miss Marx. This is Sheriff Simmons."

"I'm sorry to call you at the station, Caleb," Miss Marx said, but I didn't get an answer at the house."

Cal stifled the niggling sense of panic that reared its head. "That's okay, Miss Marx. I think Amber had some errands to run this morning." *Liar. You have no idea where she is. Or if she's coming back.* "What can I do for you?"

"Beau was sent to the office again," Cal's former teacher said without preamble. "For fighting."

"Fighting!" Cal said. "Beau?"

"Yes, Beau," she said firmly.

"I'm not doubting you, Miss Marx. But it's hard to imagine Beau fighting. He likes to talk back, and he's sneaky sometimes, but he isn't a bully."

"I'll agree with that, Sheriff," Miss Marx said. "But I assure you that he was involved in a fight, and he has the bloody nose to prove it. Unfortunately, neither he nor the other boy involved will tell me what it was all about."

"Who was the other boy?"

"Bobby Joe Milford."

Cal's heart sank. He had a pretty good idea what the fight was over.

"Bobby Joe has a history of fighting," Miss Marx said. "So I'm inclined to believe he instigated this one, but rules are rules, and I have no recourse but to suspend both boys for two days."

Cal pinched the bridge of his nose. A headache was gathering between his eyes. "I understand, and I appreciate your giving Beau the benefit of the doubt. I'll be there to pick him up in a few minutes."

Beau was waiting for him in the outer office. He had a bloody nose and his top lip was puffy. He was glaring at a kid about his age who sat across the lobby. Bobby Joe Milford—who looked uncannily like his dad—returned the hard looks as he alternately dabbed at his nose with a tissue and probed the flesh around his left eye.

"Do you need to see a doctor?" Cal asked, lifting Beau's chin and surveying the damage.

Beau shook his head. "I'm okay."

Cal signed Beau out, and they walked to the cruiser in silence. Beau stared out the passenger window while Cal drove. They were almost home before he asked, "Want to tell me what happened?"

"Nope."

"Did you start it?"

"Nope."

"Bobby Joe must have provoked you pretty bad, since you've never been in a fight before."

"He's a damned liar," Beau said to the window.

"Watch your mouth, son."

Finally, Beau turned to face him. "Well, he is. She's not like he said."

"Who?"

"Nobody."

She. Amber. Cal was beginning to understand. "He said something about Amber, didn't he?"

Beau turned to look at him. "How'd you know?"

"Bobby Joe is Joe Bob's boy. After what happened at the house the other day, it makes sense that Joe Bob would spout off a bunch of lies about Amber. Do you want to tell me what happened? It might help to get it off your chest."

"He said you two were shackin' up." Beau revealed what else Bobby Joe had said, none of which was pretty and all of which had to do with Amber's character—or lack of.

By the time he finished, Cal had pulled the car to a stop in the driveway. "Do you know what shacking up means?"

"It means you're living together and having...uh, sex."

"Have I ever lied to you, Beau?"

"No, sir."

"And I never will. Amber and I are not having sex. As a matter of fact, because she'd heard some comments about our living arrangements and she was afraid you and Claudia might hear some gossip, she's told me she'll be looking for another job."

"She's quitting?"

Beau's eyes were wide with disbelief. The shattered look on his face broke Cal's heart. "Yes. She didn't want to set a bad example for you, even inadvertently."

"When is she leaving?"

"I'm not sure. She'd like to find another job first."

"Can't you do something to make her stay?" Beau cried.

After everything Beau had put Amber through, Cal was

unprepared for his obvious distress at her leaving. "Like what?"

"You said you might have a better chance in court if you were married. Why don't you and Amber get married?"

Even though the thought had gone through Cal's mind on occasion, he'd never given it any serious consideration. He was amazed that the idea had come from Beau, who had bucked against Amber's authority since day one.

"You like her," he said, when Cal didn't answer immediately. "I know you do. She likes you, too. I saw you kissing out in the shed."

"You saw us?"

"I couldn't help it."

"Liking someone enough to kiss them isn't enough reason to get married. There should be love."

"Kissing isn't love?"

"No, Beau. Kissing isn't love. Sex isn't love. It's just a small part of it. Love is caring for a person even though they may do things that you know are wrong, or things that make you angry. It's putting the other person's wants and needs before yours."

"Like Amber getting another job because of me and Claudia, even though she needs this one?"

"Exactly."

Beau thought about that for a moment. "I don't think she'd leave us if it wasn't for people talking." He pinned Cal with a steady gaze. "And I'll bet if she had kids, she wouldn't go off and leave them the way Mom did."

"Probably not," Cal agreed.

Beau's eyes held a thoughtful expression. "Dudley says love grows. That he and Margaret loved each other more when she died than when they first met. Maybe if you and Amber got married, you'd grow to love each other."

Maybe.

"Will you think about it?" Beau asked. "Please?"

Cal's heart ached. He'd never seen Beau beg for anything. "I didn't think you liked Amber. Why are you so anxious for her to stay?"

The question caught Beau off guard. "Claudia," he said after giving the query a few seconds' thought. "She'll die if Amber leaves. She told me Amber is almost like her mother."

The pain in Cal's heart intensified.

"She likes having someone at the house when we get home from school." He gave a passable shrug of nonchalance. "And I've sorta gotten used to her being around, too. Know what I mean?"

Cal nodded.

"And I never *said* I didn't like her," Beau tacked on for good measure. "C'mon, Uncle Cal. Will you just think about it?"

"Yeah," Cal told him. "I'll think about it."

They were getting out of the car when Cal realized Amber's vehicle wasn't under the carport. Even though the principal had told him there was no answer when she'd called, he had expected Amber to be at the house when he arrived. Like the kids, he had gotten used to finding her there when he got home.

He opened the door. The house was too quiet. If it weren't for the floral scent of the air freshener Amber favored, no one would know she'd ever been there. Had she already gone? No. She wouldn't leave without saying something. Cal told himself his imagination was working overtime, but that didn't lessen the panic that unfurled throughout him as he ran down the hall to her room. He was aware that Beau followed, watching him with a concerned expression in his eyes.

As Cal expected, her room was empty. To his shock there was a box on the bed. He crossed the floor like a sleepwalker, knowing what he would find inside. The box was filled with her belongings. She'd already started packing.

Chapter Eleven

"What is it?" Beau asked, witnessing his uncle's panic.

"She's already started packing." *How could she do this without saying something? I can't let her go. I love her....*

Beau looked inside the box. "This stuff? She didn't pack it up to take with her. She brought it from her dad's last night. It's just some old yearbooks and some of her junk from high school."

Cal sucked in a relieved breath. "You looked through her things?"

Beau's face turned red. "No! I swear I didn't. When I asked her what it was, she told me. She said she thought Claudia and I might like to look at the yearbooks. She said you were in some of them."

Beau regarded Cal thoughtfully. "I'm going to get some ice for my eye. You know, Uncle Cal, you really ought to give my idea some serious thought."

Cal raked a hand down his face. Though he'd suspected

it for a while, he'd known the minute he walked in and thought she was already gone that he loved her and his life would be as empty as the house if he had to live in it without her. Did the fact that she felt sentimental about the past mean anything? Or was it simply a way to give Claudia and Beau something of their past to hang on to? It all boiled down to one question: should he ask Amber to marry him?

Cal checked in with the office and told Jimmy he needed the rest of the day off and was to be called only for the direst of emergencies. He'd decided that he should lay all his cards on the table with Claudia, which included telling her about the gossip, which was the reason for Beau's fighting and Amber's plan to leave. He wanted to know how she felt about the entire situation before he gave Beau's preposterous idea any more thought. After all, both children were an important part of his life, and he couldn't ignore their feelings about something so important to them all.

"So what do you think?" he asked Claudia when he finished. "How would you feel if Amber and I got married?"

"She'd be like our stepmom?" Claudia asked.

Cal paused. Now was the perfect time to broach the subject of Georgina, but he didn't have the heart to tell them that there might be a legal battle ahead. "Not exactly, but almost," he hedged. "I'm your legal guardian but not your father. Like I told you the other day, it's complicated."

"I like having Amber here," Claudia said. "And I think she likes being here." She gave Cal a knowing smile. "And I think she likes you, too."

"You do?" Cal asked, surprised that she and Beau had picked up on so much. "Why?"

"Hmm...I don't know. Something in her eyes when she's looking at you and you don't know it. Something...I don't know...all soft and mushylike."

"Really?"

Claudia grew serious. "If marrying her would keep her from leaving, then I say ask her."

It sounded so simple, but Cal knew that *if* he decided it was the right thing, finding the courage to ask Amber Campion to share his life would be one of the hardest things he'd ever done.

It was nearly four when Cal heard Amber's car pull into the driveway. The kids were doing homework, and he'd been pacing the floor. He hadn't heard from her all day, and he was worried sick. Relieved that she was okay, that she had come back, he reacted in a predictable male manner.

"Where the hell have you been?"

Amber, who clutched a bag from a local fast-food chicken place, stopped in the door of the kitchen, a look of surprise on her face. "I met with a couple of people and looked at some storefronts this morning," she said, eyeing him with a wary expression as she set the sack on the table. "And I've been with some carpenters and electricians this afternoon, trying to get some bids together for the bank. Is something wrong? What are you doing home?"

"What's for supper?" The words preceded Beau into the room and derailed not only the conversation but Cal's misplaced irritation.

"Chicken," Amber said. Seeing his eye, which had ripened to an ugly purple as the day progressed, she gasped and crossed the room to lift his chin. "What happened? Are you okay?"

Beau turned his head away, but more as if he were embarrassed than because he objected to her touch. "I got into a fight at school. I can't go back until Wednesday morning."

"Oh, Beau!" Amber cried softly. "What were you fighting about?"

Beau cast a questioning look at Cal, who'd always taught that honesty was the best policy. "Us."

Amber shifted her gaze from Beau to Cal. "Us?"

"It seems Bobby Joe Milford has been listening to his dad run off at the mouth. He told Beau you and I were shacking up, and Beau defended your honor. Mine, too, I guess."

Cal watched the surprise in her eyes turn to sadness. With a little cry, she gathered Beau close. Cal was surprised when the boy didn't pull away immediately. More surprised to see that he almost—almost—put his arms around Amber.

"Oh, Beau," she breathed against the top of his head. "I'm so sorry. I never meant for anything like this to happen."

Beau squirmed free and plunged his hands into the pockets of his jeans. "I'm okay. You ought to see Bobby Joe."

Amber smiled through the unshed tears glistening in her eyes. "Got him good, did you?"

"Yep." Clearly feeling that he'd faced the worst, he asked, "Can we eat now? I'm starved."

"Sure," she said. "Go get your sister."

"We need to talk," Cal said to Amber.

"I know," she told him, "but the chicken is hot, and

whatever it is that needs saying can wait thirty minutes, can't it?''

"Yeah, I guess it can."

It was a strange meal, Amber thought, lifting a forkful of mashed potatoes to her mouth. Beau ate with his usual gusto, remembering to mind his manners. Claudia was strangely quiet and kept looking at Amber with a pleased smile on her face. Cal, who loved fried chicken, alternated with pushing his food around on his plate and staring at her with a thoughtful gleam in his eyes. Amber didn't have much of an appetite, either.

When they finished, Claudia and Beau got into an argument about whose turn it was to clear the table and help with the dishes.

"You two go finish your homework and take your baths," Cal said. "I'll help with the dishes."

"Thanks, Uncle Cal," Claudia said. "I owe you one."

"I don't mind doing this alone," Amber told him, scraping chicken bones into the trash.

"And I don't mind helping."

They worked silently side by side for a while. Cal was so big he dominated the kitchen, or maybe it was just that she was so aware of him. He didn't help with the cleanup often, but he liked to drift in and out of the kitchen whenever she was there. She'd miss that, she thought, a lump forming in her throat.

"Cal, I—"

"I know what you're going to say," he interrupted. "This whole crazy thing has gotten out of hand."

She flung the dishrag into the sink full of soapy water. "I can't bear to think that people are discussing us over dinner or that Claudia and Beau are hearing talk about us—especially since it isn't true," she told him in a trembling voice.

Cal closed the dishwasher and leaned against the cabinet. "I know. I should have known something like this would happen, and maybe I did, but I never expected the gossip to be so widespread."

"There's no way I can stay until you find someone or I get my shop going," she said. "As a matter of fact, I should probably leave tonight."

"No!" he said quickly, too quickly. "The damage is already done." He cleared his throat. "There may be a way out of this."

Her eyes widened. "What?"

"I had a phone call from Marty Webb this morning. You remember Marty, don't you?"

"Marty Webb? Pompous? Arrogant? Complete jerk?"

"That's Marty," Cal said, smiling with little humor.

"What did he want?"

"He's an attorney now. A darn good one. And he's married to Georgina's sister."

"Oh." The word held a wealth of understanding.

"Yeah. Basically, she's ticked off that we didn't return her call on Friday evening and wanted Marty to call me so we could keep things from getting ugly. I explained about the dance and the party and the asthma attack, but I'm afraid I lost my temper."

"Cal, you didn't!"

"Well, he insinuated that something was going on between us, too. I set him straight about that, then he implied that I wasn't doing a very good job with raising the kids and said he and Leslie and Georgina's parents were worried about them."

"You do an excellent job with them—especially for a single man with such a demanding job. I don't know many men who could have done so well," Amber said in a staunch defense.

"Thank you." One corner of Cal's mouth hiked upward in a derisive smile. "I know it wasn't very smart of me, but I told him that if Georgina wanted a fight, she could have one."

"Good for you!"

"Yeah, but how good will it be for the kids?"

"She can't take them, can she?" Amber's concern echoed Beau and Claudia's.

"I don't think so, but in this crazy world, who knows?" Cal said. "Which brings me back to us." He paused, looked up at the ceiling and down at the floor.

"What?"

"Dudley seems to think that even though I've done everything by the book since Georgina left, I'd strengthen my chances of getting the kids forever if I had a wife."

The statement stunned and confused Amber, even as a small part of her mind had an inkling of what he was leading up to. "What does that have to do with me?" she asked in a cautious voice.

"Everything," Cal said. "I was wondering if you'd consider marrying me?"

The color drained from Amber's face, then rushed back in a flood of heat. Cal was proposing. It was her first proposal of marriage, something she hadn't dared to allow herself to dream about with Cal. But he had asked her.

Yeah. For all the wrong reasons. Love has nothing to do with it.

"You want to marry me to strengthen your chances of keeping Beau and Claudia?"

"It sounds awfully cold when you put it that way. But it would stop the gossip."

"Yes, but wouldn't that be like closing the barn door

after the horse gets out?'' she asked, still trying to come to terms with his outrageous idea.

''Maybe. But why should we knuckle under to a bunch of gossips? I think it's clear that we like each other. We respect each other. We have a mutual physical attraction.'' He paused to clear his throat.

''None of which is enough to base a marriage on,'' Amber said, her head spinning. *What about love?*

''A lot of marriages have been based on less,'' Cal pointed out. ''Look. Neither of our situations has changed. You still need a job. I still need someone to corral the kids. They like having you here. Claudia is a changed person in just two weeks. And Beau respects your authority, even if he bucks it. It can work.''

What had she missed? Amber wondered. How had Cal arrived at such a conclusion? She only hoped he was right. If she had to leave her job—and just because he'd asked her to marry him didn't mean she wasn't—it was gratifying to know she'd done some good during her brief stay.

''Kids are smart. They know when someone genuinely cares about them,'' Cal said, pressing his case. ''And even though Beau would never admit it, they've both gotten attached to you. They both want you to stay. So do I.''

Amber wasn't sure which surprised her more. That tidbit or the fact that Cal wanted her to stay, too. That gave a whole new slant to the marriage proposal. ''*Beau* wants me to stay?''

Cal nodded. ''I don't know how, but you've managed to gain his trust. He told me he didn't think you'd leave if it weren't for the gossip and that he didn't think you were the kind of person who would go off and leave their kids the way his mom did,'' Cal said with a smile.

The smidgen of hope that had sprouted in her heart died like a seedling left in the sun. The guilt and grief that were never far from the surface rose in a huge black wave. Would she ever forget? Would she ever forgive herself? It occurred to her that maybe if she told someone else what she'd done, it might ease her burden. Maybe just as admission was the first step to recovery, confession truly was good for the soul.

But if you tell Cal, he'll take back the offer of marriage. Did it matter? She could never be the kind of woman he needed as a wife. He was an upstanding citizen, a public servant with a reputation as untarnished as his heart. She was a woman with lots of baggage and a less-than-sterling reputation. She brushed absently at a tear that rolled down her cheek.

"I thought that would make you happy. What's wrong?"

She forced herself to meet his gaze. "I'd do almost anything to help you keep your guardianship of Beau and Claudia, but I won't marry you." *I love you too much to see you settle for second best.*

Dull-red crept into his cheeks. "I know I didn't ask the right way. And I know that maybe it wasn't for the right reasons. But I thought they were good reasons. Neither of us is romantically involved with anyone. Our arrangement is working out pretty well. It just seemed like a way to solve two problems."

"You'd want it to be a real marriage?"

"Yes. But not just for the sex," he added hastily. "Because I think we have something we can build on."

Amber brought her hand up to cover a little sob. Making love with Cal. Waking up beside him every morning. The stuff dreams were made of. Another tear slid down her cheek. "I'm sorry, Cal. I can't."

The muscle in his jaw tightened in a familiar gesture. When he spoke, there was a belligerence in his voice that hadn't been there before. "You said *won't* before. Which is it? Is it that you can't do it in good conscience or that you won't because I'm not good enough for you?"

"No!" she cried, reaching out and clutching at the front of his shirt. "It's because I'm not good enough for you."

He rested his hand on her shoulders. "What are you talking about. You're Amber Campion."

"A name has nothing to do with character, Cal," she told him. "You know that."

"Could you give me some sort of clue to what you're talking about here?" he asked, frowning.

The confusion on his face tore at her heart, which she was certain was slowly breaking in two. "I'm not the person Beau thinks I am," she said, throwing caution to the wind. "I'm not what anyone thinks I am. And Beau is dead wrong. I would walk away from a child. I did."

"I beg your pardon?"

"I got pregnant during college, Cal," she said almost angrily. "A common enough tale, right? But I kept it a secret from my family, and I gave my baby up for adoption, and to this day no one knows except my sister."

The anger seemed to fade as she spoke, and in its place came a weary despair. She released her hold on his shirt and smoothed the wrinkles with her palm almost absently. "You don't want me as a stand-in mom for Beau and Claudia," she told him. "Because I'm no different than Georgina, and they deserve better. That's why I won't marry you. Because of those kids."

Beau, who had no idea Cal and Amber were still carrying on a conversation in the kitchen, was on his way to get something to drink when he heard the last part of what Amber was saying. He stopped dead in his tracks, the words spinning through his mind. *"Because of those kids.*

*That's why I won't marry you…those kids…because of
those kids…I won't marry you…."*

The pain he felt was unbearable, like someone had
stabbed him with a sharp knife. He thought Amber cared
about him and Claudia, otherwise, why would she be trying so hard to… The truth hit him almost as hard as the
words he'd overheard.

He was the problem, not Claudia. Claudia was good, but
he had caused Amber nothing but trouble. He'd stolen her
cigarettes, talked back and put a snake in her bed. There
were other things, too. Spying on Claudia's friends…being
suspended from school.

He didn't doubt Amber wanted to do a good job taking
care of him. It was her job. But he understood perfectly
why she wouldn't marry his uncle Cal. No one would want
to put up with someone like him for the rest of their lives.
If he'd had a choice, his uncle probably wouldn't have
wanted it, either.

Beau swallowed hard and, turning quietly, went back to
his room. He sat down on the edge of his bed and rested
his elbows on his knees. Uncle Cal was a good man. Hard
but fair. And he loved them, Beau knew that. Uncle Cal
wouldn't admit it, probably because grown men didn't
spill their guts to kids, but he really liked Amber. Probably
even loved her, or he wouldn't have been so upset to think
she was gone.

He deserved to be happy. Maybe there was some way
Beau could pay back his uncle for all he'd done for them.
Maybe just once he could figure out the right thing to do—
make the right choice—even if it was a hard one.

It wasn't long before Beau came up with a plan that
would repay Uncle Cal for everything he'd done and give
him the chance for the happiness he deserved. He went
into the bedroom to tell Claudia what he'd decided.

* * *

After Amber left the room, Cal paced the kitchen, trying to come to terms with what she'd told him. She'd had a child by another man and given it up for adoption. Something very close to jealousy tore through him, only to be replaced by another pain. This ache was one of sympathy as he tried to imagine what she'd gone through, making the decision all alone, in a strange city, contemplating how hard it must have been for her every day since, wondering if she'd done the right thing.

It explained a lot about her, though, like the facade of hardness and sarcasm she projected to the world. Mockery and derision were fine deflectors of sorrow, just as moving thousands of miles away was a wonderful ploy to frustrate guilt. If she wasn't near her family she wouldn't have to face them daily, knowing her secret could come to light at any time. Living on the edge was a good way to forget.

But she hadn't been able to forget for long, couldn't run forever. In the end, she'd grown up, and her genuine love for her family and the values instilled by her dad and stepmother had gotten her off the road to self-destruction. Cal wasn't sure he'd seen anyone come so far as Amber had the past year.

She was a far different person than he'd known as a teenager, different from the woman he'd heard about through the Vanity gossip mill the past several years and even different from the woman who'd come back to try and escape a blackmailer. She was a woman who'd picked up the pieces of her life and was putting them back together one small shard at a time. He hoped that her revelation about her past would start to heal the gaping wound in her heart.

But knowing how far she'd come and understanding, at least in part, why she didn't feel she could marry him didn't stop the pain from overwhelming him. He wanted to go to her and tell her that it didn't matter, that none of the past mattered because he loved her, but he didn't think she was ready to listen just yet.

When Amber woke the next morning, all the tears she'd cried had left her with a stuffy head and puffy eyes. A glimpse in the mirror told her she looked almost as bad as she felt. A shower made her feel marginally better. Makeup, she thought, staring zombielike into the mirror. She needed the armor of makeup to help her face Cal and the banker she was going to see that afternoon. Maybe some coffee would help, too, she thought, opening her bedroom door and stepping into the hall.

Her foot hit something, and she looked down to see a stack of paper bound by a rubber band lying on the floor. Stooping, she realized it was Cal's manuscript. Surprised and pleased, she glanced down the hall, but it was empty. Why had he brought her his manuscript *now?* She wondered as she picked it up and carried it with her to the kitchen.

There was a note from Cal lying near the coffeepot, explaining that he'd received an early call and probably wouldn't be home until suppertime. She read the computer generated message with a bittersweet pleasure.

I hope you're feeling better about things this morning. Don't be so hard on yourself. I promised you a chance to read the manuscript and I guess there's no time like the present. If nothing else, maybe it'll give you a good laugh. Since Beau was home for the day and you had your appointment with the banker, I decided to take him with me.

Cal.

It was so like him to want to spend the time with Beau, even though she knew it wouldn't be an easy day.

She turned the manuscript over in her hands, wondering why it mattered to him that she liked his work, wondering again why he'd chosen now to let her read it. Was it because she'd trusted him enough to share something very personal with him? Was sharing his work with her a way to show he trusted her?

Feeling as if the somehow symbolic gestures had taken their complicated relationship a step in a new direction, but not fully comprehending what that might be, Amber sipped her coffee and scanned the page. The writing hooked her from the first sentence. Knowing there was no time to indulge herself at the moment, she went to wake Claudia. Once she was on the bus, Amber planned to read until it was time for her appointment.

Claudia was unusually quiet during breakfast. A couple of times, Amber thought Claudia looked as if she were about to cry, but when Amber tried to find out what was wrong, she was answered by a simple "Nothing."

Remembering her own adolescent mood swings, Amber chalked up Claudia's melancholy to rampaging hormones. Trying to show her support, Amber followed Claudia out onto the porch to wait for the bus. When it trundled to a stop, Claudia threw her arms around Amber and gave her a fierce hug. "Love you."

Caught off guard by the statement, Amber hugged her back. "I love you, too." She'd miss her, she thought, as Claudia boarded the bus. She'd miss them all.

Forcing the sadness away, she went inside, cleared away the breakfast mess and began to read. She was so engrossed, she only got up to refill her coffee cup and grab a donut for lunch. The book was good. Excellent, in fact.

But she should have known it would be. Cal was the type of man who excelled at anything he did.

As she set the manuscript aside to get ready for her meeting, she thought again of his marriage proposal. Even though her reasons for turning him down were valid, Amber couldn't help feeling she'd made a terrible mistake. There was little doubt in her mind that Cal would excel at marriage, too.

When Cal got home that afternoon, he was tired, testy and fighting the beginnings of what he knew would be a nasty headache. It didn't help his mood to walk into an empty house, even though he'd known Amber had a meeting at the bank. He'd asked her to leave Beau with Dudley when she left and told Claudia to go to Dudley's when she got home from school.

Unlike the day before when he'd gone into a near panic at the thought of Amber leaving, the singular quiet of the empty house brought, instead, the portent of lots of lonely tomorrows.

He wandered into the kitchen, wondering how he was going to get through the rest of his life without her. He found his manuscript on the table with a note that said,

Fantastic. Unbelievable. Amber.

He read the words twice before it dawned on him that she liked it. Really liked it. She was the first person he'd let see his work, and making the decision to trust her with his heart and soul had been one of the hardest things he'd done.

Lord, he missed her! Needing some tangible reminder of her presence, he went down the hall to her room and paused in the doorway. She'd hung lace curtains at the window and covered the bed with an antique quilt in muted tones of green, rose and taupe. A vase of fresh flowers picked from the yard sat on the chest of drawers, and a print of a woman smelling a rose hung on the wall in an old plaster frame. It wasn't much, but it gave the room a feminine aura it had lacked before.

The box he'd noticed the day before sat on the floor by her bed, but some of its contents lay on the quilt, among them a small wooden box, some papers and a Vanity High School yearbook. Wondering if his memory of what she'd looked like back then was accurate, he crossed the room and picked up the thin volume. The date on the front was the year Amber graduated, the year he'd been a sophomore. There was something stuck between the pages that kept the book from closing.

He flipped the book open and saw that the ''something'' was a red rose, pressed to semi-flatness and long ago dried to parchment fragility. Cal picked up the rose and glanced down at the photos. It took him a couple of seconds to realize he was looking at his class. A closer inspection found his own face smiling back at him. There was a circle around the picture and she'd written the words ''cute, but too young.''

So Amber had thought he was cute back then. Cute, but not quite good enough. Close, but no cigar. He closed the rose back inside the book and laid it on the bed. The handwriting on a partially covered page caught his eye. It was his handwriting.

Fighting the notion that he was snooping, yet unable to help himself, he pulled the paper out from beneath several others that lay beneath the carved wooden box.

The lilacs bloomed in April....

Cal's heart skipped a beat. It was one of the poems he'd written for her. Unable to believe that she'd kept it, he picked up the other pages. *I never thought it would be this way. Love, I mean...* Another one. *Yesterday's flowers and I sit forlornly... The summer beaches are empty....*

They were all there. Ten or twelve of them. Cal flipped through them in disbelief. Amber had kept them all these years, which meant that the rose was quite possibly the one he'd put in her locker so long ago. Why had she kept them? Because they meant more to her than she was willing to admit to herself? Because she'd harbored some small feeling for him, even though she'd never acted on it? And why drag them out after all this time? Could it possibly be that just as she had back then, she felt something for him she wasn't quite ready to admit?

"Dream on, buddy," he said aloud.

But the reasoning of his usually sane inner voice was sound. He knew Amber was attracted to him physically. That was obvious. But was she feeling something more, something deeper? Could she be starting to fall in love with him? Was she afraid to act on those feelings because of the past she'd admitted to him the night before?

He didn't know, but he knew that when she got home, they were going to have a serious talk. He intended to ask her about the poems, and come what may, he'd tell her he loved her.

Cal put the pages back where he'd found them. He was leaving the room when the phone rang. It was Dudley.

"I thought Claudia was supposed to come over here after school."

A frisson of apprehension shimmied down Cal's spine. "She was. She's not there?"

"That's exactly what I'm saying. But when Beau called and told me he was going with you this morning, I thought maybe you'd changed your plans and forgot to tell me."

"Beau didn't go with me," Cal said, his anxiety rising.

What the heck was going on? Had Amber taken him with her? She was meeting a banker, so it wasn't likely. And where was Claudia?

Georgina! Cal's heart plummeted, and the headache he'd been fighting throbbed painfully. Had their mother gotten her clutches on them somehow? Was she halfway across the country? Cal knew better than to get himself worked up before he found out the details, but kidnapping by a parent was a common enough occurrence for him to be more than a little concerned.

First things first. He'd get hold of Amber and see what she knew about the mix-up. Maybe she'd planned to do something with them before she moved to her dad's. First, though, he'd take some painkillers for his aching head.

He saw the note as he reached into the cabinet for a glass. A quick glimpse told him it was computer generated and had been written by him. The problem was, the note he'd left for Amber had been handwritten.

What was going on? Cal asked himself as he picked up the paper. He had his answer in a matter of seconds.

Since Beau was home for the day...I decided to take him with me.

Cal swore and crushed the note in his fist. Beau had copied Cal's note onto the computer, added the part about himself and typed in Cal's name, knowing that Amber would take it at face value. It would never occur to her that Beau had tampered with it, and knowing her, she'd blame herself for his disappearance when she found out.

Why had Beau lied? Where had he gone? Was Claudia with him? Cal didn't know any of the answers, but he intended to find out.

Chapter Twelve

Where the devil was Amber, anyway? Cal wondered, as he drove down Vanity's main street looking for her car. He'd called the bank to learn that Amber and her father had left some forty minutes earlier. They weren't at Lafourche Farm, and she hadn't returned to Cal's house as of—he glanced at his watch for the dozenth time in as many minutes—two minutes ago.

He had a whole new outlook on missing persons. Whenever he'd been involved in such a case, he'd spouted the usual platitudes about not worrying and everything being okay. He'd always believed the words helped ease the anxiety, but he'd been wrong. When someone you loved was missing, nothing short of seeing their face could allay the fears.

For the upteenth time he wondered where Beau had gone and what had been on his mind when he left the note for Amber. Cal knew Claudia hadn't gone with her brother that morning because a call to the school secretary confirmed that she'd been in class that day. So where had she disappeared to after school? He called the bus driver and asked if Claudia had been on the bus that afternoon and learned that Claudia had had a note from Cal saying she could walk to his office.

Where were they? Cal asked himself again.

Despite evidence that they had concocted some sort of scheme, Cal couldn't ignore his gut feeling that told him they were with Georgina. But how? And why? Both Claudia and Beau had been adamant about not wanting to see her.

With that thought in mind, he'd cruised by Marty Webb's office and his house but had seen no sign of the kids anywhere. It was ridiculous to imagine Marty being involved. Frankly, Cal figured the attorney would rather duke it out in court than jeopardize his career by getting involved in a kidnapping.

But counting out Marty didn't mean counting out Georgina. Hoping against hope, he'd driven by Dean and Georgina's old place, but it was locked up tighter than a drum. When he'd used the spare key Dean had given him and taken a quick tour of the abandoned house, it was obvious no one had stepped foot inside since Cal had gone to pack up the kids' stuff four years earlier.

He could drive to their grandmother Preston's farm and make a cursory look-see, but it was in the next parish, and he had no jurisdiction there. If it came to that, he'd have to call his buddy Hank Jennings to handle things.

Feeling the frustration and fear piling up, Cal fought the impulse to call Mrs. Preston and ask if she knew anything about the missing children. Two things stopped him: first, he didn't want the Prestons to know he'd "misplaced" the kids—not with a possible custody suit pending, and...there was still the chance that they weren't missing at all, and were with Amber somewhere.

With that thought in mind, he reached for his phone again. If he could just get hold of Amber....

Amber had just finished changing into shorts and a T-shirt when the phone rang. "Hello."

"Amber. Thank God."

The note of alarm in Cal's voice was distinct and frightening. "Cal? Is something wrong? Has something happened to one of the kids?"

"Is Beau with you?" he asked, without answering her.

"And why would you think he was with me when you left me a note saying you were taking him with you for the day?" The words had barely cleared her lips when comprehension dawned. Beau had done it—done something—again.

"Beau must have found my note, typed it into the computer, added what he wanted and printed it out," Cal told her.

"Why?"

"All I know is that he's missing." He spoke over Amber's shocked gasp. "And that leaving the note accomplished two things. It kept you from worrying about him, and it gave him a head start of several hours."

"Head start? You don't think he's run away, do you?"

"I honestly don't know what's going on. Dudley said Claudia didn't get off the bus at his house, either."

"You've got to be kidding!"

"I wish I were. The bus driver said she had a note from me saying Claudia wouldn't be riding this afternoon because she was meeting me at the station. They probably wrote it on the computer, too."

Amber clutched the receiver in a white-knuckled grip,

recalling the way Claudia had hugged her and told her she loved her before she got on the bus that morning. After recounting the episode to Cal, she said, "It was almost as if she thought we might never see each other again. Cal, what's going on?"

"I don't have a clue, but my gut tells me it has something to do with Georgina."

"That doesn't make sense," Amber said. "They didn't even want to see her. Why would they run away to her?"

"I don't know. Maybe she called when neither of us was around and offered them some sort of bribe. You know how kids are. Promise them a new CD player or TV and they're putty in your hands."

"Not those two. They've both been hurt too badly."

"You're right." She heard him swear softly. "Do you have any ideas?"

"No," Amber said, wishing she did. Wishing she could do something to take away the pain she knew he was feeling. "What should I do? Help you look for them or stay by the phone?"

"Stay by the phone, just in case. Now that I know they aren't with you, I want to check out a couple of things. Call me if you hear anything."

"I will."

"And Amber?"

She noticed the subtle change in his voice, a determination that said he'd come to some decision and wouldn't be denied. "Yes?"

"I found the poems you kept and I know what it means. You and I are going to get some things straight when this is over."

There was no time to think of an appropriate reply before he hung up. She recradled the receiver and went to the kitchen to make a pot of coffee. It promised to be a long evening.

Dudley brought sandwiches just after six. Amber hugged the old man and told him what she knew, which wasn't much. As they ate—or tried to—she told him about Claudia's behavior that morning. But even as she recounted the tale, her mind was divided between worry about the kids and the bombshell Cal had dropped an hour earlier.

What did all this mean? Did he realize that her keeping the poems meant she cared for him? Or did he think she'd kept them as a sick reminder of the past and mean to take her to task for it?

"That is strange behavior," Dudley said when she finished.

"What?" Amber asked, realizing her mind had wandered.

"Claudia's leaving."

"I know. It breaks my heart to see Cal so upset," she said. "He's worried sick, and I know he's afraid something like this might go against him if there's a custody hearing."

"You love him," Dudley said.

"Yeah," Amber said softly, "I do." She sighed. "For all the good it does me."

"What do you mean?"

"Oh, Dudley, Cal would never feel the same way about me. Not in a million years. When we were in school, he used to write me poems. I liked them, and I was flattered, but he wasn't one of the in crowd, so I blew him off."

"Good grief, child, that was years ago," Dudley said with a smile and a pat on her hand. "Ancient history. It might have hurt back then, and he might have resented you, but he's grown up, as I imagine you have. Cal is one of the best men I know, certainly not the type to hold a grudge for something that happened in high school.''

Listening to Dudley made Amber realize just how silly those particular fears had been. But Cal *had* mentioned the poems, so what else could he have meant about getting some things straight?

"And he's not an inverted snob, either," Dudley said. "He won't give two hoots in Hades about your money— or your family's money. The man is dotty over you."

Amber blinked in surprise. "He told you that?"

"He didn't have to. I may be old, Amber, my dear," Dudley told her. "But I am neither blind nor senile. When you're in a room together, he can't take his eyes off you. And it hasn't escaped my notice that the air fairly crackles when the two of you get within a yard of each other. Call it sexual attraction, if you will, but I saw him with his first wife, and this is something far different. I'd bet my bank account—" he winked at her "—and it is a considerable amount, what he feels for you is the real thing."

"Are you saying Cal loves me?"

"I am, but I'm not sure he knows it yet," Dudley explained. "After all, it's only been what—a couple of weeks? That's fast. And he's probably putting himself through the same purgatory you are. Telling himself things like, 'She won't want to tie herself to me because I have two kids to raise. She's used to having everything her heart desires, and I can't give it to her. She's used to the big city, and I'm a country kind of guy.'" He waved his hand in a circular gesture. "Yada, yada, yada."

"He asked me to marry him last night."

Dudley looked stunned. "Then why all the angst? Why let me go on like an old fool with all my theorizing?"

Amber's gaze held his. "I told him no."

Dudley's gaze narrowed. "Why?"

"Because he didn't say a word about love. He asked me to marry him because he thought it would put a stop to the gossip and give him a better shot in court, if it comes to that."

Dudley chuckled and gave a sage nod. "That sounds like Cal. As I said, the boy hasn't realized the love bug has bitten him—or maybe he has, but he's fighting it. However, he does know a good thing when he sees it, and you're planning to leave. He doesn't want that, so he figured out a way to keep you and his pride intact by telling himself and you that it's for the children." Dudley rubbed his hands together. "Brilliant."

The phone ringing interrupted their conversation. Amber grabbed the receiver, praying it was Cal with some good news. "Hello."

"Amber?"

The voice was so soft, it was hard to tell who was speaking. Her excited gaze met Dudley's. "Beau? Is that you?"

"Yeah."

"Thank God!" Amber said. "Where are you? Are you all right? Is Claudia with you?"

"We're at my mom's Aunt Ruth's house. Mom brought us here in case Uncle Cal came looking for us."

Amber's mind was whirling with a dozen questions that needed answers, but they could wait. First she had to get Beau and Claudia back. "Beau, can you speak up? I can hardly hear you."

"I can't," he said in a loud whisper. "They don't know I'm calling. You've got to come get Claudia. She forgot her inhaler, and Aunt Ruth has about a dozen cats."

Amber's heart gave an anxious leap. "Should I bring her inhaler or the nebulizer?"

"I think she's gonna need her shot," Beau said. "She's real bad."

Seeing the question on Dudley's face she put her hand over the mouthpiece and said lowly. "It's Beau. Claudia needs her shot."

Dudley nodded.

"Did you tell your mom?" Amber asked Beau.

"Yeah." Suddenly, Beau sounded as if he were about to cry. "She said Claudia should have remembered her inhaler, that she'd forgotten what a pain she was when she was sick and for her to stop whining." His voice did break then.

"It's okay, Beau," Amber said. "Tell me where your aunt Ruth lives. I'm coming to get you."

"No! Not me. Just Claudia."

"What! Why? Beau, you said yesterday you didn't even want to see her. Now you say you want to stay. What's going on?"

"Uncle Cal says sometimes we have to do things we don't want to do."

The statement confused Amber more than ever. "What are you talking about?" Her question was met with silence. "Tell me now, Beau, because I'm not getting off this phone until you tell me why you suddenly want to stay somewhere you didn't even want to go."

She heard a sob, and her heart broke. It must have broken the dam of emotion inside Beau, too, because the words, mingled with sobs came rushing out faster and faster. "I heard you tell Uncle Cal you wouldn't marry him because of us kids, and I knew you liked Claudia, so it had to be me, because I'm such a pain in the butt. Uncle Cal loves you, so I thought that if I wasn't here, you'd change your mind and marry him."

The pain in Amber's heart expanded with each word

Beau spoke. She realized she was crying, too. "So you ran away."

"Yes ma'am. Claudia didn't want to come, but she didn't want me to be here by myself, so she came after school."

"Oh, Beau! We don't have time talk about this now, but you misunderstood. Do you hear me? My turning Cal down had *nothing* to do with you. It had to do with me, some mistakes I made in my past. What I was telling Cal is that you and Claudia deserve someone better than me."

"We don't want anyone else," he said with a sob.

The words were some of the sweetest she'd ever heard. "Then you won't have anyone else," she said firmly. "Now tell me where you are. I'm calling an ambulance for Claudia, and I'm on my way."

Beau told her where his great-aunt lived, and Amber wrote the information down. "Hang in there, sweetheart. Dudley and I will be there soon."

"Hurry," Beau said, and hung up.

Amber was about to call 911 when Dudley's voice stopped her. "I've already called," the old man said. "I used my cell phone. The ambulance is on the way, and Jimmy Rowell is locating Cal." He held up a bottle and a packaged syringe. "I have the Adrenalin, just in case we get there first."

"I don't think I can give her the shot," Amber said.

Dudley smiled at her. "You broke down the wall Beau built around his heart. You can do anything."

Amber smiled at him and brushed ineffectively at her tears. "Will you drive? I'm having a little trouble seeing."

"Of course." Despite his arthritis, Dudley managed a courtly bow toward the door. "Come m'lady. Your carriage awaits."

* * *

Thankfully, some sort of miracle conspired that Amber and Dudley arrived at Ruth Meeker's house almost simultaneously with the ambulance. Georgina opened the door to the two paramedics as Dudley pulled to a stop. Amber saw her shake her head angrily, even as she cast an anxious look at Dudley's car.

Amber unfastened her seat belt and got out, sprinting toward the house. "Don't listen to her" she cried. "Claudia Simmons is in there, and she needs help."

Georgina turned toward Amber, her face contorted with fury. "How dare you show your face to me, Amber Campion?"

It crossed Amber's mind that even though Georgina was fashionably dressed and coiffed, she'd aged considerably. She was too thin, too tanned, too made up. And there were lines bracketing her mouth and fanning out from her eyes. Too much of the good life, Amber thought.

"And how dare you put on a pious front, Georgina, much less deny your daughter the medical help you know she needs. Now get out of these men's way, or I'm going to have to move you myself." Georgina's gaze locked with Amber's for several seconds. Finally, she stepped out of their way, and the Emergency Medical Technician team surged through the doorway.

"Amber!" Beau's voice preceded him. Seeing that Amber and his mother were glaring at each other from across the expanse of the narrow brick walkway, he skidded to a stop at the door.

"Beau!" Without a second's hesitation, Amber dropped to her knees and opened her arms. With nothing more than a cursory glance at his mother, Beau ran to her, almost knocking her over with the force of the impact. Her arms slid around his sturdy body; his closed around her neck. She felt the dampness of his tears against her shoulder, felt the wetness of her own tears slipping down her cheeks. It was one of the sweetest moments of her life. Neither of them heard the siren as Cal's cruiser came screeching to a stop.

"Amber!"

She turned her head toward the sound of his voice and saw him striding across the lawn toward them. Almost reluctantly, she released Beau and stood. He kept her hand clenched in his. Amber didn't know what she expected, but it wasn't for Cal to sweep them both into a tight embrace or for him to press a brief, hard kiss to her lips.

There was a commotion at the door, and, like a whirlwind, the paramedics whisked the gurney bearing Claudia outside. She was already hooked up to intravenous tubes and oxygen.

Seeing them, Claudia gave them a feeble wave. Cal released Amber and Beau, and they all approached the gurney as they were preparing to load her into the ambulance. Dudley joined them.

"We'll be right behind you," Cal said, dropping a kiss to her forehead. Amber squeezed her hand. Claudia smiled weakly and squeezed back. Dudley gave her arm an encouraging pat. Never much for touching, Beau held back, but his eyes were dark with pain and remorse.

Claudia smiled at him. "Thanks, Beau."

He nodded, and the paramedics lifted her inside the ambulance. Without so much as a backward glance at the house, they all climbed into Cal's cruiser and followed the wailing vehicle down the street.

None of them was aware that Georgina collapsed against the door frame, her arms wrapped around herself, her tears and mascara running like a black river down her cheeks.

Cal, Amber, Beau and Dudley stayed in the waiting room while the pediatrician who'd taken care of the Simmons kids since birth checked Claudia over. While they waited for word of her condition, Beau explained to Cal exactly why he'd left that morning, why Claudia had joined him and exactly what had happened when he reached his grandmother's house.

"I told you on the telephone that you and Claudia weren't the reason I told Cal I wouldn't marry him," Amber said. "And that was the truth."

In a voice that quavered with emotion, she sat Beau down in a chair next to her and told him about her pregnancy and how she'd given her child up. "That's why I didn't think I should marry Cal. I didn't want to be a hypocrite."

"Was it a boy or a girl?" Beau asked.

"I don't know," she said with a shake of her head. "I was afraid knowing would make giving it away harder than it already was. I shouldn't have done it, Beau, but I was young and scared and I didn't know what else to do. There isn't a day that goes by that I don't wonder about that child and if my giving it up has made him or her angry like you or sad like Claudia. And I wonder if he or she ever thinks about me, or hates me."

"Nobody could hate you, Amber."

The tears she'd barely managed to hold back spilled onto her cheeks. "Thank you, Beau."

"What do you say I take you home, young man," Dudley said. "You do have to go back to school tomorrow."

"I want to see how Claudia is."

"Dudley's right, buddy," Cal told him. "I promise I'll call you as soon as we hear how she's doing, and I'll probably be home in a couple of hours."

Surprisingly, Beau capitulated without further fuss. Amber hugged him and Dudley goodbye and watched them disappear down the hospital corridor, leaving her alone with Cal. Uncomfortable and not knowing exactly why, she turned from the doorway and went to stand in the window overlooking the parking lot.

Cal's arms went around her waist from behind. She stiffened in surprise but was too weary to object. His thighs were rock solid behind her. Unable to think of what to do with her hands, she rested her arms on top of his and curled her fingers around his.

He nuzzled the spot behind her ear. What she was letting him do was insane, but she couldn't find it in herself to tell him to stop. Instead, she closed her eyes and relaxed against him. He was warm and strong, and right at that moment she needed someone to lean on.

"We all make mistakes." His voice was a soft rumble in her ear. His breath was warm against her flesh.

"You didn't," she said, tipping her head back to glance at him over her shoulder.

"Don't kid yourself," he said, "I've made my share of mistakes. I let my marriage fall to pieces without trying to put it back together. I should have. I took vows."

Neither spoke for a moment, and finally, Cal said quietly, "I think what you did took a lot of courage."

She turned so that she could look him in the eye. "Courage? More like cowardice. I was scared, and I knew at that point in my life I couldn't be a decent mother." She laughed, a bitter, weary sound. "I couldn't even handle my own life, how could I take care of a child? And there was the very important fact that I didn't want anyone close to me to find out what I'd done."

"Why?"

She wouldn't look at him. Instead, she stared at the expanse of his chest and plucked at a button. "Because I was always in some kind of scrape or other. Believe me when

I tell you that Beau and I have more in common than you'll ever know. I didn't want my parents to be any more disappointed in me than they already were, and I didn't want them comparing me to Kim, who was so perfect.''

Cal's hands moved up and down her upper arms in a comforting gesture. ''She isn't any more perfect than you are.''

''You're right,'' Amber admitted. ''But I didn't know that back then.''

''Did the father of the baby know about it?''

''Oh, yeah,'' she breathed on a sigh. ''He knew. He told me to make a choice. I wouldn't have an abortion, so that was the end of that.'' She told Cal about her move to Dallas and entering the Art Institute there. She told him how she'd been alone when she'd given birth to her child.

''Have you ever tried to make contact with the adoptive parents?''

''No, but it was a private adoption, so I could probably find out who they are and where they live.''

''Have you thought about it?''

''Oh, I've thought about it,'' she said with a sniff, ''but it's hard to know what to do. On one hand I'd like to look him or her up and tell them I'm sorry. On the other, I'm afraid that it will just make their life more complicated.''

''Maybe as the child grows older, it will want to know more about you and decide to look *you* up.''

''Maybe.''

''Poor Amber,'' he said, trailing his knuckles along the scar that marred the creamy perfection of her cheek.

''I don't want your pity.''

''You don't have it, but you need to stop beating yourself up for what you did. It was a difficult decision and obviously one that's been hard to live with, but you weighed the situation and made the best judgment you could at the time. It's the best any of us can do. Don't you think that I worry every day that I'm not doing a good enough job with Beau and Claudia?''

''But you are!''

His massive shoulders lifted in a shrug. ''When I realized they were my responsibility, I promised myself I'd do my best by them, and I have. But I'm sure some people in town don't think it's enough.''

''Then they're wrong,'' she said looking up at him, an earnest expression in her blue eyes.

''Okay,'' he said nodding. ''I'll accept that if you accept that a decision you made more than twelve years ago was the best you could do.''

''I—''

He silenced her by putting his fingertips against her lips. ''No. No buts. I also want you to change the way you think about yourself. Don't think you aren't good enough to be a role model for Claudia and Beau. And stop feeling guilty about wanting another child, one you can keep and love.''

She sucked in a sharp breath. ''How did you know?''

He smiled, and the smile was tender and wistful and a tad teasing. ''Well, your biological clock is ticking as they say. I've watched you with these kids every day for two weeks. You love being with them, doing things for them, *being there* for them. And I saw how you were with Hannah.''

''I love them,'' she said. ''But I know I can't atone for my mistake by trying to make up for it by taking care of Claudia and Beau.''

''Exactly. So why don't you stop thinking about the good things you do as penance and start thinking about them as just doing something that's needed.'' He searched her eyes for a moment. "And maybe I need to change the way I see myself and my situation, too."

Her gaze roamed over his features hungrily, wanting to thank him, wanting to tell him she loved him, hoping against hope that he meant what she thought he did.... "What are you saying?"

Cal took her hands in his and carried them to his lips. He brushed a light kiss across her knuckles and stared at their joined hands as he spoke. "I'm saying that I still want to marry you. I can't give you what Drew gives Kim. I'll never be a wealthy man. I can't promise you a newer and better house. I have a job that occasionally gets dangerous. That's hard for any woman to deal with. And there's Claudia and Beau."

As he had earlier, she stopped him by putting her fingertips to his lips. "Why?"

He raised his head and met her questioning gaze. "Why what?"

She nodded. "Why do you want to marry me?"

She knew the moment understanding dawned. The frown between his eyebrows vanished, and the confusion in his eyes was swept away by softness. "Why else?" he said. "Because I love coming home and finding you there. I love watching you with the kids. I love *you*. More than I ever thought it was possible to love someone. And that's all I can guarantee you."

With each word he spoke, the pain Amber had carried around for so long eased a bit more. She believed that one day it might even vanish completely. She surged against him and flung her arms around his neck. With her mouth a breath away from a kiss, she breathed a fervent yes.

Neither was sure how much time passed, but the kisses were interrupted by a loud "Ahem!"

They jumped apart like two teenagers caught by a disapproving parent. Claudia's doctor stood in the doorway, a smile on his face. "I just wanted to tell you that Claudia is doing fine. As a precaution I'd like to keep her here overnight, but if she keeps improving, she can go home first thing in the morning."

Cal pulled Amber close to his side. "Thanks, doc."

The aging physician nodded. "Sure. Carry on, Sheriff."

Amber's face grew hot, but Cal just gave her a mischievous grin. "Where were we?"

"About to be tossed out of the hospital on our ear, I imagine," Amber murmured as he drew her back into his arms. She ran her finger along Cal's left cheek. "I know something you can give me."

"Anything within my power."

"Then give me your baby."

The emotions that chased across Cal's face were wonderful to behold. Surprise. Pleasure. Awe. And the kind of love she knew would last a lifetime.

His smile was back in full force. "It'll be my pleasure, Ms. Campion. We can start working on that anytime you're ready."

"We can start working on it as soon as I'm Mrs. Simmons." She laughed at the disappointment on his face. "I'm serious, Cal. For once in my life, I want to do something right."

He stared into her eyes for long seconds, then his face cleared and he smiled. "No problem. I'll have the judge pull a few strings and we can be married by tomorrow at noon."

Amber smiled and raised her lips for his kiss. "Perfect."

Epilogue

One year later

Amber opened her eyes to bright summer sunshine. Thankfully, it was a Saturday morning, a time she could sometimes sleep late, then get up and fix a big breakfast. She *could* have done that if something hadn't awakened her. The something was her husband, whose body was fitted tightly against her, like two spoons in a drawer. His breath tickled her ear and his hand moved lazily from her breast to her not-so-flat stomach. He definitely didn't have sleeping or breakfast on his mind.

"We just did this, um, some time in the night," she said, already turning toward him. "Sex fiend."

"I'm not a sex fiend. I'm trying to play catch up," he said, rubbing his nose against hers. He sighed. "I hate to tell you, but I don't think I'm ever gonna manage it."

Amber smiled. "I certainly hope not," she said, taking his hand and moving it to her breast. As usual when he touched her, her bones seemed to dissolve, and her thought processes shut down. She was capable of nothing but feeling the excitement that surged through her as his mouth moved over her body, the roughness of his beard chaffing her skin, and the gentleness of his callused hands, all working together to seduce her senses and bring her to fulfillment.

It was a heady sensation to realize she had the same effect on him, she thought, reveling in her power as she tracked the now-familiar terrain of his body. Her hands smoothed over his flesh, caressing, stroking, as if she were a blind person determined to imprint each bone and sinew to memory. Had she ever seen shoulders so broad? A stomach so hard? Her mouth followed the path of her hands, eliciting moans and mild curses and leaving her no doubt of her effect on him.

"Enough!" he said, out of patience with her teasing. He rolled her to her back and moved over her with a sureness that was still filled with consideration. She wondered, as their bodies strove together, if there had ever been a man who was so intensely masculine, yet so innately gentle....

When Cal finally rolled away from her, he cradled her close and sighed in repletion. "And I used to never like sweets for breakfast."

She gave a breathless laugh. "Tastes change."

"Yeah, they do. I used to go for brunettes, but now I sort of like mouthy bleached blondes."

"You'd better."

He propped himself on one elbow and smiled down at her. "You're so beautiful."

"I have a flabby stomach with an ugly scar."

His hand moved lower, and she gave a little groan. "Not as flat as it once was, but it's getting there." He flung back the sheet, exposing her nakedness. Before she could object, he slid down the bed and pressed a kiss to the cesarean scar just below her bikini line. Amber gave another moan.

He raised his head and looked at her earnestly. "Do you mind the scar?"

She cupped his cheek in her hand and moved her head back and forth against the pillow. "Not if you don't."

"How could I mind? It got my daughter here safely."

"Good, then, because it looks as if we're stuck with it."

Though Amber's first pregnancy had been trouble-free, two-and-a-half-month-old Calista—better known as Callie—had not only weighed in at two ounces over nine pounds, but had had the audacity to try and come breech. A cesarean section had been the safest way to go. Now everyone teased Amber about her daughter being tough enough and big enough to follow in her dad's footsteps and play football.

Amber maintained that she didn't care if Callie grew up to be a wrestler. Right now she was healthy and colic-free and incredibly beautiful. Cal yawned, pulled the sheet up over them, then rested his head against her belly and closed his eyes.

"Oh, right," Amber said, giving his shoulder a hard punch. "Have your way with me and go back to sleep when you know it's almost time for Callie's feeding."

"It's a selfish, man thing."

She couldn't help but smile. In a matter of seconds it seemed, she heard the steady rhythm of his breathing and knew he was asleep. She didn't mind. She certainly couldn't complain about Cal not taking his turn with the bottle just this once.

As a matter of fact there wasn't much in her life she could complain about. After the episode at Georgina's aunt's house the previous year, the judge had heard both sides and talked at length to Claudia and Beau. He had declared that they were old enough to have a say about whether they wanted to stay with the uncle who had cared for them or live with their mother. They had opted to stay with Cal.

Surprisingly, Georgina had allowed Cal and Amber to adopt Beau and Claudia. Marty had confided to Cal that Georgina *had* been suffering from guilt and that it had broken her heart to see Beau go to Amber instead of her, but she'd realized that maybe it was best. She really didn't have much patience with them.

He also told Cal that the threatened custody battle had been his wife's idea. When Leslie realized she would never have a child of her own, she'd asked Marty to persuade Georgina to try to get the kids back. Leslie figured it was just a matter of time before her sister grew tired of motherhood again, and this time, she planned to be the one who stepped forward to take on the care and responsibility of Claudia and Beau.

The two children seemed happy to have Amber for a stepmother, and she'd done her best by them, which, as Cal had pointed out, was all she could do. The arrangement was working just fine, though it was by no means perfect. It seemed the phone was always ringing or the house was always filled with kids, and there was never any peace and quiet.

But despite the inevitable quarrels and misunderstandings and hurt feelings and generation gaps, there was never a night that went by that the children were not told they were loved. Never a night they went to bed without a hug and a kiss.

Amber realized that none of them would ever forget the pain of their past, but they had survived it. With patience and the healing power of love, they had learned and grown from their pasts. Amber had learned that love truly covers a multitude of heartbreak. She knew that Claudia and Beau would never make the same mistakes their mother had made, though they would make others.

Amber ran her fingertip down the scar on Cal's cheek. Funny she hardly ever noticed it, any more than she paid much attention to hers. Life, she thought, was sometimes like a war. There were skirmishes and battles, and wounds were inflicted, sometimes self-inflicted. There was pain. But hopefully, if you believed in love and forgiveness and second chances, there were no noticeable scars.

* * * * *

Silhouette Stars

Born this Month

Don McLean, Buster Keaton, Clive James, Paul Hogan, Sean Lennon, Cliff Richard, Margaret Thatcher, Max Bygraves, Bill Gates, Bob Hoskins

Star of the Month

Libra

The next few months should prove challenging, you will need your wits about you and the support of those close to you. However, you will begin to feel that real progress is possible in your life and long held dreams can become reality. Finance looks good and there may be a chance for long distance travel later in the year.

SILH/HR/0010a

 **Scorpio**

A great month for relationships, you will feel stronger and more committed, by being honest with your partner you will achieve new heights.

Sagittarius

Life remains complicated and you need to sort out your priorities. Loved ones will be able to support you but only if you show real appreciation.

 **Capricorn**

You're in demand both socially and at work, you may find you need to simplify your life in order to keep everybody happy and you sane!

Aquarius

Time to sort out your priorities, by trying to please everyone you are not really achieving much. Travel plans may have to be changed at the last minute.

 Pisces

You should be feeling optimistic about the way your life is going, especially in relationships where you realise just how much you mean to that special person.

Aries

Your natural charm enables you to win over friends and colleagues to your way of thinking making this month one of progress in many areas of your life. A shopping trip could find you bargain hunting with style.

Taurus

You may feel unmotivated and not so sure where your life is heading; don't despair, changes are just around the corner. Financial matters improve and you may receive something material from an unusual source.

Gemini

There are many positive aspects around you and by being confident you can succeed in all you desire, making this an excellent month. A friend has news that sets you thinking about how loyal someone close is.

 Cancer

You could be fighting to find some personal space as the demands from work and socially get too much. Sift out the important and allow the rest to drop away, leaving you time to refresh.

Leo

You should be revelling in the attention you are receiving as a result of recent achievements but deep down you feel that someone close is not being as supportive as you would like. Whatever their motives, now could be truthtime.

  Virgo

Romance is highlighted and you will feel pleased with the way a special relationship is going. Finances are looking good and you may splash out later in the month.

**Look out for more
Silhouette Stars next month**

▼™ SILHOUETTE
SPECIAL EDITION®

AVAILABLE FROM 20TH OCTOBER 2000

BABY BOY BLESSED Arlene James

That's My Baby!

Little Georgie was Colin Garret's son, but in the year Colin had been searching for him, Lauren Cole had been caring for and loving his child. A marriage of convenience was the only solution!

HIS CINDERELLA Cathy Gillen Thacker

McCabe Men

Wade McCabe was a self-made millionaire with matchmaking parents. But Josie Lynn Corbett Wyatt wanted to prove herself and considered Wade a potential *business* partner!

A ROYAL BABY ON THE WAY Susan Mallery

Royally Wed

Looking for the brother she'd never known Princess Alexandra Wyndham ended up commandeering part of Mitch Colton's home and heart. Could their romance survive the revelation of a royal baby on the way?

YOURS FOR NINETY DAYS Barbara McMahon

Stuck together for ninety days, Nick Tanner and Ellie Winslow resolved to make the best of it, but it was awfully hard to keep their distance! These three months could be the start of a lifetime…

DADDY BY SURPRISE Pat Warren

Devin Gray had long ago resolved to stay single, although his loveable, sexy neighbour was tempting him to change his mind even *before* adorable six-year-old Emily turned up claiming he was her father!

PREGNANT & PRACTICALLY MARRIED
Andrea Edwards

The Bridal Circle

Jed McCarron had just agreed to pretend to be pregnant Karin Spencer's fiancé and her child's father. Pretending to be her beloved didn't commit him to anything…did it?

2 FREE
books and a surprise gift!

We would like to take this opportunity to thank you for reading this Silhouette® book by offering you the chance to take TWO more specially selected titles from the Special Edition™ series absolutely FREE! We're also making this offer to introduce you to the benefits of the Reader Service™—

- ★ FREE home delivery
- ★ FREE gifts and competitions
- ★ FREE monthly Newsletter
- ★ Exclusive Reader Service discounts
- ★ Books available before they're in the shops

Accepting these FREE books and gift places you under no obligation to buy, you may cancel at any time, even after receiving your free shipment. Simply complete your details below and return the entire page to the address below. *You don't even need a stamp!*

YES! Please send me 2 free Special Edition books and a surprise gift. I understand that unless you hear from me, I will receive 4 superb new titles every month for just £2.70 each, postage and packing free. I am under no obligation to purchase any books and may cancel my subscription at any time. The free books and gift will be mine to keep in any case.

E0ZEA

Ms/Mrs/Miss/Mr ....Initials...............................

BLOCK CAPITALS PLEASE

Surname ....

Address ....

....

....Postcode...............................

Send this whole page to:
UK: FREEPOST CN81, Croydon, CR9 3WZ
EIRE: PO Box 4546, Kilcock, County Kildare (stamp required)